Bound to Deceive

D.K. Greene

Bound to Deceive Large Print Edition
Published by KawaiiTimes
KawaiiTimes.com, PO Box 121, Longview, WA 98632
First Edition, February, 2024

Editing provided by Cora Corrigall, www.inkmodifications.com

where I'm at in my writing career without them. Our son, Robert, is one of the most interesting and gifted people I've ever met. I can't wait to see how he changes the world for the better. And my home support team wouldn't be complete without Chris, who shows up with joy, sincerity, and ice cream exactly when they're needed.

I am exceedingly grateful to my editor, Cora Corrigall, who asks difficult questions, and leaves hilarious commentary in the margins of my manuscripts. Likewise, Sarah Lyons Fleming is the best author I've ever read, and it is a dream come true to receive her insight as I'm writing.

My heart overflows with the help of author S. E. Anderson in character and plot development. Craft goddess Elise Berrigan brings an entertaining and informative insight to Vernonia, Oregon, where much of this novel takes place. Amber Kirkham encourages me to meet looming deadlines, while Betsy Brown brings insight and levity when I need it most.

Finally, thank you. Thank you for reading. Without you holding this book, turning the pages, absorbing the story, and sharing it with others, I wouldn't have the opportunity to travel this writing journey at all. I am forever grateful to you for giving me a life filled with stories.

One

Richard sits in the driveway, steeling himself for the trip inside the house. His muscles tense and his jaw clenches as he stares blankly through the windshield. He's too consumed with the dread of another evening at home to notice the beautiful sunset. He's blind to the golden light painting the neighborhood in sepia tones and can't appreciate the way it covers the slight imperfections of the landscape.

His stewing is interrupted by the sound of laughter. Kids play in the cul-de-sac at the end of the street, and Richard is reminded of when his own kids were young. The house felt more alive when Olivia and Josilyn were in it. Now, with Josilyn in college, and Olivia starting her own career in law enforcement, taking her licks as a street cop on the other side of the country, the house is dead, like a piece of beige furniture arranged to fill the blank page of a catalog; clean, crisp, and lifeless.

He leans his head against the headrest and drags his palms across his face before returning them to his white-knuckled grip on the steering wheel. Josie texted before he left the office to tell him that her excursion into the homeless camp was a success. She'll be home any minute.

Twenty-eight years ago, when their marriage was new, he would have been eager to see her at the end of such a difficult day. He imagines a younger version of himself bursting with anxious wonder at the sensation of holding his bride in his arms.

Those days are long gone.

Now, he's trapped between the memory of a life he thought he loved, and the miserable reality personified by the dead house looming over the nose of his ancient sedan. His shoulders are so tense that they feel fused into place around the crooked rod of his spine.

Josie has maintained her timeless beauty, caring for the homeless as she travels from rural community to rural community, feeding, clothing, and housing the masses; a mother to all. Meanwhile, he feels like each day of his exhausting career takes him one step closer to the grave. Maybe if he bothered to care about her volunteering, he could feel different, but he can never seem to extract himself from the dark web of his mind long enough to keep track of her endless endeavors.

She's working in Vernonia this week… or is it Carlton?

Richard tries to remember her last words to him before she left that morning. She'd said something about coming home for dinner, but had she reminded him where she was going? Had she smiled at him, or looked at him with familiar disappointment and disgust?

What he does recall is the sense of relief that came after she left. The well of solace in her absence. The best parts of his life have become the hours of his own work and her volunteering creating a break in the awkward dance between them.

He's being dramatic, of course. Maybe things will be different this time. He looks at the house's darkened windows, and they stare back at him like a corpse's lifeless eyes. His hand moves to the gear shift and his shoulder twitches with the urge to throw the car in reverse and disappear from this life entirely.

When the compulsion to flee draws his gaze to the rearview mirror, he catches his panicked eyes in the reflection. The weight of fear in his expression catches him off guard. What the hell is he doing? “Don’t be such a damn coward,” he whispers to himself.

Things would be better between them if he knew how to fix their marriage. In theory, he and Josie have all the time in the world to make things better. With the kids gone, and his career waning like the last light of the setting sun, there is nothing *but* time. An excess of it, in fact. Once he is fully retired, they’re going to be stuck together more often than not. Maybe he should take Mac’s advice and work on reconnecting with Josie before it’s too late. Or maybe he could simply turn the volume up on the car’s stereo to drown the thoughts of his failing relationship.

He's rolling the stereo knob between his fingers when Josie’s car pulls in beside him. She doesn’t even glance his way, seemingly oblivious to him watching her arrival. She flips her visor down to check her makeup in the mirror and runs fingers through her perfectly straight hair. She's always so put together. Flawless even at the end of another day trawling through the homeless camps for poor souls trusting enough to accept her help.

Richard wonders why she still slums around with him after all these years. She could have any man she wanted with her hourglass curves and wickedly sharp eyes. He wonders at their differences while she gets out of the driver's seat and moves around to her car's trunk. She's already hauling bags of groceries from the trunk when he unbuckles his seatbelt and eases himself out of the driver's seat to meet her.

"How was your day?" He closes his door and approaches her at her trunk. He peers inside to find neatly stacked shoe boxes, a trio of plastic totes filled with clothes and toiletries, and a black plastic trash bag filled with detritus from her activities. She's already gathered the last bag of groceries, so he grabs the garbage and closes the trunk. As the bag shifts in his hand, a stink of shit and sewage wafts into the surrounding air. It's worse than just a few dirty clothes and perished goods from the food pantry. It's musty like foul water and there's a tinge of gasoline with a slight metallic bite. Richard holds the heavy bag as far away from him as he can while he marches it over to the garbage bin. “What the hell do you have in here? This smells worse than my last crime scene.”

“A bit of this and that,” Josie says calmly as she walks up the driveway. She turns to him and smiles widely. Her teeth are as orderly as the rest of her: straight and brilliantly white beneath the deep red of her lipstick. “I re-homed a woman today. She was lovely in the end. She practically cried when I showed her the place I had found for her. It was an altogether perfect day. How was yours?”

“Fine.” Richard digs in his pocket for his keys while he follows her to the front door. On the porch, he scoots around her to unlock the deadbolt and holds the door open for her while she jostles her shopping over the threshold.

He looks her over. Really sees her. She looks small in the gaping maw of the doorway, her shoulders slumped forward under the weight of the groceries. In these moments, she almost looks gentle. He frowns. Under her fragile veneer, Josie is anything but gentle.

She disappears inside the house, and Richard hesitates on the porch. Outside, the setting sun is still warm on his back. It would be the perfect evening for a late cup of coffee on the patio. But the golden light doesn't reach beyond the threshold.

Josie's resigned sigh creeps out at him from the dark, and Richard wonders if maybe he isn't the only one tired of this charade of a marriage.

Richard pushes through the tether of dread holding him outside and forces himself into the house. Josie has already set down her bags and started switching on the lights. Soon, every nook and cranny is flooded with meticulously positioned light.

"Be a dear and put away the groceries for me? I need to get cleaned up before I start dinner." Josie doesn't wait for Richard to reply, just slips her feet from her muddy heels and glides daintily from the room. Her light step barely registers a sound when she ascends the polished wood staircase beyond the kitchen.

Before Richard does as he's asked, he retrieves the broom from a closet and sweeps the trail of crumbled soil and matted grass that Josie tracked into the house. He shakes his head as he pushes the collected debris into the dustpan. Josie is meticulous with her cleaning and normally tucks her pristine heels into the cabinet by the front door. But every so often she tromps into the house in a pair of muddy shoes, leaving a trail that she has no intention of cleaning. He sniffs at the long-dried smell of fetid water and murky soil.

It's almost like she gets some sick pleasure out of forcing me to clean up after her dirty work.

Only after the mess is cleaned does he unload the bags of groceries, opening cupboards and the pantry to hunt for the perfect place for each item. He moves slowly, taking the time to read the labels on each package before setting them on a shelf. Josie's more health conscious than he ever cared to be. Everything is organic, high fiber, low sodium, plant based, and lean. Above the rows of packaged foods sits Josie's cookbooks. Richard stops for a moment to drag his gaze across the spines. Dozens of Paleo, keto, and whole food guides; a collection of a thousand tasteless meals guaranteed to make him live forever.

"If you are looking for cheesecake, do not bother."

Richard flinches at the sound of Josie's voice. He didn't hear her come down the stairs, but now she floats into the kitchen like an irritating fairy, flitting to the stove to weave noisy magic using a spatula, bran flakes, and free-range white meat. She pulls an apron from a hook on the pantry door and slips into it before immersing herself in her cooking.

Only home twenty minutes, and Richard already feels like he's faded into the background of her life. A fixture on the sideboard collecting dust. He lets the heaviness hang in his chest for a few moments and tries to remember when they last felt like a normal couple. Back when they walked hand in hand and talked about their lives. An all-too-familiar ache tugs at his breastbone while he watches her lean against the edge of the counter. Her body lengthens as she reaches for a kitchen gadget on a high shelf, her fitted blouse shifting over smooth skin and petite joints.

"Did anything interesting happen today?" Richard sees her tense at the question, as though he's struck a nerve.

"Interesting to me, or to you?" Her tone is sharp. Irritated. She doesn't bother to look in his direction. Instead, she lowers her found gadget to the counter and moves to collect vegetables from the refrigerator. Watching her move, she loses the sheen of her grace for a moment, shoulders straining under the weight of some unspoken problem.

Despite the dark aura that fills the air, and even as he opens his mouth to try again, Richard wonders why he's a glutton for her punishment. "I'm interested in the things you're involved with."

"No, you are not. The things that interest a housewife are not the same things that absorb the attentions of her husband." Josie shuffles through the refrigerator again and retrieves a jar, handing it to Richard to open. He pops its stubborn seal and hands it back. Josie sniffs it, wrinkles her dainty nose, and drops it in the nearby garbage. Before Richard can even ask if she'd like help, Josie's retrieved a replacement from the cabinet. She's turned her back on him when she finally says, "I befriended a waif of a woman. Fed her, clothed her, tortured her with my charm, and moved her into a safer space than she had been. Then I came home. Are you satisfied, Inspector?"

He feels the distance widening between them, even though they're standing still. He knows if he lets her loose from this conversation, the gap will become too wide to breach, and she'll be lost to him for the rest of the evening. "Does the town have a shelter now?" He hopes the vague question will keep her from noticing he's forgotten where she spent the day.

It seems like she turns to him just so he can watch her roll her eyes. "No. Of course, they do not. There is no funding. But I found her a place anyway. It is what I do best. I do not know why you are asking all these questions. It has never mattered what I do before. Has it?"

Richard holds his breath in his chest, pinching off the escape of an exasperated sigh that might spark a real argument. He forces his jaw to loosen, unlocking his teeth and prying his tongue from where it's glued itself to the roof of his mouth. "I'm just trying to make this work, Josie."

"I would think in your line of work, you would have learned that curiosity killed the cat. Unless you want to come out and tromp through the mud, cleansing the world of its castoffs with me, stop asking questions." Josie glances at him, her expression sharp enough to give the phrase 'shooting daggers' meaning. "Leave me be."

Josie returns her focus to preparing dinner. Richard doesn't need to use his investigative skills to tell that she's ready to be rid of him, and he'd like nothing more than to pour himself a drink and escape to another room. But he knows his habit of running away from her and drowning his sorrows has put him where he's at. Instead of turning tail to escape Josie's frigid tension, he pulls a stool away from the kitchen island and sits down.

"What are you doing?" If the look Josie gave him the last time she glanced his way was sharp enough to hurt, the expression on her face this time could kill.

"I thought I'd sit and talk to you while you cook. We used to do that all the time. When the kids were little. Remember?" Richard is determined to take up space and leans his forearm on the counter. Josie slams the knife she's using to cut vegetables against the cutting board and hitches her shoulders up towards her ears. Maybe it's time to change tactics.

He settles into a practiced, relaxed slouch designed to disarm tense conversations. He pretends he's at work, preparing to interview a person of interest in a string of murders. It's sad how much easier that would be than talking to his own wife. He's organizing his thoughts when Josie cuts in.

"We used to do a lot of things." Her voice is morose, but the glare in her eyes might have a glimmer of interest. She stares at him for a long moment, then her entire being snaps into the role of dutiful housewife again. "Oh, I nearly forgot. I did do something a little fun. I dropped into the most adorable bookshop on my way home." She wipes her still clean hands on her apron and grabs her car keys from the edge of the counter. As quickly as she disappears out of the kitchen, she returns from the car with a shopping bag he hadn't noticed when they unloaded the trunk.

Richard pulls a book from the bag. *1001 Fun Things To Do In Retirement* shouts at him from the front cover. The sigh he's been holding back breaks through the dam of willpower, hissing long and hard through his nostrils. Josie's as bad as Mac. Why can't they leave him alone about this retirement bullshit and let him work through it in his own time?

"It may help you think about the future." Josie's voice lilts in a soft, playful way, as if she's oblivious to Richard's disgust when he shoves it back into the paper bag.

"I don't need help thinking about the future. I know what I want." Richard crumples the paper around the book, already considering which trash bin in the house Josie will be the least likely to check so he can throw it away. He knows he's overdue to retire, and Mac will be ready to take over once Ollie settles his concerns with her. As soon as the pair of them vow to be each other's eyes and ears, there will be no need for Richard to be the middleman anymore. It's like they say… all good things must come to an end, eventually. But without walking the fine line between investigation and being Ollie's eyes on the outside, how will his life have any meaning? Richard doesn't need a book of activity prompts to keep him busy. He needs to matter to someone, and he hardly matters to Josie. He looks at her for a moment and wonders, if he tried harder to be the man he was when they met, would she notice?

"Things have gotten a lot quieter without the kids around, and there is no telling what life will be like once they are married and having babies. We might not see them much between now and then. You know, young people living their lives and all. Just flip through it. You might get inspired."

"It has been quieter," Richard agrees.

"Yes." Josie's smile is tight, but it's there. She turns away to finish slicing vegetables before tossing them into a pot on the stove. "We used to throw dinner parties for the girls' friends and their parents. That was usually amusing."

Richard smiles at the memory of the kids locking themselves away in the basement for video games and movies, while he and Josie served the parents drinks and teased gossip from them in the shallow pauses between popular hits blaring on the stereo. "Yeah. Those were good times."

"Well, it is not really our thing anymore. You are always so exhausted from work, and I do not have a PTA seat to wave in people's faces to bully them into coming over." She looks over her shoulder at him and winks.

"You're right. I am tired." A weight he's held deep in his chest lifts once the admission is in the air. He gets up from his stool and rounds the kitchen island to be closer to her, placing a hand on the curve of her lower back the way he used to. He snatches a slice of carrot from the edge of the cutting board and pops it in his mouth, biting down on it with a satisfying crunch. "But Mac can handle the ins and outs of most things. I can make room for parties again."

"Maybe you can, but I do not know who we would even invite, if we had a house party. Everyone we know is retired and traveling." Josie's side eye is sharp and critical. "Everyone but us."

Richard ignores her attempt to bait him into returning to the argument over his retirement. The book she bought him is nearly enough to drive him into a red-eyed anger, and he's tired of fighting with her. He realizes coaxing her through a conversation about anything else is more work than it used to be. Maybe they're both too far out of practice. "What about inviting Mac and her husband over? They're too tame for a wild party, but maybe they'd come for dinner."

Josie's shoulders stiffen, and she freezes. He expects her to round on him, to tell him he's being stupid for wanting to invite the very work subordinate he was saying could cover his duties at the office over to dinner. The flinch of surprise that tugs at his shoulders is involuntary when she turns to him with soft eyes and a smile that grows wider as she looks him over.

"You really think they would come?"

"Mac always says her favorite meal is the last one she didn't have to cook." Richard's lungs open wider when Josie's smile bends into one that is more genuine, and he snaps a mental picture of the fleeting moment, to think back on the next time she feels like a stranger. He misses this side of her; the part that used to eat up his every word. Maybe if he could change, just a little, she would be his biggest fan again. "Besides, if Mac gives me any lip, I'll just tell her I refuse to retire if she doesn't show up."

The giggle that bubbles up and out of Josie is surprising in its girlishness. She slaps him playfully on the chest. "You will not tell her that."

It has been so long since Richard smiled at his wife, he finds himself fighting the tug at the corner of his lips. Josie has been a mystery to him since the beginning, but over the last few years she's practically become a stranger. He inhales deeply, collecting her scent in his breath and holding it for a beat before exhaling it away again. He does still ache to be close to her, the same way he had the first time he saw her. Maybe if he gives her what she wants, she'll finally give herself to him in a way that is true. "For you, Josie, I'd do anything."

Two

The edge of the bathtub presses into the back of Mac's thighs, and her bare toes tingle against the linoleum. Her fingers pinch at a headache emanating from the bridge of her nose. Isn't she too old for this?

While she waits for the pregnancy test to weigh its judgment upon her, she thinks back on the bulging women of the maternity ward where she and Richard tracked a serial killer targeting young mothers. Being inside the ward with women bursting at the seams reminded her how miserable pregnancy can be–even if some whacko isn't out to kill you. She should have pushed harder for Sam to get a vasectomy.

A lump forms in her throat, and she fishes the instructions out of the waste bin under the sink. The tiny print says it takes at least three minutes for results, and although it feels like she's been in the bathroom for hours, her wristwatch says she still has two minutes to wait.

Rapid pounding on the bathroom door interrupts her thoughts. She stumbles forward, her numb toes awakening to the sensation of pins and needles, and presses her shoulder against the door, twisting the lock to secure it.

"Mom?" Ryan pauses and Mac holds her breath, hoping he'll go away. "The cat puked on my backpack. Dad says I've got to do my homework and my biology book is in there. Will you clean it up?"

"Clean it yourself." Mac retreats to sit on the toilet. She rubs her hands across her forehead and feels her brain rattle inside her skull when he pounds the door again.

"I can't clean it, it's gross!"

"You're sixteen, not six. Figure it out!" Mac checks the pregnancy test again. A faint discoloration creeps across the indicator, and she bites the inside of her cheek hard enough to wince from the pain.

"I can't find the paper towels." Ryan's voice cracks when he pushes it into the sweet sing-song tone that pushes Mac's buttons. "Pleeeeeeease, will you help me? I'll love you forever."

Mac checks her watch. There's still ninety seconds before a clear result will show on the test. She tosses the instructions back in the waste bin, swings the mirror open above the sink, and shoves the test onto one of the medicine cabinet shelves. She slams the mirror shut and fumbles with the door's lock until she can wrench the bathroom door open. Ryan's eyes widen at the sight of her rigid shoulders and narrow glare.

"Thanks, Mom! You're the best."

Mac sniffs an irritated breath and tromps past him, through the house. He follows her to the kitchen, where she yanks open the cabinet below the sink. She grabs a bottle of multi-surface cleaner, a pair of dish gloves, and slams the cabinet door before grabbing the roll of paper towels from its stand on the counter. "Cleaning supplies have been in the same spot since the day you were born. Where's the backpack?"

Ryan drops his shoulders. "Sorry, guess I forgot." Mac rolls her eyes, then follows her son back the way they came. Mac glances at the medicine cabinet when they pass the bathroom and continue on to the next door. Ryan's bag is unceremoniously abandoned on his bedroom floor, a greasy lump of partially digested grass and kibble beside it. Bruce, their floppy-eared hound sniffs at a thin trail of goo touching the very tip of the bag's strap. Mac's chin tightens, and she can almost feel the frown lines etch into the skin around her mouth. "Bruce! Leave it!" The dog jumps backwards from the mess and looks at her with disappointment in his watery brown eyes while he hitches his way out of the room in a lumbering half-jog. Mac extends the cleaning supplies to Ryan. "Wipe it off."

"Gross, Mom." Ryan puffs up his cheeks, wraps his arms around his stomach, and pretends to dry-heave.

"Gah!" Mac blows out an exasperated breath and shoves her hands, one at a time, into the clammy rubber dish gloves. Her knee pops when she lowers herself on hands and knees to clean up the mess. She douses the backpack and floor with cleaner, though it isn't likely to make much difference on the threadbare carpet. She rips a wad of paper towels from the roll just as her husband, Sam, emerges in the hallway to watch through the open door.

"Thanks, babe. I would have, but you know." He pats his stomach, echoing their son's overdramatic queasiness.

The cat's mess is suddenly the perfect outlet for Mac's frustration. Her shoulders tighten until they ache while she attacks the stain, scrubbing as the paper towels peel apart in strips of wet pulp. "We have two teenagers, Sam. We've been through two pregnancies, two rounds of diapers, and two turns of potty training. Spit up. Blowouts. Bodily fluids of all kinds. There's no reason you can't rub a towel on some cat puke."

Mac drops the pulpy wad of paper towels in a pile and tears another grip of sheets from the roll. She wipes the backpack with enough force that tiny white flakes of paper embed themselves in the fabric, then hoists the bag up to hand it to Ryan. "It's clean. You'd better get an 'A' on that homework."

"Thanks, Mom. For real." He takes the bag and clutches it to his chest, then scurries back to the kitchen before Mac can yell at him again.

"Since when does cat puke have anything to do with babies?" Sam asks. He chuffs and scrunches his nose. "It's been so long. If I had to change a diaper now, I'd probably get sick and pass out. Woe betide the parent who asks me to babysit."

"It's been a long time for me too, Sam." Mac picks up the detritus from the sodden carpet. "So why am I the one who has to handle this?"

Sam's eyebrows pull together and his mouth turns down. "You look at dead people at work. What's a little hairball compared to that?"

Mac grunts as she struggles to her feet, the aches and pains of a thousand frustrations tweaking her spine and tugging at the sciatic nerve on her left side. She wedges the roll of paper towels under one arm, hooks the bottle of cleaning spray in the crook of the other, and carries the disgusting remains of the mess to the bathroom garbage.

"I don't understand why you're so upset. It's not a big deal." Sam leans against the bathroom doorway when Mac turns around.

"It's a big deal to me, Sam!" Mac tromps to the kitchen and Sam follows. They find Ryan hunched over his homework, pretending to be studious while Mac shoves the cleaner and gloves back under the sink and slams the paper towel roll onto the counter. "I have to work, do all the stuff with the kids, cook, clean, and apparently, I'm the only person in this goddamn house who can clean up the fucking cat puke!"

"Woah." Sam stops on the far side of the kitchen aisle and raises his hands in surrender. Laugh and frown lines intermingle while the features of his face shift with uncertainty. "Are you saying you don't want to work anymore? Because you're the one who wanted to join up with the FBI. I was fine with you staying at home."

The anger simmering inside Mac's veins boils over. Her cheeks burn and the back of her neck breaks into a sweat. "That is bullshit, Sam."

"What?" His eyebrows shoot up in surprise. "We don't need the extra money. We're fine. We're better than fine. If you're feeling overworked, just quit. You don't have to be this badass Lara Croft detective woman, chasing after killers. You could just be a mom again."

Tears prick at the corners of Mac's eyes. She's painfully aware of Ryan listening from the kitchen table and bites her quivering lip to keep from unloading every ounce of her rage in front of him. She motions for Sam to follow her out of the kitchen and back to their bedroom. As soon as Sam shuts the door behind them, her shoulders jump, her sinuses run, and an anguished sob wrenches out of her.

"I don't want to just be some mom," she warbles. "I love our kids. I love you. But I hated being a housewife. I stuck it out when the boys were little, but I gave up everything I loved to do it. I'm not some cookie-cutter, carpool chauffeur, happy-to-fold-your-underwear kind of wife. I need more, Sam!"

The laugh lines around Sam's eyes droop, and his lips turn down. He wraps his arms around her and brushes his lips against her hairline. "Mackenzie, sweetheart. I'm sorry, okay? I know you like your job, and that it's important to you. I'm just trying to help. Where is all this coming from, anyway?"

Mac snakes her arm through Sam's embrace to wipe at her damp cheeks. "It doesn't matter. I know I can quit my job, but I don't want to. I was miserable schlepping muffins to bake sales and glad-handing with parents and teachers on the PTA. I can't do all that again, Sam. I just can't."

"Okay," Sam says softly. "So, if you do decide to quit work, don't be a muffin PTA mom. Just be a yoga pants and latte mom."

The pressure behind Mac's eyes explodes, her headache scraping the inside of her skull and yanking at her spine until her shoulders reach her ears. "You don't get it, Sam! I need to make a difference. Have a purpose. My job makes the world safer, not just for you and the boys, but for everybody. It makes me feel alive. But I can't be out there every day, seeing what I see, and doing what I do, and then come home to vacuum, and grocery shop, and cook, and clean up cat puke.

"We're supposed to be partners, Sam. If you want this all to work, I need you to do your part and pick up the slack."

Sam's arms loosen and he sinks into the pile of unfolded laundry at the foot of the bed. "If I want this to work? What, so now you're leaving me because the cat got sick? Tell me how you really feel!" he shouts.

"Don't be an asshole… listen. This is how I feel. I need you and the boys to help me out here." She stares at him for a moment, watching his thoughts move across his features in a language she can't read.

"Fine. I'll try," he says. While his expression is indecipherable, Mac's must be crystal clear, because he rubs his hands over his knees and sighs. "I will. Next time the cat pukes, cleanup is on me."

Mac nods but doesn't voice the words balled up at the back of her throat. If she's pregnant, empty promises won't cut it. Things have to be different. She can't go back to the despondent soccer mom she was before, and Sam has to be more than just a run-of-the-mill husband. He's got to step up and be the partner she deserves.

"I'm sorry," he says. He holds out his arms and she reluctantly allows him to pull her close again. In his embrace, she feels a layer of anger fade away. The fight is nearly out of her when his stomach rumbles. Sam's eyes crinkle with his smile. "I don't want to start another argument, but do we have plans for dinner?"

The sound of a dying tuba rises and falls from Sam's midsection, and Mac can't help but laugh. "What do I look like, a cook?"

"You did until about ten minutes ago. Now, I'm not so sure. How about the boys and I take over cooking tonight? We can make spaghetti and meatballs."

"I've seen you eat meatballs, but I've never seen you make one." Mac squints at him. "Have you been holding out on me all this time?"

"I didn't want to use up my tricks all at once. Gotta keep some of that mystery alive." The corners of Sam's mouth lift and he quirks a suggestive eyebrow. "Maybe I don't know how to make meatballs, but I know how to look up recipes on the internet."

Mac snorts. "And here I thought you could only microwave popcorn and grill hot dogs."

"Hmm." Sam frowns. "I wonder if you can grill spaghetti. If that's a thing, I'll be all set."

Mac's belly laugh eases the lingering tension from their fight. "Please don't try. If you need me to, I can help you use the stove."

"Okay." Sam holds her a moment longer. Mac leans into his embrace, closing her eyes and breathing in the comfort of him. She remembers when they were young, and everything seemed so simple. They'd fallen into their prescribed roles in the ways they were taught, and she thought she was content for a time. But when the boys arrived, one after the other, she realized she needed more than a diaper pail and a pair of house slippers to be happy.

"Oh, shit." Mac's eyes fly open, and she springs to her feet.

"What?" Sam leans into the unfolded laundry a few inches. "Are we going back to fighting?"

"No," Mac shakes her head. "I forgot something. Go get dinner started. I'll be out soon." She swings open the bedroom door to find Robby blocking the hallway.

"Hi, Mom. Can I show you the stats on the new computer I want? It has tons of memory, a sick graphics card, and these multicolor LEDs that are *fire*. It'll be perfect for games with my friends. And homework."

Mac tries to sidestep him. "Later, buddy. I'm in the middle of something."

"But it'll only take a second!" Robby dips in front of her with his arms spread wide to block her path.

"Not right now." She gently holds his shoulders and guides him to the side of the hallway. "I'm sure it's a great computer. I'll look at it later, okay?"

A cloud of disappointment darkens his eyes and his shoulders hunch. He drops his arms, clenching his fists at his sides. "Fine."

Mac stifles a twinge of mom guilt, then rushes the short distance to the bathroom and closes the door, locking the knob. She yanks the medicine cabinet open and sees thin lines spread across the test-strip like candy stripes.

Wait. Is negative one stripe or two? She digs under the cat mess in the trash to find the instructions. The soggy paper says one band for negative, two for positive. But… *results are only valid for ten minutes*. She looks at her watch. It's been a half hour since she peed on the stick. It might be a false positive.

"Fuck!" Mac yells at her reflection in the cabinet mirror and slams her fist against the countertop. Her shoulders buck and her red-rimmed eyes shimmer in the bright vanity light. She has to get another test. Go through this whole thing again. A strange sorrow she's not prepared for twists through her, and she instinctively clutches her abdomen. Was she excited for the split second she thought the test was positive? She shakes her head. She's too old, too tired, and too close to being promoted to lead investigator. Her life is too full. She doesn't have room to hope to be pregnant.

Mac wraps the inconclusive test in its instructions and tosses the whole thing in the trash. She buries it beneath a mountain of tissues soaked in frustrated tears.

Three

The door strains on its hinges, slamming against the wall and startling Mac out of her trance. She slaps the mouse to stop the recording playing in her headphones and nearly falls out of her chair when the governor steps into the room and dumps three bulging accordion files on her desk.

She pulls off the headphones and shuts her laptop just as Richard tumbles into the room out of breath. "Governor Carter! I thought that was you. How can we help?"

Mac blinks rapidly, and the governor's salt and pepper hair dissolves in a memory of tight black curls. The camel trench coat he wears is replaced by a zip-up sweatshirt with a firefighter emblem on its breast. With years of stress and worry washed away, she recognizes him. “Tarrell!”

His arms fall around her shoulders in a trembling hug. She’s pinned into her desk chair under the weight of his awkward, off-balance embrace. Richard takes a step towards the governor, but seems to think better of it and leans heavily on the doorframe instead. Mac pats Tarrell on the back and looks over his shoulder at Richard. “What’s going on?”

“My daughter is missing.” The governor’s words sound strangled as they tumble out of him. He loosens his grip on Mac and wipes tears from his cheeks.

Her chest tightens as memories push their way through her mind, crowding out the private messages she’d received moments before the governor barged in. “Not again,” she says as she pulls back a few inches to look him over.

“What do you a mean, again?” Richard asks as he finally steps closer, reaching out to flip open the cover of the top file. Mac leans as close to the open file as the distraught governor allows. A wallet-sized portrait of a smiling young woman is fastened to the upper left-hand corner of a missing person’s report.

Mac recognizes the girl immediately. “Oh, shit. Tarrell, I’m sorry.”

The governor pulls away suddenly, using the tailored sleeves of his fitted trench coat to wipe the tears from his eyes. “You saved her once. I need you to find her for me again. Please. She’s my only daughter. I can’t believe this is happening to us again, but if anyone can find her, it’s you.”

Richard slides the file closer to Mac so she can see the details filled out on the form. Tarrell’s daughter has grown into a beautiful young woman. She’s slim, tall, and has the same kind, sparkling eyes that got her father elected to the governor’s seat in a landslide vote. To the right of the photo, the report’s header announces it came from Vernonia, Oregon, a town nearly an hour northwest of Portland.

Mac shifts her gaze back to her old friend. As governor, Tarrell has lost the active shine that poured from him when he was Portland’s fire chief. The hours of desk work and political networking have taken their toll, softening the curve of his once strong shoulders, and adding a faint bulge above his shiny gold belt buckle. “What happened?”

"That's what I'm hoping you can tell me." Tarrell tugs at his graying hair and sucks air through his teeth. The desperate look in his eye reminds Mac of the first time she met Tarrell. He drags his hands down his face and takes another breath, pulling himself together. "One of my focuses in office this year is to tackle Oregon's growing homeless problem, and Jacqueline was canvassing rural areas to find out why people have been moving away from cities, and into these smaller towns without services. She's been working the homeless camps in Vernonia the last few months, and some of the women she'd been talking to disappeared. A week ago, Jacqueline said she was going to file another missing person report, and I haven't heard from her since."

"My wife is volunteering out there," Richard cuts in. "Homeless camps have taken Vernonia over. I think she said there's something like two hundred homeless families, and no organized shelter in town."

Tarrell nods. "More than ten percent of the town's population doesn't have a home. That's why my Jacqueline was there… trying to find out why families are sleeping under tarps instead of moving back into cities like Portland where there are shelters."

Mac glances back at her laptop. Months ago, she asked her contact at the Sheridan prison for copies of any correspondence between serial killer Oliver Roberts and Richard's wife, Josie. The report came moments before Richard and Tarrell's arrival, and what little she's seen of the documents is already so much more than she expected. Several dozen phone call recordings, and nearly a hundred e-mails and scanned letters. Mac had just opened the first audio file when she was interrupted, and she's dying to know what secrets are contained in the mountain of correspondence that's landed in her lap. Josie being in a town where women are turning up missing is a giant red flag that Mac can't ignore.

Josie's correspondence with Oliver Roberts might be nothing. Mac hopes it's nothing. But if it's not, she's got to keep a lid on it until she understands what it all means, because she doesn't know how Richard will react when it comes out.

"I want you to figure out what happened to my daughter. You found her when our kids were at camp together. Find her for me again." Tarrell touches Mac on the shoulder and looks at her with eyes swimming in unshed tears. "Please."

"We'll do what we can, but missing people aren't our specialty. I'll have to call up the chain of command for clearance," Richard says. But he can't feel the way the governor's fingers tighten around Mac's shoulder, and she hopes he'll shut up before Tarrell rips the neat red stitching on her favorite Burberry trench coat.

"I am your clearance!" Tarrell's yell fills the small space like an avalanche in a fishbowl. "I'm Oregon's goddamn governor, and if I tell you to go find my daughter, you'd better damn well do it!"

Richard frowns and moves to his side of the office, where he half-sits a hip on the edge of his desk. He comes off as a cool, collected asshole inspector, but Mac sees the sweat collecting around his collar. "I'll set up a virtual conference call with Vernonia P.D. first thing in the morning. We're going to need to know what we're up against and how it fits within the jurisdiction of the FBI."

Tarrell's nostrils flare, and the space between his middle finger and thumb is becoming uncomfortably small on Mac's shoulder. The governor points to the paperwork on the desk. "These are copies of what I have access to regarding the missing women. Whether your head brass gives a shit about these young women or not, I want Mackenzie to look the files over. I hope you find something to give you a jump start on finding out what is going on out there on the Nehalem River."

"We'll do everything we can to find Jacqueline. I promise." Mac rests her cheek against the hand clamped to her shoulder. "I do hate to ask, but has Vernonia P.D. looked into any of these cases from the perspective of a murder?"

"My daughter is not dead," Tarrell says in a voice that sounds as lethal as it is strong. "I can't believe you're even implying that. It's bad enough that Jacqueline is missing. You can't expect me to think about her being…"

Richard gets to his feet and extends a hand towards the governor. "Thank you for coming in today, Governor Carter. Special Agent Mackenzie Jones and I will do our best to bring your daughter home."

"Thank you," Tarrell says. He looks at his hand as if he hadn't even realized it was there, and unlocks his fingers from Mac's shoulder, which she greedily massages with her opposing arm the second Tarrell lets go. The relief from his vise-like grip is short-lived. He leans into her again and hugs her tightly. “Thank you, Mac. I know you’ll find her. I just know it.”

The second Tarrell’s magnanimous energy is swept from the room, Mac picks up the phone and dials the Vernonia police department. In the background of the too-loud hold music screeching in her ear, Richard settles behind his desk and types a formal request to work the missing women’s case. Within a few minutes, Mac has a conference call set up for early the next morning, and Richard has received tentative approval for their involvement in the investigation.

“Well, what do you think, kid?” Richard leans back in his chair, fingers locked behind his head. “Kidnapping isn’t exactly our specialty.”

“Sure it is. Serial killers abduct people all the time.” Mac’s phone dings, and when she glances at the notification preview on her cellphone, she sees a note from her husband. “At least Sam will be happy we’ll be close to home. I think he’s fed up with our travel schedule.”

“Oh, do I sense trouble in paradise?” Richard’s eyebrows climb the wrinkles of his forehead.

Mac's halfhearted chuckle says it all. "With two teenage boys at home, we're miles away from paradise. It smells like a zoo and looks like monkeys are in charge of the housekeeping. I don't know how you managed to raise two kids and work this job. Everything is chaos."

"I had Josie." The small grin Richard wears seems a bit off, and he must feel it because he wipes it away with the back of his hand. "She always handles the household stuff. All I do is show up for vacations and holidays."

"And do you? Show up?" Mac knows the answer all too well. Oliver Roberts was a thorn in his side throughout the last holiday season, keeping him on the go through Thanksgiving and Christmas. Richard bitched about missing that time with his family for weeks afterward.

He sniffs a stifled chuckle. "Josie has been forgiving over the years. It's hard to ruffle that girl's feathers."

"Must be nice to have help at home." Mac works to keep the bitterness from her voice. It'd be nice if Sam would make an effort to help her out, but nothing has changed since her breakdown a couple of days ago.

"It was, when the girls were home. But since they've moved out, I'm the only one around for her to henpeck."

"Oh, so that's why you're avoiding retirement." Mac crosses her arms over her chest while she assesses him. "Don't want to be caught with too much time on your hands?"

"That's part of it. When I'm here, I'm racing the clock. But at home, I don't have enough to do to fill the hours." Richard glances up at the dingy white clock that watches over them from its spot on the far wall as if it will back him up. It merely ticks away the seconds, its cracked face and yellowing paper looking as ancient and weary as Richard does.

The minute hand steps forward, and Mac is reminded of the inevitable march of time. No matter what they do, it just keeps right on passing. The thought pushes her attention away from Richard's retirement avoidance, and toward the stack of files on the corner of her desk. She opens Jacqueline Carter's file and checks the date. She's been missing for nearly two weeks already. Why did her father wait so long to reach out for help? Mac looks at Richard, "Josie really didn't mention there were women going missing in Vernonia? It's a small town, and she's in pretty deep with the homeless camps there, isn't she? Seems like something she should have picked up."

"It's a small town, sure. But there are a lot of transient folks passing through there. She probably just thought they moved on." Richard picks at a cuticle before biting the resulting hangnail.

"We should talk to her about this. Ask her if she knows these women." Mac lifts the lid on her laptop and once the machine comes back to life, closes the recording of Josie speaking to Oliver on the prison telephone. There are hundreds of hours of audio to listen to. But if she can talk to Josie directly, maybe she can speed her discovery of what Richard's wife and prized serial killer are up to. "How would you feel about bringing her in for an interview?"

Richard frowns. "I wouldn't."

"What if she knows something?" Mac presses.

"She's my wife. If she knew something, she'd tell me." He squints his eyes, a tell that Mac has picked up on over the years. He either doesn't trust Josie, or he knows something and isn't sharing. The expression deepens as he turns something over in his mind. "But you know what, she mentioned she's itching to throw a dinner party. I told her I'd invite you and Sam over."

"A dinner party?" It's not the formal invitation she'd like to have, but maybe after a couple glasses of wine, Josie would be more willing to talk. She doesn't want to seem too eager over the social gathering. "That might be nice. But I'll warn you, if it's a potluck, about the only thing I'm good at bringing is booze and crackers."

Richard smirks. "It's a good thing we found you and put you to work. I can't imagine you as a domestic goddess. You don't need to bring anything but your appetite. Josie will take care of the rest. She always does."

Mac glances up at the weary wall clock. "It's getting late. No chance we can do that dinner tonight, is there? I'll take any excuse to not have to feed the kids."

"That'd be asking a little much, even of Josie." Richard shakes his head. "Let's do it tomorrow. I'll see you first thing for the briefing with Vernonia PD, and we'll come up with a plan of action for what to do next. If we make good progress, and you ask really nice, your boss might let you run home early so you can freshen up before the party."

"Damn. Guess we'll never get together then." Mac lets her face droop in a bewildered expression.

Richard's eyebrows climb his wrinkled forehead like a pair of caterpillars. "Why not?"

Mac leans towards Richard and lowers her voice. "Have you ever heard me ask nicely for anything?"

Richard laughs so suddenly, he snorts. "I'll tell Josie you'll be coming at seven. Make sure you're on time. I don't want you to make me look bad."

Mac salivates, not only from the opportunity to have some of Josie's perfect cooking, but also having unlimited access to her for questioning. Her fingers itch at the prospect of writing up notes on both the missing women, and Josie's pen pal relationship with the infamous Oliver Roberts. "Sounds good to me, boss."

Four

"Honey, I'm home!" Mac steps into the living room and tilts her head, turning the better of her two ears towards the home's interior. She holds her breath for a count of five, straining to hear even the smallest sound of life. The ice machine in the kitchen clatters noisily. The square, vintage metal clock in the dining room ticks each time its second-hand marches forward. The rest of the house is silent.

If all goes well, Sam won't be home for another hour, and both boys will be tied up at soccer practice until well into the evening. She locks the front door, drops her keys in the bowl on the entry table, but never loosens her clutch on the chocolate brown straps of her tote bag until she's locked inside the guest room that doubles as her home office.

She opens the heavy canvas bag at the end of the bed and retrieves the padded envelope that holds a slim thumb drive stuffed full of the communication records she requested from the prison between Oliver Roberts and Josie Douglas. The laptop comes out next, and she sets it up on the small desk in the corner. Finally, she retrieves the stack of missing persons files from Tarrell and fans them out across the bed, touching each of the missing women's photographs with her fingers. She wonders if any of them are still alive.

Her hand tests the door to make sure it's locked before she settles into the too-short chair pulled up to the desk. Butterflies flop against the walls of her stomach, and her chest tightens when her finger hovers over the laptop's touchpad. She'd only heard a few seconds of Josie's chat with Oliver before Tarrell burst into the office. And what she had heard made her skin crawl. It's not clear yet what their connection is, but unless Josie added prison pen-pals to her laundry list of volunteer activities, it can't be good.

There are so many files to review. E-mails, video and phone calls, scans of handwritten letters sent through the prison's mail system. Although Oliver's been in prison for decades, none of the files were more than three months old. Her contact at the prison said that's as far back as Oliver's records go. Everything else on Sheridan's servers has vanished. But she knows Josie's been in contact with Oliver much longer than three months. When she first started digging into Oliver's records, she'd received a report that showed Josie on his contact records for years.

Someone knows she's digging and is trying to cut her off. Thank God she had the foresight to print off a hard copy of that report and hide it in a locked drawer in her desk at work before the server was wiped clean.

She hovers the cursor over the file she had opened before and closes her eyes. She counts to three, taps hard on the touchpad, and when she opens her eyes again, the audio player has the selected file loaded and ready to play.

The sound of her heartbeat drumming in her ears is so loud she barely registers the front door slamming on the other end of the house. She might have questioned the thud of the heavy door, but the pitched bickering of Ryan and Robby is unmistakable.

Damn it, she should have had more time.

She closes the audio file and clicks on a scanned letter instead. She skims the letter, looking for anything important. The last few lines jump out at her.

Of course, I'm being careful. Don't worry about me becoming a thorn in your side. Richard is grooming her, and she'll be ready when the time comes. If she refuses, we'll persuade her.

Keep the faith, Brother.

J.

Mac slumps in her chair, dumbstruck. Brother? She's long wondered if Oliver Roberts' hold on people is tied to his religious dogma. Catholics and Latter-day Saints call one another "Brother" and "Sister." The Brethren movement call others in their faith familiar family names, too, even if the outside world calls them "the Garbage Eaters."

She stares at the blank wall in front of her, but sees a map of people, timelines, and questions transposed over the off-white paint. Mental copies of every document she's ever seen on Oliver Roberts hang in neat rows along the borders of the phantom evidence board. She sees his past spread in winding trails, like a long-forgotten map. Places he worked. His deceased wife. She blinks, and like a microfiche film, the map winds backwards. She sees where he grew up. His parents.

Oliver Roberts was an only child, wasn't he?

A fist lands heavy against the locked door, breaking her concentration. The details of her memories fade into a gauzy mass of unfocused vision and she blinks hard, refocusing on the speckled popcorn texture of the bare wall.

"Mom, you in there?" The doorknob trembles in its housing. "The door's locked."

"Locked, you say? Crazy. It's like I needed privacy, or something." She rolls her eyes and closes the document before opening the door. Ryan stands inches from the threshold, staring down at her. When did he get so tall?

He looks over her head at the mess of files spread across the guest bed's micro-suede comforter. "What are you doing in there?"

"Working." She leans into him until he steps backwards, then steps through the doorway and pulls the door closed behind her. "What can I do for you?"

He doesn't speak for a moment, his expression tightening with thought. His jaw works slowly, and Mac braces herself for more questions about her work. Did he see the victim's photos on the bed? He knows what kind of work she does, and that she can't give him details about open investigations. But knowing the rules doesn't stop a child from worrying about their mother poking around, looking for dead people.

"I can't find my soccer shorts." Ryan bites his lip anxiously and the skin of his forehead tightens. He's concerned, but not over the women's photos spread out in the closed-up office.

"Where did you look?"

"Everywhere." Mac lifts an eyebrow and for once he can read her disbelief. His hands fly up defensively. "I really did! Honest!"

The corners of Mac's mouth tug so heavily downward, her chin tightens and pulls back to make room. The likelihood that he's scoured the house in the few minutes he's been home is next to impossible. "Look again."

Her other son, Robby, sprawls across the couch, a video game controller already glued to his hands. "I'm starving. When's dinner?"

The thought of food sends Mac's stomach into a spasm. The mere mention of it is enough to make her sick. Her mind shifts from the missing soccer shorts to the clapping walls of her stomach. Has she eaten today? There were donuts at the office, but she'd passed on them. Her stomach twists as the pastries dance in her mind's eye. She can't tell if she's going to eat the pantry clean or throw up. "When you get up to cook."

"I'm hungry too," Ryan complains.

"As I recall, I've taught both of you how to use every appliance in the kitchen. You know where we keep the…" the images that flash in her mind when she thinks of 'food,' sends acid climbing up the back of her throat, and she searches her brain for an alternative word. "…ingredients."

Mac regrets the harshness in her tone even before she hears the boys' shocked gasps. She stops abruptly, an apology for her brusque impatience on the tip of her tongue. But she's too sick to her stomach to cater to these teenagers, who are old enough to be full-fledged husbands in some countries. She sucks in a shaky breath and lets a string of words out rapid fire while her stomach does backflips. "Turn off the TV and feed yourselves. I'm taking a shower. Whatever you put together, make enough for your dad to eat when he gets home, too."

Ryan and Robby harmonize in a teenage groan so overflowing with teen angst that Mac can almost feel her ovaries curl in on themselves. There's no time to marvel at the sensation. She tastes the acid bubbling its way up her esophagus. She sucks in a gulp of air to keep her insides in, but she looks frantically around for something to throw up in, if she doesn't make it to the bathroom in time.

She grabs her purse from the coffee table and yanks it open. She shoves her face into the opening and rushes towards the hallway, and then to the bathroom door.

"But Mom…" Robby says from behind her.

She swallows a stinging hot bubble of bile and inhales deeply, willing herself to not throw up. "Figure it the fuck out!"

Before they complain again, she's racing down the hall. The second she's inside the bathroom, she slams the door shut and spins the lock in its housing to make sure nobody will walk in and surprise her. She chucks her still-clean purse on the counter, flips the lid of the toilet upwards, and heaves. The walls of her stomach collapse on themselves, every muscle in her abdomen and lower back contracting with such force that her muscles feel like they're on fire. Mac's entire body trembles when she props herself over the toilet bowl. Disappointing clumps of pale green spittle drop from her mouth into the water.

Damn it, she can't even throw up right.

The next few moments are an agonizing mix of dry heaves and tears. When it's finally over, Mac gasps for air, clinging to the side of the toilet, struggling to keep herself from collapsing to the unwashed tile floor. Her throat and nose are raw, and her eyes water from the stink of the bile that escaped her otherwise empty stomach. Her fingers shake so badly, she can hardly hold the toilet's lever, but she manages to get the water swirling in the bowl and rests her head against the lifted toilet seat to watch it disappear down the drain.

It feels like an eternity before she finds the strength to push herself up from the toilet. She shrugs at herself in the mirror. She is already in the bathroom; may as well take her shower now. She has her shirt halfway off when her arm flails, knocking her purse off its precarious perch on the counter. The bag's contents explode across the bathroom floor. A now wasted tin of mints, half-melted lipstick, her wallet bursting at the seams. And a slim, pink pregnancy test box.

Exhausted, nauseous, and done with the day, Mac leaves the bulk of the mess for later. But she's been waiting all damn day for enough privacy to take another pregnancy test. She retrieves the box and rips open the cardboard before dumping the stick and its instructions onto the counter. The instructions are clear enough, so she picks up the stick, straddles the toilet seat, and takes a deep breath. She pushes a trickle of urine over the collection pad and prays to whatever gods are wandering the universe, that it's enough.

Mac turns the shower on full blast and tendrils of steam reach their fingers into the air while she finds her phone among the mess on the floor. Her finger hovers over the button to start the countdown timer and she glances over at the test. A wet line advances across the indicator, leaving a portion of a positive sign in its ever-expanding wake.

Not even thirty seconds in, and it's already showing positive? "Shit."

Tears come fast and hard while her mind fills with the buzz of a million thoughts all at once. She's too tired for another baby. Too old. She put her life on hold for so many years when the boys were little, and she's only just gotten used to being herself independent of them again. She has a life outside of motherhood. A job. More than a life, more than a job. She has a career with the FBI that stops the worst of the worst from hurting innocent people. Going into the office doesn't just mean pulling a paycheck. It means protecting victims and their families every damn day she clocks in.

How many mothers can say that?

Mac peels her blouse over her head and blows her nose on it before tossing it to the floor. She climbs into the shower, forcing herself to stand under the bite of the too-hot water. The sharp sting of a thousand hot droplets overwhelms her discomfort, forcing the aches and pains of the day into the background. The fog in her mind lifts a little as steam continues to roll into the room, and she turns to let the water massage her neck and shoulders.

What is Sam going to say? The question sends an alarm ringing through the back of her brain, and a new wave of anxiety screams through her veins. She's going out of her mind with worry and strife over the possibility they'll have another mouth to feed, and she'll lose the life she's fought so hard to build for herself, but he'll probably be ecstatic. But maybe there's a chance he'll understand how she feels. She can't really be the only one enjoying the freedom of having kids old enough to fend for themselves, can she?

Maybe she can reason with him. Sam's been on a journey of self-discovery since she's been back at work. Filling all the empty evenings and weekends with teaching himself to knit, learning to slow-cook meats in the smoker he built in the back yard, and going to open mic nights at a brew pub downtown. He won't want to give all that up, will he?

Mac presses her hands against the shower's tile, hangs her head, and lets the water run over her. This pregnancy could ruin everything. Zap the kids' meager college funds. Take them away from organic produce and free-range meat, and put them back on the ramen and potato diet they subsisted on when the kids were little. She looks down at the yellow and green hues of the sunflowers tattooed on the inside of her calf. What if her leg swells and it disfigures the beautiful art she finally felt free to invest in for herself?

Her tears are carried away by the hot water splashing against her cheeks. What if she doesn't tell him? She could just call her doctor tomorrow after the meeting with Vernonia PD. Make the whole mess go away. As far as everyone outside her body would be concerned, it would be like the pregnancy never happened. She turns over the idea in her mind. Could she bring herself to carry the weight of this kind of decision on her own?

She shuts off the water, wraps a towel around herself, and reaches for the pregnancy test. The plus sign hasn't gone away, despite the passing of time, and she has a feeling it's there to stay. There's no way to convince herself this one could be a false positive. The small thump of the plastic hitting the inside of its box hits her in the chest with the weight of a sledgehammer. She shoves the instructions in, too, and drops the whole bundle deep into the abyss of her purse.

Too distracted to notice her wet head dripping a trail of water behind her, Mac picks up the purse, holds it tight against the towel bunched at her chest, and carries it to her bedroom. She can't bring herself to throw the test away, but seeing it in her purse every time she goes fishing for her keys won't do, either. She checks the hall to make sure no one is lurking, then closes the door and shoves the package holding her heavy secret into the back of her underwear drawer, covering the package with a bundle of socks and panties.

With her secret safely hidden, she can finally take a full breath. She realizes how cold she is, still dripping from the shower. She quickly dries herself with the towel before wrapping the length of her soggy hair in it and putting on the fuzziest pajamas she can find.

The air carries the hint of something burning, and she follows the charred scent to the kitchen where she finds Ryan piling a mountain of overly crispy chicken nuggets on a platter. Robby scoops macaroni and cheese into bowls. Mac leans against the doorway's frame and watches Sam snap photos of his burgeoning chefs.

"What a treat to come home to. Grandma and Grandpa are going to love this when they see the photos on my socials!"

"Looks good." Mac's voice croaks over the words and she clears her throat in hopes no one will notice how close she is to crying.

"It sure does!" Sam's thumbs tap furiously away at his phone, already writing his social media post. He doesn't even glance in Mac's direction. "How was your day?"

"Long."

"Dinner's served!" Ryan announces with a grin. He picks up two bowls of macaroni and cheese, leading the way to the dining room table.

Mac and Robby help move the rest of the food while Sam moseys after them, his attention still glued to his phone. The boys dig into their dinner without another word, but Mac eases herself into her chair and sits back to watch Sam. His eyes sparkle in the light from his phone's screen, the corners of his lips turned up in a pleased grin. He really enjoys curating their lives for the world.

She can already see him hovering over a smiling baby with his phone, immortalizing every burp, sneeze, and fart for the masses. The image of a new child in Sam's arms makes Mac's stomach fold in on itself. She pushes her chair backwards, putting an arm's length between herself and the pungent odor of the processed chicken and reconstituted cheese.

"Thanks for dinner." She offers the boys as much of a smile as she can muster. "I'm not feeling well. I think I'll get a glass of water and go to bed early."

"You wan us tah save ya sum?" Ryan asks around a tumbling mouthful of food. The sight of his open-mouth chewing makes Mac's guts jump against her sternum.

"No, thanks." She stands from the table and moves past Sam, running her fingers through his hair. He breathes out a satisfied hum, and she kisses him on the head. "Have fun with your internet friends."

He sets the phone on the table beside his dinner and finally looks at her. His satisfied smile droops. "You're not eating?"

"I'm not feeling well." Mac lifts a corner of her mouth and presses her lips together. The downside of Sam's new obsessions… he hardly ever listens to her anymore.

Sam reaches up to touch her forehead, probably checking for a fever. Mac grabs him lightly around the wrist to stop him. “Not that kind of sick. Just worn out. The bad guys were rough at work today.”

Sam’s brows press together in sudden concern. “Do you want me to come with you? I can tuck you in and you can tell me about it?”

Mac lets go of Sam’s wrist and brushes her fingertips over her belly. She realizes what she’s done and sucks in a breath, hoping Sam hasn’t noticed. She’d rubbed her belly constantly with both boys, and she worries Sam might put the pieces together. “No, it’s okay. Enjoy your mac and cluck feast.”

She takes a step away from him, then remembers her conversation with Richard. “Oh, we’ve been invited to have dinner at Richard and Josie’s house tomorrow night. Are you free?”

Sam’s eyebrows lift in the same look of surprise he’d had the first day they met. “Are you asking me out on a date?”

Mac grins. “Looks that way.”

“Hot damn! Text me the deets, and I’ll see your fine ass on the flippity-floppity.” Sam’s smile is so wide, the corners of his eyes crinkle. Ryan and Robby groan in dramatic teenaged unison and Sam's grin folds into a frown. "What? That's what people say online."

"No they don't," Ryan says.

Mac walks away, chuckling to herself while the boys beg their dad to stop using whatever lingo dictionary he's found. She knows their pleas are falling on deaf ears, and he'll spend hours diving deeper into oddball slang to torture them with. That's just the type of dad Sam is.

Five

Mac runs through the FBI field office building, trying to make up for lost time. Nausea made every moment of her morning routine nearly impossible, and now she's late for the meeting with Vernonia PD. It didn't help that she spent the night pacing the house while Sam and the kids slept, blissfully unaware of her predicament. Or that she swore she heard her old midwife's voice cackle in her ear when she went to brew a pot of coffee.

"Caffeine isn't good for prenatal development! Do you want to be responsible for making a fat, diabetic, cardiovascular defunct person?"

The herbal tea in Mac's tumbler nearly sloshes straight out of its lid when she is hit by an invisible wall of stink near the break room. It smells like fish and sauerkraut have been microwaved in a mildewy sock, and it sends her stomach rolling. She covers her mouth and runs full-out down the corridor to the office she shares with Richard.

Her hand catches the latch, but between trying to keep her tea in her trembling tumbler, hauling the weight of her work tote in the crook of her elbow, and covering her nose and mouth, the handle merely snaps back in its housing. Only on the second try can she focus enough to get the damn door to unlatch, and she flings herself into the room the moment the door swings open. She glances around the room to find Richard glaring back at her from his desk with an annoyed expression, and a man in a short-sleeved button down looking at her with wide-eyed surprise standing behind his chair.

Acid suddenly burns its way up her throat like a geyser, and she coughs and sputters before finally swallowing the hot acrid liquid down. "Sorry I'm late," she stammers.

Richard only frowns, but his companion flinches as if startled by her harried entrance.

Richard looks over his shoulders and snaps his fingers to get the younger man's attention. "Ignore her. I need this computer fixed now." The man bobs his head obediently and leans over Richard's shoulder, reaching for the mouse and keyboard.

While the guy types away, Mac realizes he must be from IT. Richard watches the man's work with enough feigned interest to last the thirty seconds it takes Mac to dump her bag onto the floor by her desk, set down her tumbler of tea, and shrug off her jacket. Then he glowers at her. "Where were you? I couldn't figure out how to get logged in, so I had to call the helpdesk."

"It's been a crazy morning." Mac doesn't bother to embellish. She presses the power button on her own computer and glances up at the ancient clock on the wall. Thank God it isn't synced up to the same atomic timekeeping system all the computers and cell phones use. She knows if she checked her phone, she'd be late. But the weary office clock says she has three minutes to spare.

"All set up," the IT guy says. He stretches his back, easing out of the obviously uncomfortable position he was in leaning over Richard, and Mac is secretly glad she's too late to help with whatever problem he'd had. The IT guy catches Mac watching him and smiles. "Do you need help getting started, too?"

"No, thanks." She lifts her lips in what she hopes is a professional smile, though it is hard to tell what her face is doing with the burn still spreading at the back of her throat and her stomach turning to ash right there in her gut. She pounds her password into her computer and waves goodbye to the IT guy as he leaves the room. Her monitor comes to life with a slow glow, and she peers over at Richard. "I'll be online in just a minute."

When a notification for a critical update flashes across Mac's screen, making her computer unusable for the immediate future, she blows out a frustrated breath. "Why couldn't that have happened before the tech guy left?"

She waves off Richard's questioning look. His computer has connected to the video chat already. "Hello there. I think Special Agent Jones is having an issue. She'll be right on."

Mac gathers her files, snatches a pad of paper and a pen from her desk, and rolls her chair around the room until it stops beside Richard. She drops into the chair, scooting herself closer to Richard until she is in the camera's frame. She tries her best to hide her frustrated aggravation and smiles at Richard's poorly angled camera while she reaches out to adjust it so they are both sitting level on-screen. "Hey there. We'll just use the one webcam today."

"Good to see you," a woman says in one of the chat windows. The label on the window reads, "Detective Malone," and the man in the video window labelled "Detective Sharpe" chuckles.

Flushed with embarrassment at realizing they'd been looking at his cockeyed necktie instead of his face, Richard huffs an annoyed breath. "This is why I like phone conferences better."

Detective Malone, who Mac spoke to the day before, is a woman about Mac's age. She is wide-eyed and chipper looking, even through the lens of a digital camera. Sharpe, on the other hand, arranges a deep scowl beneath a layer of scruffy salt-and-pepper growth along his cheeks and jawline. He looks close to Richard's age, and just as rough around the edges, and Mac wonders if a similar juxtaposition is what people see whenever she and Richard enter a room.

“Thank you both for meeting with us this morning. We’ve got quite the mess on our hands. I trust Governor Carter filled you in on the details?”

“He did. We were surprised to see him yesterday.” Richard’s frown somehow manages to etch itself deeper. “Thank you for sending a fresh set of files over this morning.”

Mac hasn’t seen the complete case file yet and leans into Richard so she can better see the photos spread on the far side of his keyboard. “Do you think Jacqueline Carter’s disappearance is related to the missing persons reports she filed?”

“No.” Detective Sharpe’s frown looks like it’s trying to compete with Richards for severity. “We don’t even know if those other women really are missing. They’re beggars. Probably realized Vernonia’s a small town with light pockets and moved on.”

The way Detective Malone’s shoulders droop and face tightens belies an exasperated sigh, even if she is muted. The microphone icon on her screen changes to green and she says, “It’s hard to know if they’re related. We haven’t found any evidence either way. But it is a coincidence I’m working to better understand.”

"If they haven't 'moved on,' five women missing is one hell of a coincidence," Mac says.

Detective Malone lowers her eyes and nods. "All four of the women Miss Carter reported missing were under the age of twenty-five, were housing challenged, and were all staying in the same campground."

"Have you had any tips called in on any of them?" Richard asked. "Any Jane Does in the morgue you can match them up to?"

The look on Detective Sharpe's face shifts from disgruntled to smug. "Not a one. I'm sure they've moved on. Look, we're a tiny little town populated by a couple thousand loggers and church mice. When someone dies, everybody knows about it. It's not some mystery. As far as the tramps and panhandlers that have thumbed their way out here and taken over, we're not set up to track all their comings and goings."

"They're not tramps and panhandlers. They're unhoused families," Detective Malone mutters in a low tone that says she'd already corrected Sharpe more than enough times.

"Let's just call them homeless then," Detective Sharpe says with a grunt. "Apparently 'unhoused' is less offensive. It seems like a silly thing to get bent out of shape over, when we're talking about people who can't even get a job at Subway."

"Nobody can get a job at Subway. It went out of business." Malone closes her eyes and rubs her temples.

Richard rasps his own derisive grunt. He opens his mouth to say something more, but Mac shoots him a look and he closes it again. She turns back to the video chat. "What's your working theory on this thing if they are missing? Thoughts on motive?"

"I don't know." Malone sighs audibly this time and fatigue seems to pull the life out of her until she looks ten years older on the screen. "If these women are missing, no one aside from Jacqueline Carter has been looking for them. And, like my partner so helpfully pointed out," she glances bitterly off-screen, then lifts her shoulders in apparent exasperation, "we aren't set up to handle cases like this. A year ago, we had a half-dozen folks living permanently in tents at the campground on the edge of town. Now it feels like we have people on every sidewalk, sleeping in every doorway, and digging for scraps in each garbage can in Vernonia."

"We're not even sure how most of them got here," Sharpe adds. "There's a bus that comes around a couple times a week and drops them off. Not sure where the bus comes from, but if you believe the stories the beggars tell, they're being rounded up in Portland and dumped here."

Mac leans back in her chair. She'd just read an article about Portland's miraculous clean-up of its homeless problem. The article had painted the city as being a beacon of social fairness; moving people from the street into stable housing through programs designed to get people back on their feet. The tent cities that had covered most of downtown and filled the shadows under each of the city's twelve bridges, had all but disappeared. Filled instead with new art installations and boulder gardens designed to be both visually appealing, and less comfortable for campers.

"So let me get this all straight," Richard says. "We have the city of Vernonia being loaded up with down-and-out folks, possibly because the city is trying to get them to move. Four young women who may have decided Vernonia isn't the best place to live, and probably moved on. And then we have Governor Carter's daughter, who worries enough about the homeless people to report them missing when she can't find them, and she disappears out of the blue." Richard rubs his face while he talks, as if pushing the thoughts around in his brain will help him sort them out. "Do we know where Jacqueline Carter was last seen?"

Mac flips through the printed cellphone snapshots attached to each of the missing persons reports. Despite the tattered clothing and unwashed faces, it is easy to see the women for what they are. Young, college-aged women down on their luck and held down by a system designed to ignore the neediest victims. The colors of the photos seem to brighten as tears sting the corners of her eyes. The thought of what fates might have befallen them in the time since they'd disappeared…

Visions of dozens of crime scenes Mac has borne witness to flood her mind. What if they've been defiled like one of the countless other victims she's come across? Her nostrils fill with the stench of death and her stomach turns sour.

"Have you found any bodies?" Mac's tone is a wisp of its typical authority, but this time she doesn't bother to hide it.

"None have been reported," Detective Sharpe answers. He leans back in his chair.

"I asked around the camps and no one said they saw anything suspicious," Malone adds. "And checking social media pages was a dead end. It's not like the camp has Wi-Fi."

The air in Mac's throat solidifies until her lungs feel like they are filled with cement. Her hands shake, and she drops the reports and photos onto Richard's desk. A sharp pain weaves around her chest like barbed wire, and she mouths the words, "I'm sorry."

Richard, Sharpe, and Malone look back at her with concerned faces.

"Mac?" Richard places a hand on her shoulder. "You okay?"

The mounting tension that pulls her shoulders towards her ears makes the muscles in her neck feel like they might snap when she shakes her head. She works her jaw and pushes a breath out that feels like gravel. "I need a minute."

She gets to her feet and tries to think of something to calm herself down. Her hands shake violently now, and when she crosses her arms and shoves her hands under her armpits, it only serves to make her arms tremble. She tries to breathe through the nausea and rising bile, tries to swallow it back down her gullet, but it threatens to erupt right there in the office. She hurries on unsteady feet, out of the room, with one hand covering her mouth and the other gripping her stomach.

The bathroom stall door swings open just in time for the dry toast she had for breakfast to splat inside the toilet bowl. The partially digested mash tastes like bitter death and a tinge of acrid fear. She gags at the smell, intense pressure building inside her and fighting to get out. Mac presses her clammy hand to her forehead, searching for a fever that isn't there. She's never hoped to have norovirus before, but now she whispers a prayer to have her pregnancy mysteriously transform into a mistaken case of the flu.

Whatever parasitic cells might be clinging to her body are already making life too miserable to manage.

Hinges creak somewhere outside the toilet stall, and someone takes a few steps inside. "Mac?" Richard's voice holds a strange twinge of worry. "You okay in there?"

She peels her cheek away from the cool plastic toilet seat and waves a hand across the automatic flush sensor, thankful it didn't go off while she was eyeballs deep in the porcelain.

"Yeah, I'm alright." Her voice curls around the words with the haggard drag of a raw throat. "I'll be out in a minute."

Her partner's footsteps recede into the hallway and the heavy industrial door falls closed behind him. Mac uses a handful of toilet paper to wipe the cold sweat from her forehead and braces herself against the porcelain while she works to get her feet under her once more.

When she lets herself out of the stall, she catches a glimpse of herself in the mirror over the nearby sink. Even from a distance, she looks exactly as miserable as she feels. Her clammy skin glistens unevenly under the harsh fluorescent lights overhead. She staggers over to the faucet and washes her face with cold water, then combs her fingers through her hair.

The effort is a waste of energy. She looks just as haggard as before, but now her collar is wet with sink water, and her hair is frizzy. She trudges back to the office and Richard gives her a look of mixed concern and impatience as she slumps into her seat. She pushes the files she'd dropped onto his desk into a pile, and hands them to Richard as another wave of nausea passes through her. She blinks hard and when she focuses her attention, finds everyone watching her.

"I'm fine. Just something I ate. Can we get back to it?"

"Sure," Sharpe says, his voice tinged with skepticism at her excuse. "The last time Jacqueline Carter was seen, she was delivering food to the encampment at Rock Creek."

"Did Jacqueline volunteer with Vernonia's food bank?" Richard asks.

Malone shakes her head. "We don't have one. Volunteers come from some nonprofits based out of Portland, and a couple of churches in town will go around evangelizing to them here and there. If it weren't for those few volunteers bringing food out, everyone in those camps would probably starve to death."

Mac reaches for the stack of photos again. Each of the women Jacqueline was helping look eerily alike. They're each slender, with shoulder length hair in shades of brown or auburn. Their pale faces are gaunt, with a dark shadow of trauma painted on their eyes in shades of brown and green. If they'd all been cleaned up and stood in a row, she might have mistaken them for sisters. She scans the photos again and shakes her head. If she were twenty years younger, and these young women were dressed in choker necklaces and faded low-rise jeans instead of t-shirts and tattoos, they'd almost look like her. Thank God she's too old to fit this killer's prey list.

Only one of the photos stands out in the spread. Jacqueline, with her rich umber skin and glossy black hair, doesn't match the profile. "What if Jacqueline was right and they were taken? Look at these women. They're so similar. We might have a serial kidnapper on our hands."

"If that's the case, what do we do?" Malone's face is tense with worry, but not surprise. Mac has the feeling she's been chewing on the possibility for a while.

"It's just a coincidence," Sharpe says tersely. "We've got a good town full of good people. We haven't had a single kidnapping in all my years here. We're not about to start having them now."

"Unfortunately, you don't get to pick whether now is a good time for kidnappers, or not." Richard's tone is tight, but a sense of ease rolls off of him. He is comfortable being in charge, and he and Mac are now the expert consultants on these cases. "If we've got a serial kidnapper on our hands, it's our duty to catch the guy before anyone else gets hurt."

Richard leans back in his chair, his expression smug and self-important. He weaves his fingers behind his head and reclines a few inches farther. "We don't usually work missing persons cases. We work missing bodies. But we have resources that might help if something underhanded is going on."

Detective Sharpe nods. "I know this all falls outside your wheelhouse, but we're desperate here. The governor's daughter went missing in our town, and that's not exactly what we hope to be famous for, you know?"

Mac thinks back to before she joined the bureau, when she was nothing more than a stay-at-home mom with a stubborn streak. Her son and Jacqueline Carter were kidnapped along with an entire campground full of kids, and she'd been lucky enough to find them. She hadn't had her son back in her arms more than a half hour before the news crews descended on her, pushing her and her family into an unwanted spotlight. "We don't get to choose what we're famous for."

The glimmer of pride in Sharpe's eyes dims. It's subtle, but the veil of hope that he and his little town would be able to escape scrutiny seems to vanish. "That may be true. But if we can find her, maybe we can turn things around. Then we can all rest easy."

"I think we should start by finding out what connections there are with these other women," Mac says. "Do some real legwork to find out how well they knew Jacqueline Carter, and each other."

Sharpe glowers at her. "I know you big city folk are always looking to connect the dots, but this is a simple, friendly little town, not some back alley chop-shop. How many times do I have to tell you it's a dead end? These women got bored, couldn't find whatever drugs or cash they were looking for, and took off. Simple as that."

"Based on what I'm looking at, you've got four women who look alike, in the same age range, and missing from the same area. Looks more like a flashing neon sign than a dead end," Mac's mouth thins to a straight line and heat rises in her cheeks.

"You work with that serial murderer," Malone says timidly. "The one who tried to convert people before he killed them. Maybe he could help?"

"Oliver Roberts," Richard dips his chin. "I wouldn't say we work with him. But occasionally we consult him to understand how a killer thinks, what his next move might be." He shakes his head. "But we don't take him victim files and ask him to help us figure out why someone would kidnap them."

What Malone is proposing, asking Oliver to help them find a link between the women, is dangerous. Unsavory. Bringing victim files to him would be like bringing a trunk load of free heroin to an addict. On the other hand, if anyone in the world can tell them exactly what's attractive about a set of victims, and figure out who might be next, Oliver can. "It's a good idea," Mac says.

"Oliver Roberts is not available." Richard grips the armrests on either side of his chair until his knuckles turn white.

Mac lifts a finger, signaling Malone and Sharpe that she needs a moment, then reaches over to Richard's mouse and clicks the mute button. She looks at Richard like he's one of her boys, stubbornly defying her out of spite. "I'm sorry, I was under the impression that Oliver Roberts is a prison inmate, and therefore is free for us to call on whenever we please. I didn't realize he had a full social calendar."

"What if Sharpe is right, and the women have just skipped town? You don't know how far Ollie's reach is. If we dangle these women in front of him, it may set him off. You're the one who keeps trying to convince me he's luring other killers to do his dirty work. And you want to give him a list of lost, vulnerable women to track down?" Richard asks.

"You really think they're still alive?" Mac rests her palm on the stack of reports. "My gut tells me they're corpses. And if that's true, then you know there will be more victims. It's only a matter of time. We can either wait it out and hope Mr. Not-My-Town is right, or we can see if Oliver has some insight on what we might be dealing with."

Richard straightens his back, seeming taller and more resolute. His scowl deepens and a sense of anxious fury settles into the air between them. "We can't just show up and yank him around like a dog on a chain. When I talk to Ollie, it's on his terms, not mine."

"Maybe it's time for that to change." Mac clicks the button to turn the microphone back on.

"We've discussed it, and we'll talk to Oliver Roberts. See what he has to say."

Richard looks at her with stony frustration. His shoulders sag, then he looks at the screen where the detectives sit, watching them. "There's no harm in asking. But we'll put feelers out beyond Roberts, just in case he isn't feeling keen on helping."

"Thank you," Detective Malone says with a curt nod. "That's good enough for me. I don't really care how we find out what happened to these girls, so long as we find them."

"I think you are all wasting time with these homeless women. But we've got to get Jacqueline Carter back if we have a hope of keeping our jobs," Sharpe says.

Mac battles the urge to roll her eyes at Sharpe while Richard nods in agreement. "If she's out there, we'll find her. Special Agent Jones and I will review what you've sent, reach out to our contact, and get back to you with our findings. We'll talk soon."

Malone waves a silent goodbye and Sharpe's window in the monitor goes dark. Richard disconnects from the meeting and turns to Mac. "Thanks for volunteering us to talk to

Ollie. Next time, when I say no, I'd appreciate it if you didn't walk back my decision."

"There's no good reason not to pick his brain on this. It's been months since we've been to visit. You used to drag me down there every few weeks to sit in on your talks. We're overdue for a chat, aren't we?" Mac makes the observation as nonchalantly as possible, though the hairs stand on the back of her neck. Richard might not have been talking to Oliver Roberts, but Josie has. Does Richard know? The question teeters on the tip of her tongue, but she swallows it before it can escape.

"Fine. I'll get an interview scheduled." Richard removes his reading glasses and scratches at the three-day fuzz on his cheek. He looks like hell. The bags under his eyes are heavy, his skin patchy and dry, and his bloodshot eyes are proof he's been hitting the bottle or missing sleep. Perhaps both. Apparently, Mac isn't the only one with a tension headache tugging on her brain like an anvil tangled in a spider's web.

Richard looks back at Mac with concern. "What got into you earlier? I've never seen you run off to the little girls' room so fast. You feeling okay, kiddo?"

"Yup." Mac breaks away from his gaze and focuses on shuffling and re-stacking the case files on his desk. "Must have been something I ate."

"If you're sick, I can talk to Josie. She'll be heartbroken to put off dinner, but I'm sure we can wait."

Mac could be bleeding from her eyeballs, and she still wouldn't miss this chance to talk to Josie. See how she behaves when Oliver Roberts comes up in conversation, and plant some questions that might help her find out why Josie is in contact with the notorious killer. She is just about to say so when Richard leans closer, the worry lines etched between his eyes deepening. A whiff of burnt aluminum, steer manure, and wilted roses claws at her sinuses.

She covers her nose and mouth with her hand and leans as far away from Richard as her chair allows. "Oh my God. What is that smell?"

Richard's eyebrows scurry up his forehead and he lifts his jacket to smell under his arm. "I don't smell anything but my cologne. Sandalwood and rose, same as always."

"I think it's gone bad," Mac croaks. Her stomach climbs into her throat and she barely has time to yank the trash bin out from under Richard's desk before dry heaving.

"You're sick." Richard shakes his head. "I'm calling it. Dinner's put off for a couple days. You take the rest of today off. I won't be able to get us out to see Ollie until tomorrow, anyway. We're only running support on this Jacqueline Carter case, so it doesn't matter if you're reviewing these files at your desk, or in bed." He takes the stack of file folders and hands them to her. "I've got the digital copies, and I'll find somebody around here to help me get them printed out."

Mac wipes spittle from the corner of her mouth. "No, I'll be okay. I'll just go wash up and be right back."

She pushes her chair away from the desk and moves to stand up, but Richard grabs her by the arm. "No. Go home. I don't want to catch whatever bug is eating at your insides. We won't be any use to Vernonia PD if we're both sick."

Her shoulders drop when defeat tugs at her spine. She pushes her chair back around the room to her desk. She doesn't want to miss a second of this action, but home is the place she wants to be. Once her things are packed and her desk is locked, she flings her bag over her shoulder and turns on her heel to leave.

The floor must have tipped forty-five degrees underfoot because she keels to one side and starts to fall. She grips the edge of her desk to steady herself while Richard scrambles to his feet. He catches her by the elbow, and she leans into him, breathless, and woozy when the room turns right-side-up again.

Sweat drenches her button-up blouse, and her mouth is wet with nauseous saliva by the time the dizzy spell passes. Mac shakes her head to clear the fuzzy cotton at the edges of her vision. “Well, Richard, let’s hope this thing isn’t contagious. If you catch what I’ve got, Josie might throw a tantrum, and we’d all be having a lot of interesting conversations.”

Richard looks her over, confusion painted across his worried expression. “I don’t know what you’re talking about, but sit down. I’m calling the front desk. We’ll get a car to take you home.”

Mac sags into her chair, too worn out to pretend she feels fine. She salutes him. “Yes, Sir.”

Six

Richard side-eyes Mac where they sit at a table in a private interview room. She looks less green around the gills than the day before, but there's still something off about her. A thread of paternal worry weaves through him. She's strong, experienced, and a force to be reckoned with most days. But Richard raised two independent women of his own, and there are moments he can see the cracks in her veneer. He silently wonders who will support her through the grit of this job once he's gone.

There's plenty of time to ponder Mac's fate. They've already waited a half hour in the private interview room for Ollie, but that's expected. Nobody in the Federal Correctional Institution in

Sheridan, Oregon is ever in a hurry. Richard fights the urge to slouch sideways in his chair, the familiarity of this place resting on his bones as tenuously as in his own home. While Mac has been to the prison with him several times, she still sits stock-straight in her chair, hands folded in her lap. All business.

Will she ever feel the disturbing ease of being in this place, the way he does? After an entire career spent walking through prison cell blocks and exercise yards, the tough steel and cinderblock buildings are well within his comfort zone. The higher-ranking corrections officers are old friends, and even the elder inmates feel like lifelong companions. The realization sends a spark of restlessness alight in his belly. Despite his best efforts, he'd draped himself across the industrial metal chair as if it were as comfortable as his own leather wingback at home. Uneasy with the familiarity, he straightens his spine, plants his feet on the floor, and knits his fingers together in his lap.

Another half hour passes before sounds of movement leak through the metal door. A moment later, it swings open on ungreased hinges. Mac shifts her weight from one side to the other in the seat beside him, and Ollie shuffles into the room.

Richard nods his thanks to the corrections officer that brings Ollie through the jail. Ollie settles into the chair across from Mac and the officer leaves the room, slamming the door shut behind himself.

Ollie's soft eyes and warm smile across the table are as welcoming as a priest's at Sunday Mass. "Richard. Mackenzie. This is a pleasant surprise."

Richard reaches to shake his old friend's hand, and the cuffs still clasped around Ollie's wrists jangle against the table's edge. "How are you?" Richard's tone is too friendly, and he clears his throat to reset it. Hiding their closeness from Mac has been a tough job, and it's not one that he thinks has been successful. He lets go of Ollie's hand and wipes his palm against his pant leg with purpose, hoping Mac will see the motion as a signal of abhorrence.

"Can't complain," Ollie says with a smile. He looks over at Mac. "And how are you, Mrs. Jones?"

"Call me Special Agent Jones." Mac makes the correction without answering Ollie's question.

"Of course. My apologies." Ollie's gaze drifts to Richard. The deep wells of his pupils bore into Richard's soul, where a bud of kinship seems to bloom forever. "What brings you by this afternoon?"

"A case." The manilla folder sounds like leaves rustling in the still air when Richard slides it across the tabletop.

In the small motion of a lifted eyebrow, Ollie drops a decade of age from his features. His wrinkles smooth, his eyes brighten, and Richard feels a sense of pride at piquing his old friend's interest. "One of mine?"

"I don't know. This looks like something different. A potential kidnapper up north in Vernonia." Richard's tone softens, his voice hushed with a note of conspiracy.

"How many bodies?" Ollie asks. He runs his fingers along the file folder's spine with the tenderness of a new lover and lifts the cover with a careful touch that doesn't leave a crease in the heavy paper. Mac stiffens in her chair, and she sniffs a harsh breath, but the tension between Richard and his mentor turns almost sensual.

"None," Mac announces, the sound of her voice cutting too loud through the heavy sound of Ollie's aroused breathing. "Like Richard said, these are missing persons. Four homeless women, and a politician's daughter."

"Vagrants and elites. What a delicious combination." Ollie's voice was a whisper. He touches Jacqueline Carter's photograph with his fingertips, caressing the curve of her smiling cheek as she proudly holds a trophy up towards him. "She has outdone herself, hasn't she?"

"Outdone herself? Do you know this girl?" Mac's tone has the bite of a mother bear when she asks the questions. She leans forward and Richard rests a hand on her shoulder to keep her in her seat.

"When the homeless women were reported missing, local police assumed they'd moved on." Richard is careful not to disturb Ollie's petting of the photograph when he slides the rest of the paperwork out from under Jacqueline Carter's packet. Bringing all the paperwork to this meeting would have been a confidentiality nightmare, so he had Mac create basic profiles using only publicly available information relative to the cases. Richard hopes the limited information they give Ollie will be enough. Richard finds the page he's looking for, a timeline of Jacqueline's last known activities released on the news that morning. "When this girl kept pushing for them to find the others, she disappeared, too. Now people are asking questions. We want to know what happened to her. To all of them."

Ollie's eyes lift from the photograph, and he smiles at Mac. His pupils widen, his gaze growing sharp, and Richard feels Mac flinch as if she's been struck. Richard remembers how he'd felt in the beginning, watching Ollie transform from a slight, inconspicuous man into a predator before his eyes.

Back then, the transformation sent chills down Richard's spine and made a lump of dread sink through his gut. But now, Richard feels the room sharpen, and his mouth waters with anticipation. Ollie is about to send them down another thrilling rabbit hole, and Richard is excited to pick up the trail.

Moving so fluidly Richard might be dreaming, Ollie licks his lips and reads through each of the possible victims' profiles. "What a beautiful collection. Interesting that you are here with no bodies to show. But then, with playthings like these, I might be reluctant to let my collection go."

Mac clears her throat, bringing Ollie back from whatever twisted thoughts he's lost himself in. Ollie gingerly closes the folder and gives Richard a playful wink. He draws the entirety of the folder into his lap, below the table.

"What are you doing?" Mac asks. She braces her palms on the tabletop and rises an inch out of her seat.

"Taking these beauties back to my cell. I'll need time with them, if their souls are going to speak to me."

"We can't leave active case files with you." Mac's heavy voice drips with venom. If Ollie hears her through his predatory high, he doesn't react.

"Oh, yes. We are going to have a fine time together."

"She's right, Ollie. This isn't a game. The file is here to discuss here and now." Richard reaches an open palm across the table. Ollie looks at him, and a silent conversation passes between them. If Mac weren't here, Richard would have brought the real files, and would have had no problem leaving them behind. He hopes Ollie will understand. Until Mac is fully aligned with them, her knowledge of what normally happens within these meetings might undo them both.

Ollie's eyes flash with dissent, but when Richard curls his fingers, beckoning him to return the file, he lifts it to the tabletop with a sigh.

Mac reaches across and snatches the folder before Richard lays a finger on it.

"Keep them safe for me, will you?" Ollie says to her with a sinister smile.

Mac quickly flips through the pages, ensuring everything is still there. "In your experienced opinion, why would someone be targeting homeless women?"

"What kind of experience are you talking about, Special Agent Jones? Hmm?" Ollie brings his palms together, tapping his fingertips against one another in a slow rhythm.

He toys with Mac, and Richard glances over at her. A knot tightens in his stomach. Between the red creeping up her neck and the tightness in her jaw, it won't take much more poking to make her explode.

"Ah, right," Ollie says quietly. "You must be referencing all those people I killed. Some of them were homeless, you know. But, I confess, I'm no mind reader. Give me a week or so to play around with these ladies in my head. I'll see what I can come up with."

“Take a guess now.” Mac’s mouth barely moves when she speaks. The contours of her locked jaw strain under her skin.

Ollie’s gaze roams over her hungrily, eyes shiny like two-way mirrors. It is a knowing expression, like he’s letting a secret float in the air between Mac and himself. He licks his lips as if tasting the deliciousness of whatever words he holds back.

A moment later, it is as if the demon inside Oliver Roberts loosens its grip. His expression relaxes, the predatory light in his eyes gives way to softness and warmth. “I’d hate to give you any misinformation. Send you off the wrong way. All I have here is time. Allow me to use a bit of it to ponder your kidnapper, and maybe I can help you sort it out.”

Ollie tips his head towards Richard. “He was reluctant to work with me in the beginning, too, you know. But he realized that the information tucked inside my head is too precious an asset to ignore. I don’t ask for much in return. A little time, bits and pieces of information that I can use for my own entertainment. Richard could see it wasn’t too much to ask when I was handing him a glowing career on a silver platter. I’ll do the same for you, if you give me a chance." Ollie smiles knowingly, like a poker player holding a royal flush watching his competitors dump their pockets into the pot. "I have a good track record helping Richard. He'll vouch for my usefulness."

"I think we've spent enough time here. Thank you, Ollie." Richard pushes his chair back and stands, looking at Mac and tilting his head towards the door. "Let's get out of here, shall we?"

As Mac lifts out of her chair, Oliver reaches across the table with both shackled hands and grasps her wrist. "Wait just a moment, will you, Special Agent Jones? I'd like a private word, if you don't mind."

Mac shuffles her feet over the concrete, muscles tense and eyes wide. If she were a jackrabbit, she would bolt. But she lowers herself back to the plastic and steel seat.

Richard raps on the interview room door. If Mac is going to take over for him, she'll have to get used to being handled by Ollie on her own. Richard has protected her from Ollie for too long as it is. Time for her to be left alone with the wolf, and see if she makes it out alive.

The door screeches open, and he looks at her. "I'll be right outside if you need me."

Mac dips her chin, the only notable movement of consent in her otherwise frozen body. Richard turns to the guard. "They need a few minutes."

The guard nods and waves him into the hall. Once the door is secure behind them again, Richard nods to the next door in the hallway. "I'd like to watch my partner's interview with Mr. Roberts. Will you let me into the viewing room?"

Moments later, Richard settles into a padded office chair to watch Mac and Ollie's conversation on a large flat screen TV hanging on the wall. The camera angle is shit, but the mic is good enough to pick up the tapping sound of Mac's nervous leg as it bobs up and down under the table. For a split second, Richard worries about someone watching the video's recording, but he reminds himself there's no need. The warden will make sure anything overtly troubling is removed, same as he always has.

"Are you all right, my dear?" Ollie asks not as her enemy, but as a man who's taken a concerned interest in her.

"I'm fine." She must have broken the spell of her fight, flight, or freeze response, because she finally tugs her wrist out of his grasp. "What do you want?"

The camera angle accentuates Ollie's features. His eyes are wide, his head tilting at an odd angle. He looks more like a top-heavy bird than a man. "Special Agent Jones, I have been pleasantly surprised with your performance over the course of your time with Richard. You have a quiet power to you. Fierce. Unmovable. So unlike your predecessor."

Mac looks directly into the camera as though she can feel Richard watching her. Ollie turns to follow her gaze. "Oh, yes. I imagine he is listening. See? You're ever so much more intelligent than he was when I first met him. I understand if you're reluctant to say anything that might hurt Richard's feelings, but I'm sure we can all agree that your shining star is why he is so unenthusiastic about retirement. He doesn't want to be forgotten."

"Flattery will get you nowhere with me." Mac folds her hands together and leans away from the table.

"I never thought it would." Ollie mirrors her movements, leaning back in his seat and weaving his fingers together. But while Mac's fingers clasp tightly with tense rigidity, Ollie twirls his thumbs one over the other as if he's bored. "I'd like to offer you something, Special Agent Jones. Something of great value. It will help both of us, if you accept it."

Mac glances at her watch. The rhythm of her tapping foot quickens. "I'm running out of patience, Mr. Roberts."

Ollie's smile broadens. His bright eyes crinkle and he licks his lips, a man who delights in the defiance. "Yes, let's cut to the chase. I'm offering my friendship. I am a useful tool for someone in your position. I have connections in the dark side of society that come in handy from time to time, and the criminal insight you so desperately need for cases like the one you're working now."

"You're a convicted serial killer, Mr. Roberts. I don't think there's a world where I'd choose a friend like you."

Ollie's smile falters. "Murderer or not, you have no idea how helpful I can be. We live in a dangerous world, and you've chosen a particularly perilous position within it. I can protect you, just as I've sheltered Richard all these years."

"I have plenty of protection, thanks."

He grasps her hand in his. "It isn't enough. But I can make things easier on you. Safer for your family. Imagine what it would be like to lose a child?" He smirks when she flinches. "Oh, that's right. You don't have to imagine. You've already lost a child. Kidnapped right from under your nose. Is that why these missing women mean so much to you? Do you feel responsible for them?"

Mac yanks her hand back a second time. "I can protect my family. I don't need your help."

"It's bound to get harder with the baby coming." Ollie's voice is low, but Richard still hears every word.

Richard's gaze ping-pongs between his partner and his closest friend. Ollie appears positively beside himself with delight, while Mac's cheeks have sunken, and her eyes bulge out as if she might be choking.

"What?" Mac and Richard whisper together.

Ollie leans forward, his voice dropping to a whisper. He says a few words that the microphone doesn't pick up. Then, "… becoming a new parent at your age, and at this moment in your career. It's risky. If you're going to keep up with the bad guys, and keep that fetus growing right where it belongs, you need a friend. Once Richard finally hangs up his hat, I'll need one, too."

"I'd rather die than be friends with someone like you." Mac's voice grates with frustration and her features harden.

"That can be arranged." Ollie pauses and the space between them crackles with tension. "We can help each other. I need news from the outside, someone to be my eyes and ears. And you need someone to watch your back, to ensure you make it home to your family in one piece each night."

Richard's heart climbs into his throat. She's pregnant? Why hasn't she said anything? And more importantly, how does Ollie know? He looks her over. She looks roughly the same as always. A little thinner, and a bit more tired, maybe. He remembers when Josie was pregnant. What a toll her changing body had taken. How will Mac juggle that, and keep showing up to poke around for dead bodies?

"No." Mac springs up from her chair and crosses the room to pound on the door.

"Suit yourself. When the devil drags you to hell with her, don't come crying to me," Ollie says with a cautionary sing-song tone. "She is wicked, you know. So much more dangerous than I have ever been."

Mac pounds the door a second time. Where is the guard? Richard clambers out of his chair when he sees Ollie leap from his own.

"She'll be so happy you refused my offer," Ollie says.

The door swings open and Mac rushes the opening just as Richard grabs the handle on the viewing room door.

"She'll be in touch!" Ollie calls out before the door slammed shut again.

Richard meets Mac in the hallway. She is flushed, out of breath, and her wild eyes search the area around them. "Bathroom?" she asks the guard.

"We don't have guest bathrooms in the secure areas. We'll have to get you out to the main lobby." The guard leads them back the way they'd come in.

"She's pregnant," Richard says through the huff of his burning chest. "There's got to be somewhere closer."

Mac gives him a knowing look, then casts her eyes away. The way she stared at the camera, he knew she suspected he was listening.

What would she have told Ollie if she hadn't worried about what he'd hear?

"The nurse's office is closer. I can take you there." The guard touches a door to their right, and looks at a nearby camera, nodding once. The door's lock clicks in its housing and the door pops open.

By the time they make it through two more hallways to the prison's medical center, Mac can hardly catch her breath. Her face is blotchy, and she leans heavily against Richard's arm as if she might fall over any second.

They are a few steps from the medical bathroom when Mac looks up at Richard with red-rimmed, watery eyes. "I need to go home."

She reaches towards the bathroom door, but her fingers fall short. All at once her legs fold under her. Richard manages to get an arm around her, but she pitches forward into the metal latch of the door's lockset. The dead weight of her rag-doll body threatens to pull him down. The guard shoves the door closed, away from her sagging body, grabs her side and together they ease her to the ground.

Richard kneels beside her and feels her forehead. She is burning up. "Mac? Can you hear me?"

Someone in scrubs drops to his side. "What happened?"

Richard's tongue seems to glue itself to the roof of his mouth. He shakes his head, unable to get the words out. The woman in thin blue scrubs reaches across him to rest her hand on Mac's forehead while she lowers her face to her chest. Before he knows what happened, he's been pushed aside while the medical technician tells the guard to call for an ambulance.

Ollie told her if she didn't take his side, she'd regret it. And not ten minutes later, she's blacked out inside the prison that holds him. Richard breaks out into a cold sweat. He had thought he was doing okay, all the years he's served Ollie. All the lies he's told, crimes he's ignored, and people he's hurt along the way. Ollie had saved his skin more than once. Gave Richard a career that brought fame and recognition. But what if Richard had made another choice?

His head hangs low and his shoulders sag. Mac isn't willing to sacrifice herself for Ollie's cause, and that might cost her everything. The wolves will be after her. And she has no idea just how many of them are out there.

Seven

Mac gags on the antiseptic stench seeping into her lungs. She wags her head back and forth but the mask strapped around her head only seems to pull itself tighter. The gurney beneath her rises with a jolt and snaps into place high above the painted concrete she's been lying on for the last half hour.

She hooks a finger around the elastic strap tangled in her hair and pulls the mask from her face. "This is unnecessary. It was just a fall." The EMT at her head looks at her with a passive expression, but she can see derision in his eyes.

"You hit your head when you fell. It's possible you have a concussion." The technician's eyes wander to her hairline.

“I don’t have time for a concussion.” Mac touches the throbbing spot to find a lump has formed. The dull soreness intensifies to a hot ball of agony and she hisses with equal parts of pain and frustration. She wants to find Richard and tell him to get her off the gurney. But when she tries to push herself onto an elbow, pain blossoms through her side. She bites back a groan, not wanting to admit that her fall has done her in for the day.

“Let’s get your mask back on.” The prison nurse who’d sat with her until the ambulance arrived leans over her with a maternal authority that even Mac can’t ignore. She is careful but firm when she readjusts the mask into place. But the way she ratchets the elastic strap down, it’s clear she’s not going to give Mac a chance to argue. Mac wonders if her firmness is a result of triaging unpredictable prisoners, or if she’s always been that way. The woman slips a hand over Mac’s middle, fiddling with something at the side of the mattress, but Mac’s attention is drawn to the ambulance technicians loading all matter of medical supplies back into their bag. Had they needed all of that just to check a bump on her head?

The EMTs wheel her casually out of the prison and into the parking lot where an ambulance sits idle at the front door. There are no spinning lights or racing anxieties. Just a fall and a bump on the head. No need to hurry.

But underneath the too-loud sound of flowing oxygen and plastic encased breathing, Mac's heart is pounding. Oliver Roberts knows she's pregnant, before her own husband does. How?

They push the gurney to the back of the truck, folding the legs up below her while they shove her inside. Richard and one of the crew clambers in on either side of her, and the doors slam shut, encasing them in the small, too-cramped box.

Richard appears from somewhere outside her view, and squeezes himself onto a waiting bucket seat, his knees pressing tight against the edge of the gurney. Everywhere Mac looks there are cabinets climbing down from the walls, and tools reaching towards her from their hooks and pegs.

The technician looms over her like an ancient tree threatening to fall over in the next gust of wind. Heat rolls off his body and when he leans in with an IV in hand, Mac feels like her skin will catch fire. The medical technician presses a needle into her and hooks the fluid bag on the claw above Mac's head.

Her chest tightens and white lights pop in her vision. Even with the oxygen blowing on her face in a cool, dry wind, she can't manage to take a breath. She didn't see where the IV bag came from. Had the technician pulled it from the truck, or had it been in the prison's infirmary? What if Oliver had access? He might have tampered with the bag. Will she die like the pregnant women at the St. Christopher Medical Center case she worked just a few months ago? Mac grabs the IV bag and twists it around, trying to find a label.

There are so many dead, and Mac is sure Roberts was a guide for Liam Miller's hand. Her heart bashes against her ribcage, fighting to get out. The words on the bag are fuzzy and the bright spots in her vision are in the way. She tries to suck in a breath, but her lungs won't expand. The damn face mask isn't working. Where is the oxygen?

"Stay still," the technician commands. He pulls the IV bag out of reach. "You can't touch that."

"I have to..." Mac tries to explain, but her words come out in a whisper. She must get closer to him so he can hear. When she tries to sit up, she is caught by a strap around her ribcage. They've tied her down. How had she missed that? She wriggles under the binding, an ache growing just under her ribs. Maybe it has always been there, this tightness in her belly. The wrenching of her heart. The twinge in her back. The sheer agony of her spine holding her together.

She fights against the restrictive belt. "Sam can't find out. Not like this," she mumbles into the mask.

"Can you get her to stay still?" the technician asks Richard.

He lays a heavy hand on her shoulder and presses her into the mattress. A blinding wave of helplessness rushes through her. She wants to scream, but when she opens her mouth, only a tired wheeze makes it through. A heavy crack splits between her eyes, so painful it makes her stomach flail against her other organs.

"I'm trying," Richard complains through an immovable scowl. "Mac, just lie down, will you?"

"We've got a fighter," the technician calls up front. The ambulance picks up speed, wobbling left and right as it weaves through traffic. Mac wants out. Out of everywhere. She battles the strap. The IV. Richard and the technician until the ambulance slams on its brakes and the doors fly open, letting in the light and air of the glorious outside.

Mac's stretcher is heaved from the truck, legs slapping the pavement, and then she's pushed through the open doors and down a hallway. Voices murmur behind the wall of sound from her heartbeat drumming in her ears. None of it makes sense until someone says two words: panic attack.

The vise-like grip on her lungs breaks free enough for a shallow breath. She holds it in and counts to four, and blows it out again. Panic attacks were a constant challenge when she was pregnant with Ryan. She knows what to do. With closed eyes, she takes stock of her body. Her head hurts like hell. Her neck, too. Every muscle in her body is tight, her hands and feet are freezing. Breathe in, count to four, breathe out.

"It's going to be okay," Richard says. Mac is glad she can hear him over her racing heart. "I called Sam. He's on his way. He'll be here to hold your hand in a little while."

"What?" Mac's eyes snap open. Sam is coming? She cranes her neck to look down the length of her body, focusing on the wrinkled fabric bunched around her middle. She imagines the tiny cluster of cells multiplying and mutating inside, an unseen bundle of threads arranging themselves like an arm and reaching up to flip her the bird.

Fucking great.

Eight

"Stay in that chair." The nurse checking Mac into the ER peers down her nose at Mac from across the intake counter. "You're a patient today, Mrs. Jones."

"I'll keep her in line." Richard palms the grips behind Mac and the wheelchair shifts.

Mac crosses her arms over her chest and bites her tongue. She'd fainted. So what? It's not like she can't walk right out of here if she wants to. Shouldn't the nurse be more worried about the person groaning in agony from the back corner of the waiting room?

The nurse scowls at Mac and then shifts her gaze up to Richard. "You'd better. If she bolts, you're responsible for catching her and bringing her back."

As if the hospital gods can hear Mac's internal complaints, a man enters through the sliding doors, coughing up a storm. He can barely stop his hands from shaking long enough to loop the elastic bands of a mask over his ears. His flesh is yellow from nose to nail, the color tinting his eyes and palms. People shouldn't be mustard colored. Someone should get *him* a chair. But he's allowed to walk to the other end of the waiting room without a second glance.

"How long is this going to take?" Mac asks.

"As long as it takes," the nurse answers. She turns her attention back to her computer, transcribing Mac's insurance card into the system. "You may as well get comfortable."

Once a hospital band is secured around Mac's wrist, Richard wheels her around and pushes her towards a bank of chairs in the center of the waiting room. Mac grabs at the wheels, hissing at the burn of the rolling plastic against her palms. She turns towards a sign with an arrow pointing towards the vending machine promised land.

"Where do you think you're going?" Richard asks, fighting for control of the chair.

Mac yanks herself forward and Richard sets the brake. He leans over her shoulder to see her better. "You heard the nice nurse lady. I'm under strict instructions to make sure you stay put."

"I'm hungry. I haven't eaten today. Bet that's why I fainted." She nods towards the sign. "I want to toss a few bucks in the machine."

"You sure you're not just trying to escape? Let's get you checked out. I promise, when they cut you loose, I'll take you out for a burger and shake." Richard's phone rings and he fishes it out of his pocket. He swipes at the screen to answer. "Sam? Hi. Thanks for calling me back…" Richard plunges a finger in his ear to hear better and turns away from her, taking a step closer to the windows to their right.

Mac tries to wheel herself away from him, but she can't reach the brake. What's the deal with this hospital making it so hard for a person in a wheelchair to get around? She slouches against the chair, heart sunk to her knees, and stomach threatening to erupt. Richard is giving Sam the play-by-play of her fiasco at the prison. "I gotta go," Mac says, though Richard isn't listening. She peels herself out of the oversized plastic chair, pulls the IV bag off the hook, and makes a mad dash towards the bathroom.

Richard shouts her name as she yanks the bathroom door open. The stale, chemical-laden waiting room was nothing compared to the sterile bleach-soaked air of the bathroom. The smell knocks into her like a punch to the face, stomach leaping in protest. Mac flings herself toward the counter and leans heavily on the sink's rim, gulping air, and willing her insides to stay put.

The nausea's edge dulls after a moment and Mac sets the half-empty drip bag on the counter before she turns on the faucet. A splash of cold water on her face pulls her back to her senses and she looks at the mirror while she steadies herself. The face looking back at her is gaunt and tired. The harsh fluorescent lights make her eyes appear sunken into her skull and highlight the dark circles beneath them. She looks like a ghost.

She holds her hands under the faucet and lets the water run until her knuckles ache from the cold, a stark contrast to the frustrated heat that burns through her veins and makes her body shudder like a volcano about to burst. Her knees threaten to buckle beneath her, and she grips the edge of the counter again while her heart races.

Behind her, the bathroom door groans on its hinges. In the mirror, Mac sees a woman in scrubs lean through the gap of the partially open door. “Mrs. Jones, we’re ready for you.”

“I’m not ready.” Mac’s shoulders sag and she splashes more water across her cheeks. She feels the woman staring at her back, which only adds to the fire of annoyed embarrassment raging inside.

“Vitals only take a few minutes, then you’ll have time to rest.” The nurse’s voice carries a tone of authority that needles Mac’s bristling nerves.

“I know you’re just doing your job, but you don’t understand.” Mac shuts the water off and forces herself to turn to face the nurse. “Me being here isn’t good. I can’t go with you. Once I’m back in the room, you or some other helpful person will figure out what’s wrong with me and everybody will get all worked up…” She sighs heavily and pulls a paper towel from the dispenser, letting the words hang while she dries her hands and dabs the water from her face. Why does she feel like unloading her burdens on this woman, when she can’t tell her own husband? “I already know what’s happening to me.”

"Oh?" The nurse lifts her eyebrows in a placating expression that isn't fully curious, as if she is used to humoring self-diagnosing patients.

The weight of Mac's secret is so great, it feels like she'll be pulled through the floor if she doesn't let it go. Her shoulders droop and her spine bows behind her ribcage.

"I'm pregnant." Mac forces the words past a lump in her throat. Her eyes sting and she blinks to keep her tears from spilling over. "At least, I'm ninety-nine percent sure. And I can't deal with that right now. You know what I do for work? I investigate serial murders. It's not a fun time. And now, my friend's daughter is missing, along with four other young women, and I'm supposed to find all of them. What if they're dead? I'll have to look my friend in the eye and tell him every horrible thing I find out about what happened to his little girl."

"But as messed up as that would be," Mac's voice rises, and cracks when she tries to manage it. "It'll be worse if my husband finds out I'm pregnant and tries to convince me to quit working so hard. Who's going to find those girls then? Inspector Douglas out there might have been the world's greatest investigator at some point, but these days, he can't find his way out of a paper bag without someone leading him by the nose. But if this case isn't solved, if those girls do die, it'll give him grounds to block my promotion for another million years. My case, my friend's daughter, my career, my entire life will be over if I can't show up a hundred and ten percent all day every day. I can't handle that right now!"

"Have you taken a pregnancy test?" The nurse's voice is soft, her expression neutral.

A laugh scrambles its way through the vibration of Mac's hysterics. She catches a glimpse of herself in the mirror. She looks like a crazy person, losing her damn mind. At least her insides match her outsides. "Yes."

The nurse pushes the door open a bit farther and enters the bathroom fully, closing it behind her. She looks at Mac with dark eyes and a thin-lipped frown. "Listen, I know how pissed off I'd be if I got pregnant right now. I'm six months away from finishing my doctorate. I'm ready to start my own private practice, not sit on my ass through maternity leave."

"You get it, right?" Mac laughs again, but this is a chuckle of relief. "I already have two teenagers at home. They're finally independent enough that I can work without feeling guilty every minute of the day. I can't have another baby."

"I understand. But pretending a pregnancy doesn't exist won't make it go away." The nurse hooks her thumbs in the pockets of her scrubs and studies Mac with thoughtful hazel eyes.

The sting behind Mac's eyes intensifies and her bottom lip trembles. "I know."

Tears push through Mac's stubborn will, cascading down her cheeks in swift tumultuous rivers. The nurse pulls her into an embrace. "Oh, honey. You don't have to do anything you don't want to. There are options we can discuss, and you can choose what's best for you."

Hearing the words out loud that have been tumbling around in the back of her mind dissolves Mac's joints in an instant. She collapses against the nurse, and all her angst and worry pours out of her in the form of anguished tears. She's been thinking about abortion in silence, and hating herself for it. But receiving the option from another woman clawing her way through an unforgiving world makes it all the more concrete in her thoughts.

Shame and guilt well up inside her. What will Sam say if she willingly terminates a pregnancy? Will her boys still respect her?

Could she live with herself knowing she'd been so unthinkably selfish?

"It's okay," the nurse says, patting Mac's hair. "Look. You're here. Let's get you checked out. We can confirm whether you're pregnant, or not, and make sure your body is doing okay. Then, once you have all the information, we can talk about your options."

"I can't do this. Not now. I don't want to have to listen to options and make decisions."

The nurse pulls back and looks her in the eyes. "Maybe you aren't pregnant at all. It could be a false positive. Happens all the time. Maybe you'll get lucky and find out you've had a stroke instead." Her mouth lifts in a compassionate smile. She reaches behind Mac for a handful of paper towels, handing them to Mac. "But I wouldn't be doing my job if I let you leave without finding out."

Mac snorts. She dabs her eyes with the paper towels. "A stroke sounds great. I haven't told anyone about this. Not even my husband."

"It might be nice to have that weight off your shoulders."

"He won't understand how I feel." Mac presses herself back against the counter and grips its edge. She plants her feet, feeling ridiculous like a toddler refusing to get ready for bed, but the reality of her situation makes her too afraid to leave the safety of the bathroom. Once Sam knows she is pregnant, he'll push her to stop working. How will she find Jacqueline Carter and the other missing women then?

And Oliver… he already knows. She'd walked out on him, making it clear to him what she thinks of being his ally. What will happen to her family if she leaves the protection of the FBI?

The nurse's nose wrinkles as if she's smelled something sour. "I can tell this is hard for you. But you can't just ignore it. The sooner you know what you're up against, the sooner you can make some decisions to protect your health."

Mac straightens her spine and lifts her chin. She has to face this. It isn't like she can live out the rest of her life in a hospital bathroom. "Fine. I'll come with you on one condition. Don't tell my husband."

"You have my word. You don't even have to let anyone in the exam room with you. No one will know if you don't want them to."

Begrudgingly, Mac peels herself from the counter. The nurse picks up the IV bag and Mac follows her to the waiting room like a toddler on a safety leash. Richard is there, the lines of his face written over with questions, but she settles into the abandoned wheelchair without saying a word.

The nurse hangs the IV drip bag back on the post at the back of the chair and wheels her to a cubicle behind the check-in desk. Mac answers dozens of medical questions while her vitals are taken.

"Your blood pressure is low, and your heart rate is elevated. Feeling a little stressed today?" The nurse asks the question casually, as if they haven't just had one of the most terrifying girl-talks in bathroom history.

Mac barely has the energy to shrug her shoulders, and is relieved to hear her name called from deeper within the triage center. "Guess that's me." She looks at Richard, appearing lost where he stands in the waiting room. "I'm going back by myself," she says with a voice raised loud enough to be heard across the cubicle wall.

"You sure?" Richard steps toward her.

She considers her life; the choices she has made. She'd always considered herself an intelligent woman, but she holds a battery of guilt instilled in her by growing up in a conservative religious family. Her mother had always told her that raising babies was her only purpose, and now here she was, torn between chasing the most dangerous men in the world, and bringing a new person into it. "I'm positive. I want to be alone."

While she is wheeled into an examination room and left to wait for a doctor, Mac loses herself in her thoughts. She hadn't become a determined person, someone who knew what she wanted and went after it, until she'd joined the FBI. Maybe that was a mistake. Who might she have become if she hadn't been so closed off to possibilities of a life beyond family? Been willing to take more risks?

Maybe it was a good thing she'd been groomed for motherhood from the start. If she had been allowed to follow her dreams… hell, if she'd been allowed to *have* them from the start, maybe she wouldn't have become a mother at all.

But parenthood had seemed like the only path open to her when she was young. She'd been blissfully unaware of this life filled with puzzles, excitement, even danger. A life she chose for herself.

She hears footsteps outside her door just before it swings open. A man in blue-green scrubs carries a tray with a needle and a pair of vials. Mac's face must show her discomfort because he grins. "Don't worry, I do this all day. You'll hardly notice a thing."

"My veins are probably hard as concrete. I haven't eaten or drank much of anything." Mac shrugs, "Wasn't exactly expecting to be poked and prodded today."

"Not a problem."

Soon, Mac has a fresh bag of intravenous fluid dripping into her arm, and a row of paper cups full of water lining the counter beside her.

"Your husband arrived a few minutes ago. Do you want him to come in?" the nurse asks.

A gasp catches behind Mac's sternum. She looks at the clock, noting she's been here nearly two hours already. The walls lean in above her head, and it feels like the floor has dropped out from beneath her, the narrow hospital bed was the only thing keeping her from falling into the abyss. "No."

It's another twenty minutes, three cups of water, and an empty IV fluid bag later before the needle goes into her arm. The nurse attaches the first vial when Mac feels a mounting pressure in her lower abdomen and has a sudden urge to use the bathroom. "Do you happen to need a urine sample? I'm ready to pee, if you do."

The nurse breaks his focus from the blood draw long enough for a short chuckle. "I don't think so. Bloodwork is more accurate. I'll show you where the bathroom is when we're done."

Mac glances down at the needle. Her blood splatters into the vial, splashing against its walls with each beat of her heart. Her breath shortens, and the overhead lights swim across her vision. "Damn it, not again."

"What?" The nurse's voice is quiet as if it's travelling through wads of cotton. He holds the vial in one hand and reaches for her with the other. She overshoots his palm, grasping his forearm as a hot blindness overtakes her.

When she comes back around, she lies on the hospital bed, Sam standing beside her and gripping her hand. He wears a weary, somber expression.

"Sam," she croaks. "How did you get in here?" She tries to prop herself up on her elbows.

He squeezes her fingers in his. "I came as soon as Richard called. They wouldn't let me come in at first, but when you lost consciousness again, I pestered the staff until I found someone who would help me." He leans forward, watery eyes filled with worry. "Babe, what's going on?"

"Nothing. I'm fine." She pulls her hand from his grip and presses it against her forehead. She's irritated. No, furious. How could they let him in now, before she's come up with a plan on how to tell him their lives might change forever, all over again?

Sam looks bewildered. He pulls an empty chair to her bedside and lowers himself into it, palms up in his lap. "Seriously, Mac? You've passed out twice now, and you're lying in a hospital bed with an IV stuck in your arm. You're not fine."

The way his unkempt salt and pepper hair flops across his forehead while he searches her face with his brooding green eyes pushes her over the edge in a way she doesn't expect. She's saved from having to answer him when two knocks rap on the door. Mac hopes it's the nurse coming to take Sam away again, but she deflates like a lost balloon when a doctor lets himself in without waiting for an answer. He pushes a computer on a trolley into the room and stops it at the foot of Mac's bed. His eyes smile at Sam over his medical mask. "Mr. Jones?" Sam rises to his feet and shakes his hand. "Congratulations! Your wife is pregnant."

"His wife is right here, and is the patient in question." Mac doesn't bother to keep the grating irritation from her voice. She grips the bed sheets so tightly that the starched fabric stings her fingers.

Sam's face goes slack, and his eyes widen. He looks rapidly from the doctor to Mac, and back again. "She… she's what?"

"Pregnant. Going to have a baby." The doctor moves to the computer and types a few keys, then looks past the monitor at Mac. "Everything looks just fine. You came in very dehydrated. You've got to watch that, especially now that you're expecting. No coffee though, we don't want caffeine mucking up the works. Just drink lots of good old-fashioned water, and make sure you're eating more regularly. That should clear up the fainting spells. Any questions?"

"Yeah, what happened to doctor-patient confidentiality?" Mac's knuckles ache and she works them loose from the sheet only to slam her fist into the stiff mattress. "You weren't supposed to just announce it, for anyone and their husband to hear. This was supposed to be a private room!"

Sam rubs her shoulder and grins. She hates it when he glosses over her frustrations like this, eyes shining with excitement instead of registering any of the big red flags Mac is waving that say she's upset. "Babe, it's a miracle! Another baby! I didn't think it was even possible at your age..."

She squeezes her eyelids shut and flops back on the pillow. Tears burn at the corners of her forty-three-year-old eyes. She slams her fist into the mattress a second time. "This isn't a miracle. It's a nightmare, Sam."

"She's just in shock," Sam says to the doctor. "It's amazing. I'm going to be a dad again!"

"You're not listening. I can't do this." Mac groans and forces herself to sit up to look the doctor in the eyes. "Doc, I'm not wired for motherhood anymore. And I don't *want* to be."

"Yes you are," Sam says, his grin drooping on one side. His eyes wander over her distress with an expression of confusion. "You've been through this. Having another kid running around will be just like before."

The uncertainty in his voice breaks her heart. “No. It can’t be like it was before. I’m not letting anyone take my life away from me again. I’ve worked too hard to get to where I am. Too many people depend on me. I can’t stop now. Not for you, and not for this…” She waved a hand across her abdomen. “… collection of cells.”

Tension fills the air in the cramped room and the doctor clears his throat. “I have another patient to take care of in the next room. Mrs. Jones, I’ll start your discharge paperwork and refer you back to your regular doctor. They will handle whatever choices you and your husband decide to make.” With an uncomfortable wave goodbye, he pulls the cart from the room, and closes the door behind himself.

The door latches and what was left of Sam’s smile falls. “Didn’t we just talk about what it would be like to have more kids the other day? This is great news, babe. Take as much time off work as you need to. You’re always complaining that Richard’s not in a rush to retire. Use that to your advantage.”

Mac could feel her face tighten, her ears ringing with the rising fluid behind her eyes. She couldn’t tell if it was the hormones, exhaustion from the day of discomfort at the hospital, or if the world was really crumbling around her. But a hard, fast, ugly cry was on its way. "I'm not giving up my work, Sam. It's my life. I can't have a baby."

"Come on, Mac." Sam clasps her hand tight. "You can't be serious. What's so bad about having another kid wandering around? The other two are alright."

"Are you going to raise it?" Mac shouted the question and glared at him with defiance. "Are you going to stay at home every day for years on end, waiting for this kid to grow up the way I did with Ryan and Robby? Spending every cent we have until we're back in the poorhouse because of diapers and formula, throwing away all the plans we've made for once the boys move out?"

Sam's face darkens for a fraction of a second, but he recovers and pushes his lips into an unconvincing smile. "You're tired. It's been a long day. We don't have to figure all this out right now. For now, let's break you out of this joint so we can go home and celebrate."

"It figures I'm the only one who sees this as a problem." Mac tosses the sheet off herself and swings her legs over the edge of the bed. Sam's right about one thing, she's ready to get the hell out of here.

"You are. What could be better than being a mother again?" The smile lines around his eyes harden, and the way his body tenses in preparation for a fight knocks the wind out of her.

Mac wants the best for him; wants him to be happy. But doesn't she deserve to be happy too? "I don't know, Sam. Some days, I think anything would be better than being a mom."

The cheerfulness drains out of him, and he stares at her somberly for a moment. He shoves his hands into his pockets and moves towards the door. "I'll get out of here so you can have your space while you wait for your discharge. Meet me in the waiting room when you're clear, and I'll take you to pick up your van at the office." He hunches his shoulders and tugs the door open, shuffling out of the room without looking back. The door's hydraulic arm hisses as it slowly closes behind him, as if even its enthusiasm is bleeding away.

Sam Jones. Her Sam. The best friend she's ever had. Her husband, a man she's loved for most of her adult years, had turned away from her as though witnessing her reluctance for another round of motherhood had ripped him to his core. Why couldn't she just be excited to upend their lives the way he'd been a few minutes ago?

She'd been caught up in her own depressed paranoia and fear. She'd lashed out at him. God, what an asshole she was.

This was exactly what she'd been afraid of… him knowing she viewed the start of this new life as a death sentence for herself. But if she doesn't see the pregnancy through, it might be the end of their marriage. No matter what she decides, this pregnancy could be the thing that finally breaks them.

Mac looks around the stark room for anything to take her mind off her own misery. The room she's in isn't an overnight suite, but it does have a television on the wall. She feels the hospital frame beside her until she finds the attached controls and turns the set on. A local newscaster flashes on the screen.

More bad news tonight for residents of Columbia County as a combination of rainfall and snow melt has flooded the Nehalem River and nearby Rock creek. We're on the scene in Vernonia, Oregon, where city officials say the river has risen above the highest watermark on record, which happened back on December 3rd, 2007. We'll have more on what residents are calling the worst flood in history after the break...

Nine

It's a quarter to midnight when Mac's headlights peel up the driveway. Sam's car is already parked, dark and empty, and his sister's car is nowhere to be seen. The tangle of tension wrapped around her lungs unwinds with a heavy sigh of relief. It means his sister isn't inside waiting to needle her with questions. She takes another moment of silence before having to face him.

She shuts the car's engine off but leaves the radio playing. She hums along to *Before Love Came to Kill Us* and allows the dark neighborhood to envelop her, clinging to the solitude for a few more minutes.

After the doctor dropped the pregnancy bombshell, it was another two hours before Mac was finally released. By then, the potential risks of middle-aged pregnancy had settled in, and Sam had taken on the role of the paternal white knight. He dropped into full-on protector mode; talking to the medical staff on her behalf, demanding the nurses bring her dinner from the hospital café, and nagging anyone who would listen about her discharge paperwork. He'd been so instantly overbearing; he'd even tried to walk back his offer to pick up her van.

When he'd threatened to take away access to her mom-mobile, she'd put her foot all the way down. There was no way she was going to allow herself to feel trapped without an escape vehicle.

Her peace is broken when a curtain is drawn away from the living room window. Before she can even unbuckle, Sam is opening the front door, and trotting over to tap at her window. The moment she's out of the car, he cups her elbow in his hand and guides her up the walk to the front door.

"Hey, let me shut things down, will you?" Mac pulls her arm back and waves Sam backwards to give herself some space. She leans into the van, flicks off the headlights, pulls the key from the ignition, and takes a deep breath. The way he's hovering makes her plant her feet firmly on the pavement. "You really don't need to do this whole savior thing. I'm not an invalid, you know."

The lights mounted on either side of the garage highlight his pinched expression. "You've had a hard day. Why wouldn't I give you some extra love?"

"Because it's stupid!" she snaps. She sidesteps him and makes her way to the rear door to gather her things.

"I'm worried about you." The wound in his voice digs at her, and she's glad she can't see the full depth of his puppy-dog eyes in the dim light.

Mac hoists her work bag from the back seat. It's heavy with her laptop, case files, and the weight of Josie and Oliver's secrets. "Remember this morning when I was a fully functioning FBI agent? I'm still that person."

He shakes his head and guides her towards the house. "We need to talk about what happened today."

"I already told you what happened."

"You're holding something back. I can feel it." Sam fumbles the doorknob the same way he did the day they moved in together, more than twenty years ago.

"I'm trying to hold back the bridge-troll funk I'm feeling right now, that's for sure. I need a shower and a fresh change of clothes. If you want, you can interrogate me more after I get cleaned up." The door swings wide and Mac steps inside and lets the heft of her bag slide off her shoulder and land on the sofa.

"Okay," Sam concedes. "I'll make you a cup of tea while you shower. Help you wind down from your wild ride today." He picks her bag up from where it just landed and carries it to her makeshift home office. A few seconds later, he moves to the kitchen where banging cupboards and running water announce he's already begun the quest for tea.

Mac trudges through the house towards the bathroom. She notices there is no light bleeding from the crevices beneath the boys' bedroom doors, and she's tempted to crack their doors open to check on them. She doesn't know what Becca told them about why she'd come to the house, and she's not ready to face whatever fears, judgements, or criticisms the pair of teenagers might have for her. She decides to let them sleep in hopes that she'll be more prepared to face them in the morning.

Tiptoeing the rest of the way to the bathroom, she closes the door slowly and winces when the hinges creak and the door's latch clicks loudly in its housing. She turns the water on to let it heat and avoids her reflection in the mirror while she undresses. She doesn't have to look at herself to feel the heavy bags under her eyes, or the film of sebum and dried sweat caked over her unwashed skin.

When she's ready, the heat of the falling water envelops her. She turns her face upward, leaning into the soothing warmth pattering against her skin, and letting it drown out the rest of the world. Though she tries turning to let the water massage her back, it does nothing to soothe the tight muscles straining beneath her skin. Her shoulders ache and her neck feels like it's made of iron. It'll take more than a bit of hot water to wash this day away.

Mac leans against the shower wall and her mind wanders through the events of the day. A muscle in her neck tightens so much it might snap when she thinks back on her conversation with Oliver. He knows she's pregnant. But how?

The shower knob is loose, one of a hundred little house projects that has been put off for another day, and Mac holds it firm in both hands to push and twist in just the right way to shut it off. She pulls her towel from a nearby hook and breathes in a tinge of mildew while she rubs it over her face.

Damn it. Why didn't she swap out a fresh towel before she started?

She drops the musty towel atop the dirty clothes strewn across the floor and pulls her bathrobe from the hook on the door, wrapping it around herself. She shoves her hands in her pockets, and something crinkles in her left pocket. A wrapper from a Kit Kat candy bar she snuck in to eat during her last bath. When she goes to toss the wrapper in the garbage bin below the sink, she finds it is so full, it's close to spilling over.

Of course, no one has emptied the small plastic trash bin. It's yet another task on the long list of things only she ever does. The last time she'd emptied it was before she'd taken the first, inconclusive pregnancy test.

Mac stares at the bin, thinking about what Oliver said. He must have been guessing she was pregnant. There's no way he could know. She hasn't told anyone. And it's not like Oliver has eyes in her bathroom.

Does he?

With the care of an archaeologist, she peels away the layers of refuse from the bin. Empty toilet paper tubes, disposable flossers, wads of tissues from her bouts of crying. She removes a used-up toothpaste tube and a pair of holey socks to uncover the bottom of the wastebasket.

The inconclusive test and all its packaging are gone. Mac's heart skips a beat and her stomach clenches. No… maybe someone did empty the trash. Maybe she did, and she just doesn't remember because she's been so busy. That tracks, right?

She scoops up the trash from the floor and shoves it back in the bin. She still has the second test. She wouldn't have thrown that away.

Picking up her musty towel and dirty clothes before rushing to check the other test comes so naturally. It's automatic despite the ice freezing in her veins. She hurries to her bedroom, dumps the dirty laundry in the basket and opens her dresser drawer. She shoves both hands in, pushing the underwear aside and searching for the cardboard box and thin applicator.

Nothing. Where the hell has it gone?

There were two of them, right? She replays taking the tests in her mind and tells herself the tests have to be here. She pulls everything out of her drawer now, tossing panties on the floor until she sees the bare wood at the back of the drawer. She's been on Sam and the boys to do laundry for years. Maybe they picked today to start folding and putting clothes away for her and found it? No, Sam would have freaked out if he'd found a positive pregnancy test in the house. He would have texted, or called, or said something at the hospital.

She thinks back to the one in the garbage. It's got to be there. Maybe it's stuck to the wastebin's liner. She hurries back to the bathroom and picks the wastebasket up to turn it over. She shakes it automatically, willing its contents to fall out, but freezes when she sees a canary yellow envelope resting inside the bathroom vanity where the garbage had sat.

Her lungs freeze and time stands still. It's the same brilliant yellow as the envelopes they'd found during the maternity ward murder investigations. Mac fights her natural instinct to grab it, instead rocking back on her heels and tucking her hands into the folds of her robe to give herself distance from the ominously cheery envelope.

There's a first aid kit in the cabinet above the sink, and she carefully unfolds herself from the floor, groaning from the effort of standing without touching anything. Damn, she's touched so much already. Not to mention whatever Sam, the kids, and Becca have manhandled. Her mind goes blank, all worries about Sam and the pregnancy erased to make room for the catalog of doorknobs and countertops her skin as contacted since she's been home. While the list manifests in her mind, she carefully pulls a hand towel from the hook near the sink and uses the fabric to swing the medicine cabinet door open and pull the first aid kit from the shelf.

A moment later, her trembling hands protected by the medical gloves from the kit, she picks the envelope up. There's no name written on it, but she knows it's for her. It's a sure sign Oliver, or someone under his influence, has been in her house. Has stood where her feet are currently planted.

The drum of her heartbeat thunders in her ears and her palms sweat inside their gloves. She slides the letter into her robe pocket and scrambles back to her feet. Somehow, Oliver reached right into her bathroom and plucked away her sense of safety. There's no telling who he has on his side. And where are they now? Are they watching her?

Dark fingers creep at the edge of her vision and she smacks herself in the chest to get her lungs working again. The rapid shallow breaths that come aren't enough to keep herself upright, and she can't afford to pass out now. She has to get out of here. Save her family. Save herself. She wheezes a thread of a breath in and fumbles with the doorknob. She blinks away the flecks of white light that float across her vision and pounds her fist against the wood.

Mac's knees buckle and she slides down against the door, her fist still pounding the wood as she folds into a heap against the linoleum.

"Honey?" Sam shouts from the other side. The doorknob turns and the door opens a crack, but it's stopped by Mac's hip and knee. "Are you okay in there?"

She's sure she only blinked, but when she opens her eyes again, she's lying on her back,

Sam kneeling over her, his nose an inch from her own. "Oh God, you're back! You passed out again. I had to push you off the door to get in here. Are you hurt?"

"Oliver was here." Her voice is small and sounds like it's coming from somewhere outside herself, but the way the creases around Sam's eyes tighten means that he heard.

"Oliver Roberts?" Sam asks. Mac nods her head in reply.

"Impossible. You saw him at the prison earlier today. He's locked up." Sam's voice cracks with doubt.

A crash and shriek cut through the house. Adrenaline rushes through Mac's worn down body, bringing it back to life. Sam looks over his shoulder toward the hallway. "What the fuck?"

"It's him!" Mac shrieks. "He's in the house!" Her hand reaches for the gun at her hip, but all she grips is her terrycloth bathrobe. The alarm inside her head screams at her. She grips Sam's forearm, and he helps her to her feet while she pushes through the fog in her mind. Where did she leave her gun?

The hospital. Richard took it before she was admitted. He must still have it.

Robby and Ryan's doors pop open in unison, and both boys tumble into the hallway.

"What's going on?" Robby asks.

Mac and Sam wave the boys into the bathroom. "Home intruder," Mac says. "Get in the bathroom, lock the door, and don't come out until I come back for you." She pushes both boys into the bathroom and pulls the door shut while Sam ducks into Robby's room. Mac doesn't turn away from the bathroom door until she hears the lock click, then she turns to see Sam emerge from Robby's bedroom with a baseball bat.

"Where's your phone? We need to call 9-1-1." Mac pats the empty pockets of her robe as she asks Sam the question and he shakes his head.

"On the kitchen counter," Sam says. "Where's yours?"

"In the living room." Mac kicks herself inside for holding off getting the kids their own phones, leaving them to manage their teenage lives with the single landline in the kitchen.

Sam presses himself against the hallway wall, and Mac follows. She has nothing to defend him with. Hell, she's barely even clothed. But despite Sam's manly two-handed grip on their teenaged son's baseball bat, she's the one with defensive training. It would be suicide to go up against an armed intruder bare handed, but she'll do whatever she can to protect her family. Her fingers curl into fists, and she bites her lower lip.

They round the corner into the living room when a loud bang from something falling in the kitchen makes Mac leap out of her skin. The sweat across her neck turns cold, and a shiver runs down her spine. She prays they make it out of here alive.

All is quiet while they tiptoe through the dining room, but Sam erupts with a warrior's cry when they make it to the kitchen door. His voice is hard as steel against the silence.

A brown and grey blur tears out of the kitchen, Bruce's wild eyes and untrimmed nails clattering against the hardwood floor while he slides around the corner. He gets his pads under him and tears off across the house, disappearing from sight.

Mac and Sam stare at one another for a moment before they rush the final few feet into the kitchen. Sam is tense as a rubber band stretched to its extreme, ready to swing the bat at anything that moves. He tromps around the island, looking for someone hiding on the other side. His tense, red face lengthens, the tightness in his shoulders ease, and he lowers the bat to his side while erupting in wild laughter.

While Sam hunches over, shoulders jumping as he tries to breathe through his hysterics, Mac takes the opposite route around the island to cut off their intruder. She stops at the opposite corner from her husband. Between them, a broken platter smeared with frosting and the final dregs of a cake lay scattered across the tile floor.

"Bruce!" Ryan yells from the living room. A moment later both boys scramble into the kitchen and stare at the empty island. Ryan hoists himself up on the countertop and peers over the other side. "He ate mom's cake!"

"It was the dog!" Sam shouts through a laugh. He sets the bat down and wipes the tears from his eyes. "Holy moly, I thought we were all goners."

"I told you to stay in the bathroom." Mac's words may be griping, but her tone is filled with exasperation and relief. Tears prick at her eyes, and she pulls her robe around herself like a plush hug.

"I told you we should have put it in the fridge," Robby says, trailing his words with a groan. He looks at Mac. "Dad said you were in the hospital, so we baked a cake for you with Aunt Becca."

Adrenaline drains from Mac's body, carrying all her strength with it. She takes a step back and leans against the refrigerator. "I thought Oliver was here."

"You had me going there for a minute." Sam's grin slips when he looks at Mac. She must look as exhausted as she feels because he breathes through the end of his laughter and the burst of humor flattens under the weight of her gaze. "Even if that psycho did get loose, I'm sure he'd have better places to be than hanging around this mess. I haven't seen Bruce run like that in years." He pokes a large shard of the broken platter with his toe and pushes it into the pile of green frosting. "Hope it tasted good."

The minor shift in the pile is just enough to waft the sickly-sweet scent of sugar and cream cheese frosting Mac's way. The hint of chocolate dessert folds her stomach inside-out. Closing her eyes and blowing out a heavy breath does little to distract from the tremors deep within her gut.

“Mom! Are you okay?” Ryan is on her before she opens her eyes, grabbing her by the shoulders with his broad hands and squeezing her too hard, as if he isn’t aware of his own strength.

Damn it, she wanted to put off talking to the boys until tomorrow. Or next week. Maybe forever. She opens her eyes to find both teenagers and Sam staring back at her and knows she can’t keep quiet about what’s going on with her health, even with the threat of Oliver hanging over her head. “No, I’m not okay. I’m pregnant.”

Ryan lets go of her and his face drops. “Pregnant… with suspense and mystery?”

“Not pregnant with literary genres, unfortunately. But I’m glad you’ve been paying attention in English class.” Mac reaches up to pat him on the head, the way she would have when he was younger. She looks Sam in the eyes. “The tests I took here at home are gone.”

“You took tests, with an ‘s’? That’s plural, Mac. Damn it! How long have you known?” His eyebrows climb to his hairline, and the ruddiness of his cheeks deepens as he freezes before her eyes, wounded.

The moment she hunches her shoulders and sags against the refrigerator she wishes she'd done anything else. Sam's features darken and he balls his hands into fists before folding them over his chest.

"Just a couple of days. I wasn't ready to tell you. I didn't know how I felt about it. And the first test was inconclusive, anyway."

"So, we're having a baby, or aren't we?" Robby asks.

"I don't know," Mac says at the same time Sam says, "We are." Sam's neck and cheeks turn crimson and the tension that floods the room presses down on Mac enough that she feels like she might pass out again.

"We'll talk about the baby stuff tomorrow. Right now, we need to call the police."

"Why do we need the police? We already know the noise in the house was the dog," Sam says with a tone tinged with anger.

Mac looks at her hands and realizes she's still wearing the gloves from the first aid kit. She slips her hand into her robe pocket and pulls the envelope from its depths. "Oliver Roberts left a note inside our bathroom."

Ten

The crackling sound of police radios, shuffling of cloth booties, and low voices fill every corner of the house. Sam and the boys sit shoulder to shoulder on the sofa, squeezed together like sardines in a tin, answering the interviewing officer's questions.

Mac leans against the opposite wall. Richard is red-eyed and bleary, but still came over when she called. Despite it being after one in the morning, he'd made record time, arriving before the glow of police lights even touched the edge of the neighborhood.

"This is overkill, isn't it?" Mac comments while she watches a dozen people in dark blue uniforms poking around her house, some carrying boxes of possible evidence to a waiting SUV outside. The breeze sneaking in through the front door teases the hem of Mac's bathrobe. She did think to put on some real clothes after Sam called 9-1-1, but the underarms of her white and navy star field pajamas are damp with sweat. The cold evening sends a shiver through her. "A break-in only needs two or three officers to respond, right?"

"Special circumstances." Richard yawns, then lifts a corner of his cheek in an attempt at a weary smile. "It's not every day a Bureau agent has a break-in."

"Oliver Roberts is still behind bars?" Mac knows the question is unneeded, but the ball of fear jumping through her like a pinball hunting for a high score makes her ask anyway.

"After our interview, he went right back to his pod. Stayed in sight of the cameras all day, according to the warden."

"He has someone working for him outside." It isn't a question for Mac, even though she still hasn't formally floated the idea to Richard yet.

Richard looks at her and sucks in his cheeks. He licks his lips and looks around the room. "I wouldn't put it past him."

He shuffles his feet, like he's anxious to say more. Does he know his wife is involved with Roberts? Mac busies herself watching the surrounding chaos. There's just no smooth way to ask your partner if he knows his wife is flirting with the devil.

"How is Josie doing?"

Richard's forehead wrinkles at the sound of his wife's name. "She's fine. Why are you asking about her?"

Mac presses her tongue to the roof of her mouth to keep herself from blurting out that maybe Josie is the one who broke into her house. If she is, maybe they'll find her prints on the doorknobs. Of course, it would be great if they found her prints on the envelope, but Mac couldn't be sure she hadn't messed that up during the race to find out Bruce had eaten her cake. She clears her throat and glances at the clock hanging on the dining room wall.

"I was thinking we could do that dinner party. Forget this whole fainting episode and get out of the crime scene that is now my life. With this burglary mess, I imagine we'll stay with Sam's sister for a couple of days. Even if they decide to release the house, I'm not going to sleep here." Mac sighs. "I'm grateful for her opening up her home to us, and the kids never complain, but my sister-in-law is a terrible cook."

"Josie will be glad to have you. I'll let her know you've turned in an RSVP, and we'll see you and Sam tomorrow around six?"

"I'll make sure the kids are busy so it can be just us adults." Mac turns her head to watch an officer walk by with the yellow envelope in an evidence bag. "Whose arm do you think we'd have to twist to get them to let us read that letter?"

A breathy chuckle escapes through Richard's nose. "You picked it up. Why didn't you open it before they got here?"

"It didn't even cross my mind. Blame it on the pregnancy. They do say pregnancy turns women into hysterical creatures," Mac says.

"Speaking of hysterics, I think it would be best if you take a couple of days off work. I can get a copy of the letter sent to you." Richard yawns and rolls his head around on his shoulders. "Sound good?"

"No, it doesn't. We're in the middle of an investigation, remember? Those women aren't going to find themselves, Richard. I can't just walk off the job. Not now. Tarrell would never forgive me if I just walked off his daughter's case." The way his eyes glaze over, she can tell he's not listening. She can't let his attention slip. "Did you hear about the flood in Vernonia? The news says it cut right through town and broke a record."

Richard shrugs his shoulders. "All I heard was some rain fell and the rivers are high."

"I saw footage. Half the city is underwater. If there is a killer out there, that flood is going to be a boon for hiding evidence." Mac wishes she'd insisted on walking around the homeless camps the day the governor first brought up his missing daughter. With all the rain since, both Rock Creek and the Nehalem River had flooded. The newscaster had made it seem like anyone wanting to wander Main Street would need diving suits.

"Malone and Sharpe invited me out to walk the high ground and see the layout of the town. Sharpe said it wouldn't be hard for someone to hide out in the timber." Richard smirks at Mac's tense expression. "I might find it in my heart to show you my notes when you come over for dinner. Give us something to do while we wait for Josie to tell us it's time to eat."

"Sounds like my kind of date."

Eleven

Richard rolls the window down, letting the stale dampness of his beat-up, rattling rust bucket fill with the greasy wetness of the early Portland morning. Once celebrated as the City of Roses, Portland now reeks of decomposing tents and trash. The scent of a rotting corpse of a city is enough to make lifetime residents pack up their worldly possession and seek out a fresh start in parts unknown.

He pulls out of the city and heads westward through the countryside. The winding two-lane road is protected in turns by picturesque fields of sheep and cattle. The scattered trees in the fields move closer together, melting into the close-knit shadows of leaning evergreens in the dense wooded Oregon wildlands.

It's mid-morning when he pulls into Vernonia, a tiny one-stoplight town where the hardware store doubles as a liquor store, and the streets are lined with brightly colored cottages built atop over-tall foundations. It takes less than ten minutes to find Hawkins Park, and he pulls into the edge of the lot where detectives Sharpe and Malone wait for him.

"Richard." Malone greets him once he's out of the car. The detective peers through the windshield and squints. "No Special Agent Jones this morning?"

"She's not feeling well today." Richard reaches out to shake both detectives' hands. "Your call sounded urgent. Where did you find her?"

"About a quarter mile from here. We can hike down." Sharpe gestures towards the water. "Care to take a walk?"

The narrow beach drops away under a steep riverbank covered in Oregon blackberry, and thick trees lean over the dark water. The smell of decay is stronger here, a mixture of gutted fish and rotting logs heaved ashore from the fast-moving water. They follow the water from the high ground of an elevated field, but the ground is soggy and littered with trash.

Richard casts his gaze over the refuse. It gets thicker and heaps together in clumps farther up the riverbank. Beyond the largest trash mound, he sees the flutter of a loose tarp.

They round a curve in the river, to find a knoll covered in the huddled blue and tan domes of dozens of tattered tents.

"Is that your homeless camp?" Richard asks.

"One of them," Sharpe says. An exasperated breath escapes him. "We'd hoped when the river flooded, they'd get the hint and move on. But they've just claimed higher ground. There's two more out in the woods, and even more folks squatting in the recreational camp areas outside of town."

"Where we're walking was under water just a couple of days ago," Malone says. She gives her partner a sideways glance that Richard imagines he isn't supposed to notice. Based on his time working with Mac, he imagines Malone has an uphill battle on her hands where technology and changing social norms are concerned. "We haven't had this much water since back in 2007."

"Beat the record by four and a half inches," Sharpe adds proudly, as if having the town underwater was a personal achievement.

They trudge through the sloppy mud to a strand of yellow tape, though whatever crime scene it protects looks like it was ripped apart by the previous night's winds.

"Which girl is this?" Richard asks.

"We've identified her as Jacqueline Carter," Malone says so low that Richard almost misses it.

"The governor's daughter?"

"Yup, the big fish. The one that can make or break our careers." Sharpe grins like he's won the lottery. He pulls a pack of cigarettes from his coat pocket and tamps one out.

Malone points upstream past the dead-end pavement of a dreary-looking neighborhood on the opposite bank. "Another girl was found over there. We haven't identified her yet, but we suspect she's one of the women Jacqueline reported missing."

"And behind door number three," Sharpe holds his cigarette between two fingers and juts it in the direction they just came from, "Another body was found stuck in the grating of the kiddie pool an hour ago."

"The kid's pool?" Richard looks back downriver but doesn't see any buildings aside from a couple of private homes and the park's small event center.

"It's cut into the riverbank, below the lot where we parked. In the summer, the city puts up a dam to raise the water enough to fill the pool, and in the fall, they break it all down again to protect the wildlife downstream. A kid that works for the city was cleaning up some deadwood caught in the pool. Pulled on what he though was a branch, but ended up being an arm." Malone's face turns green as she's talking, and Richard wonders if she'd ever dreamed she'd be hanging out with three dead bodies at once when she got hired in this little town.

How is she going to react if they find the other missing women? Richard silently hopes they don't find even more bodies than they're expecting.

"Any idea where they were first dropped in?" Richard looks at the rushing water and wonders how far its current might carry a bundle of dead weight.

"All four of the women Jacqueline filed reports on stayed in the same camp on the other end of town," Malone said. "But they can't have been dumped in the river there. No matter how unpredictable flooded rivers are, they don't ever flow backwards."

"The governor is about to be one pissed father," Sharpe said, scratching the stubble at his jaw. "Not only is his daughter dead, but when the water washed out their original camp, the squatters moved onto a lot that's supposed to be developed into a planned neighborhood. Apparently, the governor is a major investor in the development."

Richard pushes his hands into his pockets, hoping to warm his frozen fingers. The damp chill of the wind cuts through his fleece jacket, lapping at the sweat from the hike out to the site and pulling away any warmth he might have felt. "Have you seen the bodies yourselves? How do they look?"

"The M.E. says the decomposition is varied. He said they'll be busy for a while, sorting them all out. But he thinks they were killed before they went into the water. Whoever is doing this seems to be hitting victims on a regular schedule and has a place where they keep them until they start to rot."

“Have you gotten any leads?” Richard looks back and forth between Malone and Sharpe, and neither has a positive expression.

“The homeless camp is a dead end. Our city cops have been pushing them around for months. None of them will talk to us.” Malone’s face has turned from green to white, and her breathing has slowed. Richard would never hope for anyone to get used to the sight of death and decay, though in this case, it would be better for everyone if Malone got over her queasiness.

A quick breeze picks up over the water, sending a fresh chill through him. He lets his gaze drift over the poorly secured scene. “No chance you’ve found a calling card from our killer?”

Malone and Sharpe look even more downtrodden than they had a moment before. Malone exhales a quick sigh of frustration. “We’ve been looking for footprints, tire marks, anything.” She gazes down at the heaps of trash vomited out of the river. “The entire riverbank has turned into one churning dump. Even if the killer left a neon sign with his name, address, and photograph, it’s still like trying to find a needle in a very disgusting haystack.”

Richard reflects on the recent visit he and Mac paid to Ollie. "We talked over the kidnapping files with our... expert. To get his impression of the victims."

"What did he say?" Malone asks.

"He didn't have an immediate answer beyond young women making for a nice collection, and mentioning whoever is doing this is smart, dangerous, and we'll be surprised when we find them. Basically said he'll think it over and get back to us. Has anyone inserted themselves into the investigation? Anyone from the community being exceptionally helpful?"

Malone shakes her head. "Everybody in town is happy to ignore the homeless, and I'm sorry to say they haven't seemed too torn up by a couple of panhandlers being absent from their corners."

"I'll circle back with Mr. Roberts and see what he's come up with." Richard shifts his gaze from Malone to Sharpe. "Serial killers tend to work on some type of schedule. They can suppress their urges for a while, but eventually they lose that internal battle and start prowling again. If our guy is on the clock, that puts us in a tight spot. How long has it been since Jacqueline Carter went missing?"

"A little more than two weeks," Sharpe says. He looks downriver and squints his eyes. "She'd been coming in to report a new girl missing about once a week, or so."

Richard's eyes follow the gnarled roots of a log bobbing through the rushing water. A weight tugs at his spine, telling him the next girl is already taken, killed, and hidden somewhere along the river. She simply hasn't surfaced yet. He searches for something positive to say, but comes up short. "He's late."

"Maybe," Sharpe says, pulling his shoulders towards his ears. "Or we might be lucky enough that the flood ruined his fun and he's moved on."

"Didn't you say the same thing about the three women you pulled out of the river today?" Richard narrows his eyes on Sharpe. "I think it's time to realize you're not that lucky."

Twelve

The pull-out sofa bed in Becca's living room might be more comfortable than the floor, if it weren't for the metal bar pressing against Mac's ribcage through the thin mattress. She reaches out for Sam, but finds the far side of the mattress is empty. Quiet voices trickle into the living room from the kitchen, so she rolls to the edge of the mattress and hoists herself out of the sagging bed. It takes a minute to find her slippers in the mountain of luggage and loose clothing piled against the nearby recliner, but once her feet are tucked inside their thick fluff, she shuffles towards the conversation.

"Thanks for letting us stay the night." Sam leans against Becca's kitchen island and grips a coffee mug with both hands as if it might grow legs and run away.

"Any time, broseph." Becca looks up from the bowl of lumpy mush she's stirring, and winks at him. "So, how long do you think you'll stay?"

"We can go back today," Mac announces. She makes her way to the coffee maker and pours the last dribble of brown nectar into a nearby mug. "The police said they pulled everything they could, so it's no longer an active crime scene."

"They also said whoever broke into the house might come back. I'd rather not be there if they do," Sam says.

Becca's eyes widen and her mouth tightens. She redirects her attention to the bowl of goop, pouring a lumpy spoonful onto a still-cold pan before turning on the burner. Mac checks her watch. The boys will be late for school at the rate Becca's moving.

"Since Richard told me I can't work today because of the…" Mac bends her fingers in air quotes, "… 'stress', or whatever, maybe we should all take the day off."

"Oh!" Becca's cheeks crease in an over-exuberant grin. She leans over to pat Mac on the belly. “That’s right, you have an extra bundle to worry about now, don’t you? Congratulations!”

Mac grabs Becca’s wrist and holds it tight. “Don’t touch my stomach like that, Becca. It wasn’t okay when I was pregnant before, and it sure as hell isn’t okay now.”

She hadn’t wanted to tell anyone about the pregnancy. She isn’t even sure if she is keeping the damn cells multiplying inside her. The fewer people there are who know, the better. But Sam had called everyone on their contacts list before she’d even been discharged from the hospital, and now she has to deal with people like Becca patting her belly like some good luck charm.

If Becca is put off by Mac’s shortness, she doesn’t show it. “You think you’ll get another boy?”

“I hope not,” Ryan says from where he and his brother sit at the kitchen table, waiting for breakfast. “I don’t want another little turd following me around.”

“Hey!” Robby reaches across the table to punch his brother in the shoulder, and Ryan responds with a weak slap. A split second later, they leap out of their chairs to grapple with one another, knocking dishes off the tabletop, their chairs screeching across the linoleum and toppling over.

Sam shouts, but it does nothing to stop them, only adds to the noise. Mac lifts her coffee cup to her lips and takes a drink, watching her family turn into a bundle of arms and legs, tumbling from the tabletop to the floor.

It feels like yesterday when Ryan was taken from her. Her entire world shattered the day he was kidnapped. She thought she had reclaimed some of her security by joining the FBI and pulling the worst kind of bad guys from the street, but now, with Oliver getting access to her house, and aware of her pregnancy, she wonders if her family will ever be safe again.

Ryan yanks Robby's shirt upward and over his head to blind him while Sam grabs at both boys' arms to pull them apart. Mac sighs, her face passive despite the terrible thoughts rattling around in her mind. "I don't want a boy or a girl. Do you see these kids? I'm hoping for a quiet goldfish."

Becca laughs. The frying pan has finally warmed enough for a few bubbles to form in the batter, and she grabs a spatula from a utensil holder on the counter. It's warped to hell and looks like someone sawed at the flat end with a pair of scissors. She holds it off-kilter enough for the flat end to touch the pan, then tries to flip the watery pancake over. She fights with the beige pancake skin until the inside of the pan looks like a monochrome impressionist painting, then pushes the goopy mess to the center of the pan with her spatula. “Will you be here for dinner?”

“No,” Mac and Sam say in unison. Mac meets Sam’s eyes. He’s holding the boys at arm’s length, one in each hand by their shirt collars. He grins and winks at her, acknowledging their jinx.

“Sam and I have a dinner party to go to. A work thing, so we can’t take the boys. Can they stay here for dinner?” Although at sixteen and seventeen, Ryan and Robby have been old enough to hang out without a sitter for years, based on the way they kick their feet around Sam to get at one another, she’s not sure they’ll ever be emotionally ready to be left alone together.

“Sure,” Becca says with a smile. She turns back to her pan, where the pancake smolders, and she forces the spatula beneath it to flip it over. It’s as black as the bottom of the pan.

"I think your pancake is done," Mac says, scrunching her nose at the smell of burning batter.

Becca scrapes the burnt food from her pan and puts it on a plate. Sam has managed to get the boys back into their chairs at the table and she slides the plate in front of Ryan. "I'll be back in just a minute with yours, Robby."

Sam watches Ryan douse the carbon on his plate with syrup. Mac can tell he's trying to be polite, but the tip of his nose wriggles and his nostrils creep upward in disgust. "I'll leave you money to order a pizza for dinner. We'd hate to make you cook all day."

"That's totally not necessary," Becca says cheerfully while she pours a puddle of batter into the smoking pan. "I love to cook! It's no problem for them to be here for dinner."

Ryan saws at his breakfast with a butter knife. When he scoops a bite into his mouth, his eyes pop and his cheeks deflate like a balloon that hasn't been tied. Crumbs splatter across his plate until he swallows and chases the scorched pancake down the hatch with half a glass of milk. Becca looks at him with raised eyebrows and doe-like eyes while he scrapes his tongue against his teeth and smacks his lips. Finally, with watery eyes, he looks at her. “Thanks, Aunt Becca.”

“Let me take over,” Sam says. He glances at the clock on the back of the stove. “You should be getting ready for work anyway, right Becca?”

Becca drops the spatula in the pan, and it sticks in the still-doughy batter. She nods and wipes her hands on the towel hanging on the oven’s handle. “Good call, bro. I wasn’t watching the clock. You all have everything you need?”

The Jones family nods all around and Becca flutters out of the kitchen. Mac, Sam and the boys spend the rest of the morning doing the awkward dance of living life in someone else’s home. Sam calls off work and busies himself with taking the trash out and cleaning the kitchen. Though they’ve given the boys permission to play hooky from school, Mac insists they finish their homework from the day before.

With everyone’s attention focused elsewhere, Mac extracts her laptop from her work bag and sets it on the hide-a-bed to boot it up. She fiddles with the Wi-Fi settings until she gets it to connect and opens the secure desktop to access her email. She hunches over, sick to her stomach when she reads the subject line of the first message.

Previous Roberts penitentiary records—urgent.

Mac has barely scratched the surface of Josie's connection to Oliver. Was this more evidence of their correspondence from before his transfer to Sheridan?

She's so absorbed in the question that she doesn't feel Sam's presence behind her.

"What are you doing?"

Lightning shoots up Mac's spine and she slams the lid of her laptop closed like a middle schooler caught looking at hentai during health class. She looks up to find Sam's frown hanging over her.

"I was checking in on work."

"You're supposed to relax today. The doctor said it would be better for you and the baby."

She breathes deep, feeling the air fill her lungs and letting it out slowly. "Sitting around twiddling my thumbs, wondering if someone else will make the connections I could be making before another woman goes missing doesn't sound relaxing. I'm not going into the office; I'm just reading my e-mail."

"I'm not asking you to sit there. You'd feel more relaxed if you did some of that self-care stuff you're always saying you don't have time for. Take a hot bath, or go for a walk. If you want, I could give you a massage…" Sam waggles his eyebrows suggestively.

Mac rolls her eyes and her shoulders droop under the weight of her aggravation. Although Sam was quick to leave their home after the police searched the house, and he's in no rush to return until he's sure it's safe, he doesn't seem to grasp the danger of Mac walking around a strange neighborhood with a serial killer, or at least one of his minions, on the loose. And while she has seen the faces of this killer's victims, there's no way for him to feel the weight of responsibility she feels for the women she's never met, or the potential horrors that might be unveiled when she finds out more about Oliver and Josie's history together.

Since her first day on the job, she's made it a point to not discuss her work with her family, thinking it was best for their safety and her sanity. But now that the job has literally followed her home, she's not sure that division was for the best. Maybe if Sam knew about the terrible things she saw day in and day out, he'd take her desire to stay in the loop more seriously.

She drops the irritated tone from her voice and softens her expression. "Okay, how about this? Give me thirty minutes to scan these e-mails. It'll help me out tonight, so Richard won't have to bring me up to speed over dinner. That will make the evening better for everyone." She touches his forearm gently. "When I'm done, I'll log off and you can give me that massage, even though I'm pretty sure a 'massage' is what got me into this pregnancy mess to begin with."

Sam frowns and the worry lines across the bridge of his nose deepen while he considers her.

"How about I sweeten the deal? It's not like I'll be drinking, so how about I volunteer to be your designated driver tonight. You can tie one on with Richard. I won't even complain when it smells like a bar died in your mouth in the morning." She wiggles her own eyebrows at him, copying his suggestive tease.

His mouth twitches, and his eyes regain a playful twinkle. "I'll say one thing about this job. It has made you a much better negotiator." He winks at her the way he did when they first met, and for an instant he looks twenty years younger. He glances at his watch. "I'm timing you. I'll be right back here in thirty minutes for my massage."

Mac slaps him across the butt when he turns to walk away. "Hang on one minute! You said you were giving *me* a massage."

"Huh, that's not how I remember it." He flashes her a smile before retreating into the kitchen. He's found her out, and there's no sense being hunched over the laptop on the bed, so Mac gathers her laptop and charging cord and follows him.

"How does a massage get a woman pregnant? I don't remember them covering that in sex ed." Robby looks at Ryan with a wicked grin while he shudders and groans disgust.

"Leave me alone." Mac takes a seat at the table and plugs her laptop into the outlet on the wall behind her. She opens the lid and taps the track pad, grumbling about having to go through the steps to log in again. When she gets back to her e-mail, a new message from Richard tops the list.

Hey Mac,

I would have called, but figure Sam wouldn't let you answer. We're not looking at a kidnapper anymore. Walked the river with Sharpe and Malone this morning. Three bodies found so far. We'll see if they find the other two missing women in the mess the flood left behind.

One of the women they found was identified as Jacqueline Carter. Vernonia PD are notifying the Governor now. They're still working on IDs for the other two.

See you tonight! Don't bring anything. Josie has everything covered.

- *R*

"Shit," Mac mutters under her breath. She doesn't have her phone on her, but calling Tarrell about his dead daughter while her own family hovers wouldn't do any of them any favors. She opens a fresh e-mail and types a quick note to the governor, telling him she's just received an update on his daughter, and she promises to do everything in her power to find the person who hurt her. She sends the e-mail, even though it feels like a half-assed condolence. She'll speak to him as soon as she can, so he knows she's there for him.

Mac is sure Richard got on the phone with Oliver the second bodies started popping up. The convicted killer will salivate over the new bits of information, the way a hungry dog drools at the sight of a bone. Oliver Roberts is a special breed, and not one she has any interest in replicating.

Before she gets too lost in her discomfort, she scans the subject lines stacked inside her inbox. She deletes some, opens and reads others, trying to get through as much as she can before Sam's timer goes off.

She comes across an e-mail that is about Oliver, but not his killings. She clicks on the bold **urgent** and sucks in a breath while the page loads.

Special Agent Jones,

I reached out to previous prisons that have held Oliver Roberts to find his prior correspondence. Deer Ridge Correctional Institution lost hard copies of inmate correspondence in a fire last year.

However, Mule Creek State Prison forwarded a summary of their records. The person you're curious about, Josephine

Richards, appears in his correspondence logs six hundred and fifty-six times. Please follow the link below to the secure site where scanned copies of all of Roberts' letters can be viewed. Login instructions will be sent separately. Happy hunting.

- X

Mac doesn't have time to go through more than six hundred letters, but she can't help clicking on the link and digging through her e-mails to find the instructions so she can read one or two. The remote server takes forever to load, but when it does, she skims through the documents until she finds one from Josie. Just like the other letter she'd read from his recent correspondence, this one from years before has the same tone. Familiar, encouraging, and intimate. What is Josie to Oliver? Some kind of religious fanatic, fancying herself as his faithful servant?

"Time's up!" Sam reaches over Mac's shoulder to close the lid of her laptop. She brushes his arm aside.

"I need just a few more minutes." Mac closes the scanned letter and opens another.

Sam squats at her side and leans in. His expression is tight. “Mackenzie, you promised. You and I both know that you’ll be asking for a few more minutes every time I come check in, until you’ve been here all night.” He reaches out and rests his hand on the laptop again, threatening to close it.

“Shit. Fine. At least let me shut everything down.” She wishes she could argue with him, but he knows her too well. She bats his hand away and clicks the laptop’s track pad to close the e-mail and disconnect from her secure connection. Reluctantly, she powers the laptop down.

Sam hovers over her, resting his broad hands on her shoulders. She can feel the warmth of his skin through her shirt and his thumbs press into the soft tissue between her neck and shoulder, seizing the tension she holds there. His breath flows over her neck when he leans closer, tickling the small hairs with his exhale and sending a shiver down her spine. “How about that massage?”

She leans into his touch, breathing in his familiar scent, remembering how easy it was to be close to him before there were teenagers, careers, and all the other trappings of life getting in the way. It feels like now there are so many obstacles to overcome, including the lack of privacy now that they're couch-surfing. "You sure this is a good idea?"

"It's not like you can get more pregnant," Sam whispers in her ear.

Mac looks across the table at her two teenaged sons, both of whom look like they're witnessing a busload of commuters getting decapitated on the freeway. "Boys will you go out to the garage and find Aunt Becca's lawnmower? I think she'd appreciate coming home to a mowed yard."

"I don't want to," says Robby.

"It's raining," complains Ryan.

"Do we have to?" they say together.

"Yes," Mac and Sam answer in unison.

The boys scrape their chairs against the floor when they push away from the table, the noise of their belabored movements reminiscent of their fight earlier in the morning. Ryan and Robby share the same dissatisfied glare, and grumble together at being ousted from the house. When they finally disappear, the garage door slams behind them.

Mac rises from her seat and Sam takes a step back, pulling her chair away from the table like a gentleman and gesturing towards the living room. "I have prepared the pull-out sofa, milady."

The intensity of his gaze makes Mac's cheeks burn. She hopes he recognizes how he still lights a fire in her after all these years. He guides her into the living room where the hide-a-bed looks exactly as messy as it had when she sat on it with her laptop before. She's about to ask him exactly what he's prepared when Sam dives into the sheets like a swimmer plunging headlong into the shallow end of a pool.

He spreads his arms and legs like a starfish, taking up the entire, sagging mattress. "I'm ready for you," he says, his voice leaking through the mound of pillows covering his head.

Mac heaves an oversized sigh and rolls up her sweatshirt sleeves. "Fine. But you're doing me next."

Thirteen

Richard has been on hold with the administration office at the Sheridan prison for nearly twenty minutes. Ollie wields his limited power from inside by deliberately dragging his feet and wasting people's time. Getting him on the phone on an unsecured line is always a lengthy task, and Richard distracts himself from the suffocating feeling of being one of Ollie's pawns by shuffling through the paperwork on his desk. He reminds himself the delay is worth it. The warden allows Ollie to speak to him on a private line in the admin building, so their call won't be recorded.

If Mac walked into the room right now, she'd assume his ruffled feathers meant he was busy. He's adept at keeping anyone from knowing his busywork is designed to distract from anyone suspecting that he's not looking for clues… he's waiting for directions from Ollie.

No one has ever questioned him about it, and he takes their willful ignorance as a permission slip to keep going.

It isn't until his boredom drives him to open a game of solitaire on the computer that the line clicks and his closest confidant's voice seeps through the receiver.

"Inspector Douglas. To what do I owe the pleasure?"

"Thank you for taking my call. I hope I'm not interrupting anything important."

"It's all important, Richard. Every interaction, each turn of phrase. Today, I'm recruiting," Ollie says with a low chuckle. "A promising young man was delivered to my doorstep this morning. Not a particularly interesting case on the surface, just a run-of-the-mill triple homicide. Very messy. But with a shift in mindset, and a bit of focused attention, his violent streak may be harnessed in a good way."

"You're just the person to set a lost soul on the right path," Richard says politely. He'd taken this job to make the world a little less scary, but early on, he'd become a conduit for a killer's unlimited reach. There had been a time when Ollie's admissions would have made him cringe. Over the course of their entwined careers, Ollie's openness about certain aspects of his operation had faded into the background; just the cost of doing business.

But the last disciple Ollie sent into the world reignited the worry deep in Richard's bones. His victims hadn't been greedy assholes or drug-addled hustlers. They'd been young mothers; some of them young enough to be called children themselves.

After they caught him, Ollie had assured Richard that Liam Miller was a wild card. A bad actor who'd gone off-script. But that explanation didn't sit right with Richard. Not when it came from a man who was meticulously organized and had only slipped up once in his killing career.

It only took once to get caught.

"Indeed, I am blessed to be the shepherd of these lost souls," Ollie says with the pride of a Sunday minister. "Would you like to know more about him, or is this simply a social call?"

"I have some new information about the women we talked about the other day. I thought it might help you give me a little insight on what I need to be looking for."

"Ah, so it is a social call! I do love a bit of gossip. What's the gab floating around the watercooler? I'm all ears." Ollie's broad smile leaps through the receiver, and Richard can imagine him reclining in a padded office chair, comfortable and eager to chat.

"Three women were found, Ollie. Vernonia was underwater because of all the rain, and when the flood receded, three bodies turned up on the riverbank. The first two had fewer open wounds, and the M.E. believes they were strangled before whatever else happened to them. Their deaths look quick, disorganized. But the third woman suffered more. She was carved up with a variety of different blades, and was choked, but not enough for strangulation. There was water in her lungs, indicating she drowned."

"This third woman… she's our high-profile prize?" Ollie's voice was slick with pleasure.

"Yes, she is. Listen, Ollie, I've got to come back to these detectives with a trail to follow. Not so much for them, but for Mac. The people in Vernonia don't appear to care too much about a few homeless girls dropping out of the game. But Mac isn't going to let it go until she finds the other two missing women and gets some answers. And one of these young ladies…" Richard almost blurts out that Jacqueline Carter went to summer camp with Mac's son, but he bites back the words. Although Mac's family was plastered all over the news when she cracked the case and found all the kidnapped campers, back then Governor Carter was nothing more than a firefighter with a bright smile. Ollie might not know how tight Mac is with the governor, and Richard thinks it might be best for her if it stays that way.

"Yes?" Ollie asks, impatience strangling his tone.

"I need to know if this guy is one of yours." Richard hears someone outside his office door and holds his breath. If they come in, he'll have to hang up, and that's certain to make Ollie irate.

It's never good to get on a serial killer's bad side, no matter how close of friends you might be.

"This one girl they're concerned about. Do you think she was mishandled? Or was she drowned as part of the show?" Ollie breathes the questions over the line, but he's talking to himself. Richard stays quiet, waiting for him to give his answer. “If the third woman was drowned, that would be an interesting escalation. One I hadn’t expected, and I’m not surprised much after all these years. But where are the fourth and fifth girls hiding? I could ask them to shed light on the change.”

A lump of dread forms in Richard’s throat. Between the flood, and the Vernonia townsfolk glad to see the homeless population suffer, they may never find the other missing girls. And what if there are more that they don’t know about yet? Anxiety yanks on his sternum, tugging him forward in his chair. “Do you know who’s doing this?”

“How should I know, Inspector Douglas? I’m locked away in concrete and steel. You’re the one out in the world, meeting people.” Ollie’s words are aloof, his tone papered with dry disinterest. But Richard is sure he knows more than he’s letting on.

“If these women aren’t coming out of the water because of one of your disciples, then I guess I’ll have to figure this out the old-fashioned way. And if I’m doing that, I’m not going to feed you details about the case.” Richard swallows hard. His stomach gurgles and palms break into a sweat. These unmonitored talks with Ollie are the secret moments that have made Richard's career. But his direction always comes with some personal cost, and Richard won't know what that might be until after the dust settles. The weight of what Ollie's help might cost feels heavier now that Mac might be the one to pay for it.

"Do you have any suggestions on where to look next? How to stop him from taking another woman?"

"I'm afraid I cannot help you with this one. Not yet." Ollie's knowing smile drips through the phone. "Have any bodies been recovered away from the river's flood zone?"

"No, but we're keeping an eye out." Richard glances at the calendar hung at the edge of his desk. Mac keeps pushing him to use the digital calendar she's set up for them to share, but something about the physicality of the paper hanging from the dingy gray wall makes him feel grounded.

The scribbled over grid makes him wonder if the killer is late picking up his newest victim, or if there's simply no one left who cares if another homeless woman goes missing. Maybe the upheaval of the town during the storm has put him off his hunt. Or perhaps law enforcement combing the river has scared him out of the small town altogether.

"It's a shame there aren't more treasures to study in this case. It's easier to feel what demons my peers are working through when there are more data points." Ollie laughs at himself. "If we give them a long leash and sit back and wait, I'm sure there will be more bits to pick up later."

The discomfort balls in the back of Richard's throat and creeps down his spine. He wonders where he'd be if he hadn't married himself to Ollie all those years ago. There'd undoubtably be less talk about serial murder and data points. Would he and Josie be happier? It's too late to ask those questions now. Here he is, still drawn to The Godless Killer's power like a moth to a flame.

But this game is exhausting, and Richard is nagged by the threat of wearing out. He feels less spry and willing to jump through Ollie's hoops for a scrap of evidence. For the moment, he's still willing to play the part of the moth, the glow of faith, fame, and heroics are still bright marks on his maturing career. But he senses the time to pass the torch to Mac is growing near.

"I gave you all the information I can. If you get any ideas of who is behind this and how I can track them down, I'd like to be the first to know. This guy is killing in my wife's neck of the woods, and I want to keep her out of the crosshairs."

"You don't give Josie nearly enough credit," Ollie says. He sniffs. "I'm sure she won't come to any harm. She's far too clever for that. Good luck on your hunt, Inspector."

"Thank you, old friend." Richard pulls the phone's receiver away and hovers his thumb over the red "End" button.

"One more thing before you go," Ollie's voice shouts through the tiny speaker at the side of the phone. "You'll be put out to pasture before this is all over. Don't be afraid to have fun at your dinner party tonight. Let loose and live a little, before it's too late."

Richard smiles at the friendly suggestion. "I hear you. Thanks for the advice."

He hangs up the phone and his grin widens. Leaning back in his chair, crisscrossing his fingers behind his neck, he turns in his seat.

The dinner party. Shit.

Richard's smile falters. Did he mention the dinner party to Ollie during their call? He searches his memory but comes up blank. But he must have. How else would Ollie have known?

Fourteen

Mac presses her eye to the peephole and breathes a sigh of relief when she sees Sam walk into view. She pulls back to make space for him to open the door and he pulls a rolling suitcase across the threshold, kissing her on the cheek as he moves past her. She shuts the door and throws the deadbolt the second the door settles into the frame.

"I walked through the entire house. It doesn't look like anything's been touched since yesterday."

"Is there still an officer posted out front?" Mac asks while she trails Sam into the living room like a lost puppy. There's a hole in her gut where a sense of security used to sit, and the river of helplessness that pours into it seems to have no end.

Sam hoists the suitcase onto the crumpled bed sheets on the hide-a-bed, unzipping it to reveal bundles of haphazardly packed clothes punctuated by the spines of a half dozen books. "I didn't see a car, but maybe they have someone undercover?" Sam's lifted brow and crooked smile do little to dissolve the knot of pessimism in Mac's tired brain.

"Not likely." A shiver runs through Mac, and she hugs herself, trying to ward off the deepening well of unease drilling its way through her. She ignores the prick of tears in her eyes and begins the task of unravelling the contents of the suitcase. Sam packed enough clothes for the family for the next couple of days, and she's thankful for his efforts. But she still has to bite her lip to keep from complaining when she pulls out the rumpled blouse, and slacks covered in pet hair that he brought for her to wear to Richard's house for dinner.

Everything is wrinkled as hell, and nothing he shoved into the bag matches, but there's no use in nagging his efforts. At least he was able to get in and out of the house without any bother, and more importantly, he didn't get hurt along the way. She had wanted to go with him, knowing it would be safer for him not to go alone. But he'd insisted she stay at Becca's, as if her constant worry wasn't as hard on the pregnancy as a run-in with a phantom burglar might be.

While Sam settles into a nearby armchair with one of Becca's health and wellness magazines, Mac sorts and refolds the rest of the clothes and places Sam's books on the end table on his side of the sofa bed. The suitcase stands empty, not a dress-shoe in sight, and she decides Richard won't mind her turning up in sneakers. Josie, on the other hand, will notice her wardrobe's deficiencies. She might still have a pair of boots floating around the mess in the minivan. They're not quite what she'd like to wear to dinner, but boots are better than the bright blue glow of her sneakers.

Becca's laundry room has an iron to straighten out her blouse, and Mac finds a roll of packing tape on the shelf above the dryer that will serve to peel the pet hair off her slacks. There's no way Mac is going to be a picture of perfection this evening, but at least she'll be wrinkle-free and markedly less fuzzy.

Mac delivers the boys' clothes to the guest room where they've holed up with video games. They're keeping out of her way to avoid any more chores, and she pretends not to notice Robby's side-eye when she sets their clothes on the end of the full-sized bed. "Dad brought you clothes. He and I are getting ready to leave, and Aunt Becca will be back from work soon. How about the two of you take turns showering and get dressed in something clean? Aunt Becca might like it if you didn't smell like dirty socks when it's time for dinner."

"Gee, Mom. You say the nicest things," Ryan says. He leans over to his brother and sniffs. "Robby doesn't smell like socks. More like week-old garbage."

Robby smacks his brother and Mac gives him a warning look. He shrugs and goes back to his game. She leaves them to do, or not do, what she's asked.

If only she had controlled her anxiety better while Sam was gone. It would have been easy to take another look at the letters Josie sent to Oliver, and now she doubts she'll get another chance before she and Sam head over for dinner. As if he can hear her thinking about him, Sam meets her in the hallway dressed in a pair of wrinkled slacks, and a button-down shirt with a pinched crease trailing over his left nipple. The tie in his hand looks like a drunken sailor got hold of it, a tangled knot cinched at its middle.

"Help me with this?" he asks through pouting lips.

"Sure." Mac forces something resembling a smile. After all these years together, Sam isn't quite the gorgeous boy she chased after as a teenager. He's softer around the edges, with shallow creases tucked into the corners of his bright eyes. A dusting of gray hairs gives him a salt-and-pepper maturity that is sexy in its own way.

Her fingers work the knot until the tie is undone, and deep pink creeps up from under Sam's collar when she casts it around his neck and weaves it into a neat Half-Windsor. He smiles sheepishly while her fingers smooth the silk fabric, tucking it under his collar. "You look nice," she says softly. "It's been a rough couple of days. It's good to see you smile."

He kisses her cheek and heat rises where his stubble grazes her skin. It's not an uncommon display of affection between them, but something about the complexity of the break-in, the lack of privacy at his sister's house, and the pregnancy hormones hammering throughout her bloodstream ignites a fire deep in her belly.

Before she gets lost in the swooning feelings brewing inside her, she pulls herself back to her senses and finishes straightening his necktie.

Although she found Becca's iron, the ironing board is elusive, so Mac lays a towel on the floor of the living room and kneels on aching knees to iron her slacks, blouse, and the black trench coat with smart red stitches that she'd worn to the prison the day before. It reminds her of how she used to iron when she was nineteen, in her first apartment, when she hadn't had anyone but the Sunday congregation to impress.

As the wrinkles fade, her mind wanders. She wonders what it will be like to spend the evening with Josie. Will she blurt out that she knows Josie is in contact with Oliver? That would make for an interesting conversation, but depending on their connection, it could be dangerous to play her cards too soon. Mac could turn the conversation to cults and religion. Would Josie take the bait and inadvertently share something to confirm Mac's suspicions of the killer's views on faith?

The possible outcomes of both scenarios send a wave of nausea through her. Maybe she'll chicken out. It would be nice to have a simple, calm, normal dinner with her husband among friends, even if one of those friends might be under the thumb of a mass murderer.

Mac straightens the cuff of her slacks and presses down on it with the iron. One way or another, she's got to come back from dinner with more information than she's arriving with.

Once the iron is set back in the laundry room to cool, Mac carries her mismatched clothes to Becca's bedroom to dress. She's standing in front of the full-length mirror when Sam finds her again.

"Hey, good looking. You ready to go?"

"Ready as I'll ever be." Mac frowns at her reflection one last time, wishing she'd pushed Sam to let her go with him to the house earlier. She could have put together a more fitting outfit for the evening. She turns around. "Give me a minute to say goodbye to the boys."

The kids haven't moved from where she'd left them before. Their clean clothes are still piled at the end of the bed, and neither teenager bothers to look up at her when she enters the room. "Bye guys, be good for Aunt Becca."

"Bye," they answer in unison.

"I'll miss you, too," Mac mutters under her breath. She doesn't miss the extra work of toddlers in the slightest, but at least when Ryan and Robby were little, they acted like her absence was a terrible inconvenience.

Sam waits with the minivan, keys in-hand. They head out, double-checking the door is locked before they leave.

"Shouldn't we bring a gift to this dinner thing?" Sam asks while he looks over his shoulder to back down the driveway. "Bottle of wine? Crackers? Chinese takeout?"

Mac slaps his shoulder. "We're not bringing a sweet and sour platter to Josie's big dinner. Don't worry. Richard says Josie's a great cook."

"I'm not so sure." Sam grimaces. "Remember those vegan pinwheel sandwiches she brought to your company picnic a couple of summers ago? The plant 'meat' tasted like rotten eggs, and I swear whatever that 'cheese' was made of, reset the function of my spleen."

"You can't blame Josie for that. It was a hundred degrees outside, and nobody told you to eat a half a dozen pinwheels." Mac rolls her eyes. "But to answer your question about actual gifts, Richard said not to bring anything other than our appetites."

"I guess even rotten pinwheels will be better than eating whatever Becca makes for dinner. I feel bad for leaving the boys there to suffer her cooking." Sam's grimace returns and he sucks air through his teeth.

"They'll be fine. Besides, we deserve a night out without kids getting in the way. And there's no safer place for us to be than at Richard's, right?" Mac absentmindedly rubs her stomach. "If I have this baby, we're going to have a serious lack of adult time for the next decade."

"When you have that baby," Sam corrects her. He winks. "There's no if's about it."

Mac looks out the window at the passing scenery. How can she tell him she feels like she's dying every time she thinks about her pregnancy? The car ride to face Josie and her secrets isn't the best time to talk about the impending doom she feels wrapped around her uterus. There has to be a better place to bring the topic up. A way to help him see her side of things before it's too late.

She bites her lip when they pull up to a four-way stop, and a woman pushing a stroller jogs past the nose of the van. She's young and beautiful, with high cheekbones and a taut ass tucked into purple yoga pants. But she's also tired, mouth tight between sunken cheeks, shadows of dark circles poorly concealed under a heavy layer of makeup.

"Aww, did you see that baby? I can't wait to see you pushing a stroller again." Sam watches the woman all the way to the far corner of the intersection, waiting until she's pushed the stroller all the way onto the curb before taking his turn through the intersection.

The seatbelt tightens around Mac like a vise, pulling her deep into the minivan's upholstery like the mommy mobile is hugging her to death. She'll find the right way to tell him she never wants to push a stroller again. Won't she?

Fifteen

"Come in and make yourselves comfortable." Josie holds the door wide, pressing her slim frame against the hinges to make room for her guests to enter. She looks past them, up the block to where an unfamiliar dark grey SUV is parked. The interior of the vehicle is in shadow, and she has trouble seeing inside with the glare of the setting sun. It is not so out of place, she supposes. Just looks like another neighbor having their own set of company.

She returns her attention to her guests. Richard already has them gripped in the niceties of a conversation. Once the door is closed, left casually unlocked, she drops into place beside

Richard, clasping her hands at her waist. The model of patience and hospitality. It is so difficult to listen to their small talk with her plans for the evening buzzing around in her brain.

Richard shifts topics to their newest case while Mackenzie sets her purse in an armchair and shrugs out of her jacket. Josie looks at Sam, visibly uncomfortable with the discussion of river-churned corpses and the murky details of missing women.

Josie touches Sam's arm. "Want to help me finish getting dinner ready? Might save you the trouble of hearing all the gory minutiae of their case and ruining your appetite."

"Sure," Sam says with a limp smile. He kisses his wife on the cheek, but she is so engrossed in Richard's description of a drowning victim that she hardly reacts to his touch. Josie makes note of the detached interaction, and adds it to the list of things she detests about Richard's so-called protégé. If she had been more malleable, Richard could have passed the reigns to her years ago. It would make Josie's life so much easier if Mackenzie could accept the status quo.

Sam clears his throat, recovering from the unease of Mackenzie's snub quickly, and Josie leads him through the living room and into the kitchen. She opens the pantry door and hands him a neatly pressed apron. "You should put this on. We would not want to get any stains on your delightful tie. What is that? Silk?"

Her wink is playful, but still, he eyeballs the starched pink frills. "Are you sure I need one? I'm not that good of a cook."

"You will do just fine." She loops the apron around his neck before he has time to protest any further. She relishes the feel of the apron's thick straps sliding through her fingers and the way his body goes rigid as she reaches around to tie a knot behind his back. He hardly breathes until she backs away, and then his eyes meet every surface of the kitchen except her face.

His expression tightens even more when his eyes land on the kitchen island. The entire surface is arranged with a collection of pots, pans, and casserole dishes, each hiding its own secret treat.

"Did you invite someone else over for dinner? It looks like you're catering a wedding."

The compliment causes a giddy laugh to bubble up from Josie's chest. "I suppose it does.

It has been a while since we had dinner guests, and I wanted everything to be perfect. Do you think I overdid it?"

Sam shrugs and she delights in his discomfort. It is true; Josie has gone all-out, preparing a varied selection of appetizers, three main entrees, and both a decadent chocolate cake and marionberry pie for dessert. This may very well be Mackenzie Jones' last meal, and Josie has ensured it feels like the final supper of a royal facing the firing squad at dawn.

She steers him to a double boiler already on the stove and turns the burner on. "How about you make the Hollandaise sauce for me?"

"I don't know how," he says while his eyebrows knit together in worry.

"It is a lot easier than you think. The big secret is, to not stop whisking once you get started." Without waiting for a response, she directs him to separate the egg yolks. When his attention turns to cracking eggs, Josie pulls a vial from the cabinet and pours a healthy dose into the upper pot.

She cannot help but smile when he dumps the egg yolks into the puddle of clear liquid, whisking the concoction together, and nearly loses herself in a fit of giggles when the remaining ingredients are added to the pot.

While he is engrossed in stirring and watching the sauce thicken, Josie finishes setting the table. The dining room has been transformed from its day-to-day blank slate to a menagerie of color and texture. The table set for four is burdened with heavy linens, crystal and China dishes, and a centerpiece erupting with perfectly arranged flowers.

Josie carefully places formal flatware beside each of the four place settings and returns to check on Sam.

"Help! I don't know what to do!" he croaks when she enters the kitchen.

The bottom of the double boiler is bubbling like mad, steam rising into the air around him. Josie hurries to turn off the stove and looks in the pot. The texture of the Hollandaise is off, but the color is fine. She dips a spoon in, tempted to taste the lumpy yellow sauce to make sure the flavor is there, but hands the spoon to Sam. "Every good chef tastes his handiwork. Tell me, how is it?"

Sam wraps his lips around the spoon and his eyes close gently. He pulls the spoon away with a soft smile. "Wow. That's so much better than the powder mix we get at the grocery store."

The murmur of Mackenzie and Richard's voices grow louder. They enter mid-conversation, crowding the narrow galley kitchen. Richard inhales the rich scents of the kitchen deeply while Mackenzie shrinks into the corner near the pantry, a strange expression accompanying the color draining from her face.

"Dinner will be served in a few minutes," Josie says with her brightest smile. She lets the joy she feels at Mackenzie's cringe shine through and hums while she picks up a waiting bottle of wine from the counter to hand to Richard. "You three go on to the dining room. I will finish up and have the first course ready before you know it."

Sam wrestles himself out of his apron. "Sounds good to me. Thanks for letting me help. It was fun."

Josie curtseys to Sam in a playful way and then ushers the three of them out of the room. Alone, she fishes two cellphones from her skirt pocket. She sets the pink one on the counter and plugs it into a waiting cable to charge, and cradles the other in her palm. This one, a simple black cellphone, is like so many others Richard has never known about.

Plan in motion. Are all players ready?

She fills four bowls with mixed salad and arranges them on an ornate silver tray. The phone vibrates on the counter, and she swipes to read the reply.

Ready.

The phone slides easily back into her skirt pocket and rests against her thigh like the soft presence of a lover's warm hand. The lift of her cheeks and pull of her lips is genuine. This evening is going to be fun, even if she does have to play the doting hostess through it all.

Picking up the tray, she gracefully slips into the dining room. Richard and Sam talk about the latest political scandal while Mackenzie slouches in her seat, fingers tapping against her water glass like an annoyed teenager.

"Is everything alright?" Josie sets the first salad down in front of Richard, then weaves her way around the dining room to serve their guests. Her skirt swishes with each movement, its hem tickling her calves in a way that feels freeing. Seeing Mackenzie's weary eyes drag up to meet her makes Josie feel like twirling through the room in a manic dance.

"Everything's fine," Richard says. "We were just discussing that senator who was caught using campaign donations to support his collection of mistresses overseas. The way the fraud charges are stacking up, it looks like he's got a few rough years ahead of him."

The salad dispersed; Josie sets the serving tray on the sideboard beneath a framed family photo. Richard, their two grown girls, and a visage of Josie's past self, are all professionally arranged, smiling at her with straight white teeth. Thank God for the photography studio's image correction service. She would have died if Richard's tar-stained smile had hung on their wall.

"I still don't think the scandal will stick," Sam says. "Have you ever seen a politician ruined in this country over an affair?"

"One? No. But a half dozen?" Richard shakes his head.

Josie delicately sweeps her hands down the flowing skirt at her backside, tucking it neatly beneath her when she settles into her seat.

Mackenzie sighs from across the table and Josie watches her bored gaze wander the room, settling on the window. The poor woman looks like she would like to throw herself through it. Josie's smile does not falter, she would love to see Mackenzie try.

But she will be gone soon enough.

Richard has already poured her a glass of wine and Josie takes a dainty sip, enjoying the bite of the red wine against her tongue. She licks her lips, savoring the way the flavor mingles with the velvety feel of her lipstick. "Mackenzie, Richard told me about your trip to the hospital. I do hope you are feeling better."

Josie freezes her face in an expression of concern, holding back the smirk desperate to surface. Mackenzie's shoulders hunch when she folds in on herself, and her face loses another shade of color. Her hand shakes when she picks up her water to take a sip.

"Call me Mac, please."

"Oh, but Mackenzie is such a beautiful name!" Josie pretends to miss the irritation in her voice. "And then you had that break-in, after all you had already been through. So terrible."

Mackenzie chokes on her water and Sam pats her on the back while she gasps for air. "It's been a rough couple of days," Sam says over his wife's spluttering. "We appreciate you going to all this trouble. We needed a break from it all."

"Yes," Mackenzie finally says, her voice gravelly. "Thanks for putting all this together, Josie."

"Did they find the person who broke in?" Josie leans forward in her chair. Although she knows he has not been found, and never will be, she does not have to feign rapt attention. She is curious to see how it will all play out.

Mackenzie shakes her head and picks up her fork like she is going to shove a bite of salad into her mouth to stimy the conversation but cannot seem to do more than pushing the greens around in her bowl.

Sam rubs her shoulder, the circles moving ever more slowly as his wife's breathing settles. "Nobody has told us much, yet. I thought they'd be open with Mackenzie about their suspicions, but if they know anything, we haven't heard."

"Maybe they are intimidated, working a case involving such an important FBI agent." Josie smiles at Mackenzie's green-gray face and delights in the way Richard's partner keeps cutting her gaze away like a child whose confidence has been stripped bare. Josie follows the broken woman's dark eyes when they dart back towards the window. The tree in the yard waves its branches in the darkening evening, sending an ominous shadow across the glass.

Richard's fork clatters against his empty bowl. "Maybe we should switch topics. What's next on the menu, Josie?"

"A whole smorgasbord of options. Turkey and gravy, chicken parmigiana, or poached salmon with Hollandaise sauce made by Sam himself." Josie gestures at Sam and bows her head while Sam perks up with a proud grin and Mackenzie's cheeks turn to ash.

Josie is about to ask for everyone's order when the sound of Dvorak's sixth symphony tinkles from her cell phone ringing in the kitchen. "Richard, will you take everyone's order? I have to get that call."

Ever the dutiful husband, Richard nods and Josie excuses herself to hurry to the pale pink iPhone plugged in at the edge of the kitchen pantry. The screen shows a number she does not recognize, but she is used to answering calls from numbers she's never seen before.

"Hello?"

"Um, hello." The woman's voice sounds like it is falling through a network of mail tubes in a postal sorting facility. She pauses, and it takes a moment for Josie to recognize the rising and falling sighs in the background as fast-moving traffic. “Is this Mrs. Douglas?”

“It is. Who do I have the pleasure of speaking with?”

“My name is Sarah Myre. I don’t know if you remember me. I was hanging out by the food cupboard at the church on North Street a couple of weeks ago, and you gave me your number. You said to call you if I ever needed help?” The woman’s voice is tentative. Scared. And she lifts the last sentence in question, as if she is unsure if calling Josie is the right decision.

Josie’s already wide smile stretches until her cheeks burn with the effort. She closes her eyes and pictures the jagged edges of the woman standing on the broken pavement of Vernonia, her auburn hair darkening with the setting sun. Long, slender arms tucked into her starved body in a futile attempt to stave off the cold. Her t-shirt and ripped jeans hanging off her frame like the stained drapes of an abandoned house.

“Of course, I remember you, Sarah. What is going on?”

"I've been camping on the river with some people, and everything was going fine until we had to move. There was a flood."

"I heard about that," Josie said, and the corners of her grin dip with the frustration that attempts to poke through her giddiness. The flood had caught her off-guard and washed away enough of her work to be more than a nuisance.

"Yeah, we had to move our camp to a place where the bank was higher. It was a pain in the ass. Then today while I was in town trying to get some money, the cops came and tore down my tent." There is a hitch in Sarah's voice when she talks, but when she mentions the police, her tone turns hard as stone. "They threw everything I had in a dumpster. My sleeping bag, my clothes, everything. I was picking up bottles and cans to recycle for some cash, but they took all of that too. It took me weeks to fill my tent with all those bottles and cans! I was saving up for a hotel room or something, but now I've got nowhere to go. I know it's asking a lot, but you said if I hit rock bottom, you'd be there for me."

Richard wanders into the room and Josie waves him away. He scribbles something on a scrap of paper and disappears.

"Now, here I am." Sarah's voice seeps back into the hum of the background, quiet and distant. "Rock, rock, rock bottom. The rockiest bottom I ever saw."

The desperation in Sarah's voice makes Josie's heart flutter. After finding out the campers were moving, she had urged neighbors all around Vernonia to call and report the campers pitching tents on high ground around town, hoping they would push young women like Sarah over the edge.

Josie's skirt dances around her calves when she wiggles in a silent celebration. The timing of Sarah's predicament is flawless. "I am so glad you called. Helping women get off the street is what I live for. I am working closely with the city of Vernonia to raise funds for a new shelter, so there will be a safer place for women in your position. Everyone deserves a place to go. We even have a big fundraiser gala in a couple of days, and we hope to break ground on the shelter's construction next year. How lovely would that be?"

While she talks, Josie plucks Richard's list from the counter and begins arranging everyone's order onto white and gold Vera Wang plates, carefully placing each meal so the food does not cover too much of the delicate floral pattern. It's all about the presentation with quarry as precious as Mackenzie Jones. She doles out the dangerously prepared sauces over each entrée, leaving her own meal dry.

"I mean… sure. That'll be great for people next year. I'm calling because I need help tonight." Sarah's tone is heavy with anxiety and Josie scrunches her nose in delight.

"Listen, I am in the middle of something right now. It will be hours before I can get to you. But I do have a quiet place there in Vernonia where you can go to get warm. It may not look like much, but there is a small office where you can get out of the cold."

"Where is it?" Sarah asks, her tone lifting in hopeful question.

Josie's lengthy pause is calculated. "Actually, I do not want everyone in the homeless camps to know about it. There is plenty of food, and a cot for one, but if you tell anyone about it, it will get overrun."

"I won't tell anybody, I swear!" Sarah's voice cracks as if the threat of losing a couple of bags of chips and access to a dry cot is too much for her to bear. "None of the assholes I'm camping with tried to get the cops to leave my shit alone. Not even my friends. I'm not gonna share with people who are too chicken shit to stand up for me. I've got to look out for myself. I'm not telling anybody where I'm going."

"I really want to help you." Josie lets the statement hang as if she is contemplating some perceived risk. She is careful to not let the smirk on her face carry through the worry in her voice.

"I swear. You can trust me!" Sarah breathes so heavily into the phone that Josie can almost feel it.

It is easy to manipulate someone as desperate as Sarah into her web, but Josie relishes the moment, anyway. "Okay. Okay. I trust you, Sarah. Be a good girl and take down this address." She rattles off the street address without bothering to wait for Sarah to say she has nothing to write it down on. "The entrance is covered by an awning. Wait there and I will send someone to meet you in a few hours."

"But aren't you going to meet me?"

"Like I said before, dear. I am busy." Josie punches the button to end the call and slips the phone into her dress pocket while she admires the meals she has prepared. Everything looks exquisite, and even with the drug infused sauce, the taste is sure to match the presentation.

Humming, she loads the plates onto her serving tray and carries it to the dining room.

"There she is, Miss America!" Richard sings the beauty pageant tune off-key and his mouth slips drunkenly around the words as the Rohypnol from the wine works its magic.

"I still can't believe you made all this food just for us." Sam speaks more clearly, but the glassy gleam in his eyes tells Josie he is not too far behind Richard where the drinks are concerned. A few bites of dinner are all it will take…

Josie serves her beautifully arranged dishes to each of the diners. "On our first date, Richard took me to an all-you-can-eat buffet. He had one of everything, and I guess feeding his love of variety has stuck with me. Besides, with the work I am doing in Vernonia, I have a never-ending supply of mouths to feed. Trust me, none of the leftovers will go to waste."

Mackenzie, clear-eyed and stoic, stares across the room at the Douglas family portrait. "How did you two meet, anyway?"

"She rear-ended me." Richard draws out the e's when he speaks and gestures to Josie with the pepper grinder before blackening the salmon and hollandaise on his plate with a hailstorm of pepper.

“A happy accident,” Josie says with a grin. She presses her skirt neatly down and lowers herself to her chair before her naked chicken breast and dry slice of bread.

“It’s kinda funny story.” Richard takes his bite and dabs at the corners of his mouth with a loosely held napkin while he chews. “I’d just left my first Godless Killer crime scene. Gruesome find. I was tryin’ ta get outta there before anybody saw me puke. I swore I looked around before I put it in reverse, but I must’ve been deeper in my head than I thought.”

Mackenzie leans forward in her chair, sniffing at the gravy drenched turkey and potatoes on her plate. Her hands hover over her silverware but when the color drains from her face, she sets her hands back in her lap and leans back against her chair, redirecting her attention to Richard. “Was that the Henry Sanchez case?”

Richard’s nod is off-kilter, and it bobs like a novelty toy on a spring. “Thaz the one. It was a mess. Body’d been kept inside a wall of a Baptist church, well preserved ‘nough to paint a clear picture of the torture Sanchez endured. Ollie tattooed a note on the victim’s inner thigh.

But even with the vic clean as 'e was, took us weeks of trawling through missing person's files to ID the guy."

His chin dips too low in a moment of silence, then he jerks his jaw upward and looks at Josie with shining eyes. "I'd gone to th' scene to poke around. Get a feel for what happened. Never knew some jackass'd rear-end me and change my whole life."

"I think I was more damsel in distress than a jackass. Different perspectives, I suppose." Josie winks at him playfully and the curl of her lip is genuine as she remembers their first meeting.

Richard takes another big bite of fish and chews sloppily. "This woman gets out of her little cream-colored Fiat and starts cussing me out! I argued with her 'til she reached into her purse and threw her drivers' license at me. 'I'm gonna lose my job if I'm late again!' She was cryin' an' carrying on. I felt bad for her, so I pushed her car back into its space and drove her to work." A lazy smile crawls across his lips and his cheeks redden. "I got chewed out by my director for the whole fiasco, but Josie met me for coffee after we both got off work. Totally worth pissing the boss off."

Josie's smile lifts until her cheeks cut into her vision. "Speaking of beginnings, Mackenzie, Richard told me you received some big news after your fall at work the other day." She looks across the table at Richard's partner, even though she has known about the pregnancy since the day she stole the first test.

The hand Mackenzie uses to lift her fork trembles too much for her to hide. She uses it to cut a miniscule bite of gravy-drenched turkey. She tucks the bite between her teeth and chews slowly before answering. Her ashen face glistens with sweat. "Sorry, I need to use your bathroom."

"Let me show you where it is." Josie rises from her seat and leads Mackenzie through the kitchen, directing her down the hallway. "First door on your left."

She takes a step to the side, allowing Mackenzie to move past her. Up close, it is easy to see how exhausted Richard's partner is, as though it has taken up all her energy to make it this far. Drooping eyelids hover over eyes saddled with dark circles buried beneath thin makeup. Josie sizes her up, instantly glad for the helping hands waiting to move Mackenzie's stockier body from the house.

The evening is far from over. Josie will share her prey in a few short hours. Although it will be convenient for a fresh set of hands to join her in manipulating Mackenzie's corpse later, she could have been fine on her own. She has ways of moving even the heaviest flesh to-and-fro when she wants to.

Josie turns on her heel, ready to leave Mackenzie to a few last moments of privacy, when the younger woman stops in the middle of the hallway. She stares at another family photo hung along the corridor, a puzzled expression on her face.

Mackenzie turns to look at Josie, a fire blazing in her weary eyes. "It must have been easier for Oliver to follow the investigation with you romancing Richard."

"I am not sure what you mean." Josie cocks her head to examine the picture herself, reaching out to straighten the frame by a degree.

The photo is of Josie, Richard and their two girls when they were toddlers. Josie sits in an armchair with a girl on each knee. They rest their heads on her shoulders, and her arms wrap around their waists in a practiced pose that might look like protection to anyone who did not know better. Richard stands to the side of the chair an arm's length away, his placement awkward, as if adding him to the portrait had been an afterthought.

"They have Oliver's eyes." Mackenzie's voice is low, as though she is afraid of the words.

A spark of electricity dances through Josie's chest. This game of cat and mouse is fiendishly delicious. All these years of Richard being too blind, afraid, or stupid to recognize Josie's relationship with his star offender has made Josie complacent. But in Mackenzie, a feeble, pregnant woman in her last hours, the game has truly begun.

"How long did you follow Oliver before you met Richard? Or did your affair start after you and Richard were dating?"

The laughter ringing between Josie's ears tinkles like rain over the accusation. "*His* follower? Hardly. Though our mother never did like the way we got on. She said our connection was unnatural. Her jealousy forced our father to send me away."

Silence grows between Josie and Mackenzie like a cancer. The agent's eyes are piercing and thoughtful, and the gears turning deep inside her mind bring Josie an amount of satisfaction she had not anticipated. Mackenzie had sidestepped the truth and giddiness at the missed mark bubbles inside Josie. Josie leans forward to close the gap between them.

"When we were children, we went on grand adventures together. Oliver would capture pets around the neighborhood for me. Soft little creatures that would follow a child to the ends of the earth, just as happy as could be." Josie's lips curl so completely, her jaw aches with pleasure. "I took them to the woods behind our house and played with them in my own way. I taught Oliver what to do. He loved me so much; he would do anything I wanted him to do to them."

Josie sinks her hands into her pockets, playing with the phones hidden there while Mackenzie folds into herself. The great FBI agent trying to fill Richard's shoes looks ready to puke. "Bet you never read any of that in your reports."

"Oliver Roberts' sister has been missing for forty years. She was abducted from her adoptive family's home." Mackenzie's shallow breath rattles her voice while she pushes the words out. Her hand rises to her chest.

"Well, look at that. I just solved a cold case, did I not? What a pair we make, Special Agent

Mackenzie Jones." Josie winks and gestures to the bathroom. "Didn't you need to powder your nose?" She shoves her husband's partner and Mackenzie stumbles backwards over the bathroom threshold, an expression of utter shock written across her face. Josie flicks on the light and leaves the agent inside, closing the door between them. She listens to Mackenzie vomit and ignores the urge to make sure she made it into the toilet. Instead, Josie fishes the black cellphone from her pocket.

She is nearly ready.

The toilet flushes and water runs at the sink before the door swings open again. Josie smiles. "Feeling better?"

"Sam!" Mackenzie shouts. "We're leaving!"

Mackenzie shoves Josie's shoulder and marches with purpose back the way they came. Josie feels the weight of the phone in her hand. Her men are waiting on her, and the thought gives her renewed strength. Mackenzie Jones is about to disappear like everyone else who has ever gone against Josie or her brother. She trails the wild-eyed woman through the house, telling herself it will be fine. The men should be under by now…

"Did you know she's Oliver Roberts' sister?" Mackenzie starts yelling before she is even through the door to the dining room. She sweeps an arm backward and grabs Josie by the sleeve, dragging her into view.

Josie yanks her arm back and straightens her dress, as gentle and demure as ever. "I do not think Mackenzie is feeling very well. I heard her throw up in the restroom."

"What?" Richard's eyes are glassy and his focus wanders between Mackenzie and Josie. "Olvr's sister is dead."

"They never recovered Kristin Roberts' body." Mackenzie grabs Josie by the elbow, squeezing like a vise. "Kristin didn't die. She just reinvented herself. She's right here."

"Sam," Josie keeps her voice light. "I think the strain of the last few days has pushed Mackenzie beyond her limits. Surely, that is not good for the baby."

Mackenzie's husband stands from his chair but does not lift his palms from the crisp white tablecloth. He lists to one side, knocking his silverware to the hardwood floor.

"What's wrong with you?" Mackenzie's voice is shrill as an alarm. Her husband's elbow bends awkwardly, and he stumbles where he stands, shoulder hitting the table edge before he falls backwards into his chair.

"I dun feel so gud," Sam mumbles. He squints hard. "D'you think it's tha wine?"

Richard's shoulders slope unevenly. He rocks backwards in his chair. "Did Olivr make Kenzie keep tha baby?"

"Not if I can help it, Dear," Josie answers.

Mackenzie's face glows. She balls her free hand into a fist and wrenches it backwards, only to throw it lightning fast towards the bridge of Josie's nose. Josie does not have room to duck the blow, and her sinuses crackle with the fiery explosion of an instant hemorrhage.

"You drugged them!" Mackenzie screams when Sam's eyes roll into his skull and his head drops to his shoulder.

Josie elbows Mackenzie's ribcage and wriggles her arm, trying to break loose from the woman's grasp before she strikes a second blow. But Mackenzie follows Josie's every movement and punches her below her left eye. She can hardly see, her brain is on fire and her nose feels like it has shattered into a thousand pieces, but somehow Josie wriggles her way backwards into the kitchen. Mackenzie lunges for Josie's throat, but is interrupted by the metallic flash of a handgun sweeping overhead, knocking into her right temple.

Mackenzie's grip loosens and her fingers slide away from Josie's arm while she slumps against the countertop. Groaning, the agent traces a hand across the painful impression in the side of her head.

Triumphant, Josie snatches a dishtowel from its hangar beside the sink and presses it against her nose. There is a whistle when she inhales, and she feels the blood bubbling into the towel with her sigh. She stares at one of her men through eyes narrowed from anger and swelling. His features are obscured by a black ski mask, but the way he moves and the hatred in his eyes tells her enough of who he is. "Damit, Carl. Took you long enough."

Sixteen

The shadow that passes over Mac might be a person, though she can't decipher the shape through the gauzy haze of her vision. But the searing pain that radiates from her shoulder when her arm is yanked upward, hoisting her body upright, is unmistakable. Her tongue catches between her teeth when she clenches her jaw, but the angry grunt that tries to escape is caught behind lips sticky with blood.

She's pulled against a tall, lean body, her arm flung over the figure's shoulder. Up close she can see their head is covered in black, turning them into a faceless monster. Anxiety grows in her chest, but a wall of anger beats the worry into submission. Hatred engulfs her like a wildfire, and she vows not to lose whatever sick game is being played. A sharp pain pierces her jaw when she finally works it loose. “What the hell do you think you’re doing?”

The arm around her ribs tightens like a vise until a second body slides under her opposite shoulder. Her toes drag across the checkerboard tilework stained with what Mac can only assume is her own blood. Her heart bangs off-kilter in her chest, and she can almost feel the adrenaline seeping into her bloodstream. When the person on her right slips, dropping her against the kitchen counter, everything jumps into focus.

“Surely you big, burly men can get her out without making more of a mess.” Josie is hunched over, opposite the kitchen island, tipping a bottle of soda water into a towel and dabbing it at a dark stain splashed across her chest. On a good day, Mac would reach her in three long strides, and rip the wretched woman’s hair out. But right now, even though Josie is mere feet away, her voice is distant, worming its way into Mac’s ears through the thundering irregularity of her heartbeat.

“I’ll get out of here myself,” Mac splutters. Her tongue is swelling, and the words come out like broken glass. Josie’s eyes rise to meet hers.

"I would rather you not. Carl, be a dear and tilt her head backwards for me?"

Before Mac can argue, fingers tangle in her hair and yank her head backwards until her eyes are filled with the bright white of inset lights against a cream-colored ceiling. A second hand wraps around her jaw and the pain in her cheek blooms, sending the metallic taste of blood down her throat. She coughs, gasps, and the ceiling spins like an unhinged merry-go-round.

Fear douses the fire of hatred within her, and her veins fill with ice. It can't really end like this, at the hands of a couple of goons and an egotistical housewife… can it?

Mac squeezes her eyes tight against the swirling room and drives her focus to her other senses. The bodies to her left and right hold her tight when she fights against them, though her battle is short-lived when her chin is squeezed tighter and the fingers in her hair twist until it feels like her scalp is ripping away from her skull. The feathery scent of tulips and thistle mingles with the ruddy blood in Mac's sinuses. Josie must be close.

Her mouth is pried open, and Mac opens an eye to see Josie's delicate hand pour a cool liquid between her lips, any flavor it might have is not strong enough to wipe out the wet-penny taste of her squirming tongue.

"Are you backed up to the garage, like I asked?" The small glass vial and Josie's hand disappears from Mac's weaving vision, and both grips on her head loosen. Mac lowers her chin and watches Josie drop the vial into a kitchen drawer.

"Yes, ma'am." The voice is familiar, scratching at the back of Mac's mind. An echo of a memory she can't recall. "How long 'till she's out?"

"Give it a few minutes. She already had a head start over dinner." Josie's smile weaves across her face like a mirage over asphalt on a hot day.

Whatever was in that vial was strong enough that Mac's reeling mind slows to a crawl, and though she wants nothing more than to grab her gun and fight for her life, her body won't answer her call for action. No amount of blinking can stop the dimming of her vision, or the weight of the pull of gravity on her slackening limbs.

"I'm gonna..." Mac fights over the words, losing her train of thought before it leaves the station.

Josie laughs and says something in response, but the words come into Mac's mind upside-down and backwards. Her eyelids draw themselves closed, erasing the world as her body is jostled, and then dropped, falling in a direction she can't decipher.

Soon Mac feels like she is nowhere at all.

Seventeen

Richard lifts his head from the pillow and the room tips on its end like a ship threatening to capsize, listing to port until the deck touches the sea. He breathes deep, willing himself not to vomit. If he soils Josie's starched white sheets, imported rug, or the hand-waxed hardwood floors, there'll be hell to pay much worse than any hangover.

His movements are slow and measured when he rolls onto his side but no matter how gingerly he turns himself over, the searing pain behind his eyes still feels like he's been hit with a fire poker. He attempts to open his eyelids, but the resistance of his eyelashes knitted together is too much to bear.

"You and Sam had quite the night." Josie's harsh tone splits Richard's head in two, pounding a mallet of misery that is nearly as unbearable as the disdain dripping from her words.

"I didn't think it was that much. Two glasses of wine, at most." The way Richard's lungs cling to his breath, only allowing him to pulse shallow exhales without turning his stomach over tells him otherwise.

"The two of you were insufferable together." Josie sniffs her disapproval and Richard knows better than to fill the silence. The weight of her pause punctuates her hatred of him. "No wonder Mackenzie dragged him home halfway through dinner."

"They left?" The confused scrunch of Richard's nose shifts to a wince of pain. He can't figure out why everything hurts so much, or what he and Sam could have said or done to piss Mac off. Maybe it wasn't as bad as Josie is saying and Mac's hormones made her overreact.

The gluelike grip of his eyelashes finally breaks free, and he opens his eyes to find Josie tucked into her side of the bed. She's surrounded by a nest of pillows, a pad of Post-it notes and colorful gel pens arranged in her lap. She turns the page of a new home decorating magazine and bites her lip as she devours the print. An ache behind his ribcage fills him with the impulse to reach for her, to answer the yearning need to curl his body around hers, to let her warmth sooth him. But they haven't shared an intimacy like that in years, so he shoves the urge back into its cage. Without her affection, it's up to him to ease his own discomfort.

"How long have I been passed out?" Richard asks the question while he turns himself around again and inches towards the edge of the mattress. The room swims around him, but he's determined to get his feet under him. Maybe if he leans against the waving walls, he can walk it off, find his phone and call to smooth things over with Mac.

"Only about a half hour, I suppose. Not nearly long enough." Josie peels a Post-it from the stack in her lap and places it carefully on the page. She selects a purple pen to write her note, then sets it back in the pile and turns the page of her magazine without offering to help him up. Oh, shit. He must really be in it deep.

A quiet clunk deep in the house forces the muscles in his neck to twist towards the bedroom entrance. "What was that?"

"There's a storm coming through. It's probably the wind. You look ill. Why don't you get back in bed?" Josie tilts her head with an expression of mock concern that Richard knows well. But she reaches to the nightstand for a glass of water, stirs it gently with a spoon, and hands it to him.

He takes a sip. The cool liquid feels like a balm on his raw throat and soon he's downed the entire glass. "Sorry," he says. "Didn't mean to drink all your water."

"It was not mine. I had it just for you." Josie's smile softens the edges of her harsh gaze.

"I'd better call Mac. Make sure everything's okay." Richard tries to get his feet under him, but dark foggy fingers wriggle at the edges of his vision. Closing his eyes, he settles back onto the mattress. Maybe if he rests a while, he'll have an easier time checking on Sam.

Downstairs, a door shuts and Richard's eyes snap open.

"Damn it," Josie mutters. She sets her book on the bedside table and quickly stacks her reading supplies beside it. When she uncovers herself, she looks like she's dressed to go for a nature hike, not spend the night between the sheets. Richard blinks furiously at the sight of her, so out of place. Where are her pajamas? He shakes his head, deciding she's right. He must really be out of it.

She rounds the bed, heading for the hallway, but stops at his feet, expression shifting to a cold, dead-eyed glare. "You stay right there."

He shifts his weight, about to try to follow her, and she steps towards him. He suddenly has an overwhelming fear that she'll smother him with a pillow. Could he pull himself together enough to fight back if she does? He wrestles his arms into a defensive position over his chest, palms towards the ceiling, as if they'll do anything to deflect her when she leans over him.

Relief washes over him, cooling his flushed cheeks when she gently pushes him towards the center of the mattress and tucks the blankets tightly around him like a mother putting a child to bed. Without a word she leaves him there and he listens as her footsteps fade down the hall. Hears the creak of the staircase and then her voice drifting through the air from somewhere far away.

Who is she talking to? He tries to sit up, uncover himself and get up from the mattress, but the effort of pushing himself upwards sloshes the blood around in his brain and the pressure of his eyeballs resting beneath their lids is too much to bear. The bed slides out from beneath him, and the floor rushes upwards, catching him with his face pressed into the curled fibers of his woolen slipper. With hands pinned between his torso and the floor, he feels curiously free from pain. Two slow blinks and his brain releases him from the boundaries of his body, and he sinks into darkness once more.

Eighteen

The ground beneath Mac shudders like an earthquake. She jostles against rough fiber with the motion, and when she inhales, lint and a suffocating putrid rot fills her nostrils. A scratchy, dense fiber fills the space where air should be. She tries to push and pull herself away from it without success.

Her tongue is heavy in her mouth and her jaw feels like it's split in two. She must be on her side, though the dark tunnel pressing in from all sides makes it impossible to tell for sure. One shoulder presses more firmly against the material than the other and she guesses it is the side resting against the quaking ground.

She searches for an opening but doesn't find one until she tilts her head backwards as far as she can, fighting the friction of the material tugging at the loose hairs of her mom-bun. By pushing her chin into the grit of the material, she can create enough of a pocket to breathe.

The mass encompassing her smells like a low-rent crypt's decomposition. She's too weak to move what she realizes is a cocoon of something heavy like carpet, and she's walked through enough crime scenes to know this doesn't bode well for her future health.

Whatever Josie poured down her throat left her brain foggy, and her body too worn down to make any headway in loosening the material. Sifting through her mental files, trying to remember any victim who escaped a similar situation, her focus breaks when the world slides to a halt. The momentum rolls her against something hard, and while worry filled her mind before, now that she knows she can roll around this place and her arms won't budge from their straight-to-the-hip placement, ripples of hopelessness shatter her calm like a rock thrown in a pond.

A pair of muffled thumps come from somewhere outside the cocoon, and then Mac's tiny world returns to silence. Even the sound of her breath is absorbed by the scrappy threads of carpet. Mind fuzzy, muscles tense, the skittering spiders of panic crawl under her skin. She won't be able to do anything if she can't breathe. She blinks furiously in the blackness, breath fluttering in her chest so rapidly she hardly feels like she's getting any oxygen at all.

"Breathe, Mackenzie." Her words have nowhere to go, which makes them feel even more important. She tilts her head, pushing her nose into the small bubble of open space above her head and forces herself to draw a slow, fetid breath. Mac curses to herself. The air trapped in the carpet is thick with dust and mire, causing a dull ache in her lungs that makes the effort feel pointless.

A million things race through her head, none of them pleasant. She waits for something to happen. Has she been dumped somewhere? Or is someone watching the bundle she's in, looking for a sign she's alive? The incremental way her ribcage expands and contracts with each half-breath feels like dying a fraction at a time, and the pressure over her diaphragm feels like it's growing tighter by the minute.

She could asphyxiate right here, rolled up in a rug like a burrito, easy to dispose of whenever, and wherever, Josie and her crew decide.

Heart thudding against the prison of carpeting, Mac's breath comes sharper. So loud that it fills the space between her ears. She always thought death would be silent. But the wheezing struggle for oxygen clamors through her like the rattling percussion of a brass band, vibrating every bodily cell in a feral roar for survival.

Her brain buzzes louder with each recycled breath. She's trapped. Has she been here five minutes? Hours?

Her own critical voice cuts through the clamor inside her mind. "Why the hell haven't you been counting your damn breaths?" She puts herself to work, focusing on the count to have some way to track time, and keep herself busy.

There's a sound nearby, like a warped door swinging open in a neighbor's apartment. The rug shifts around her, and something presses through the layers of the rug against her shins. Her legs rise up a few inches, but she hardly has time to register the odd angle of her twisted legs before a sharp pull on the rug moves the entire bundle wrapped around her.

There's a pause before the next tug, and the carpet scrapes its cheap, plastic fibers against her exposed skin when it shifts again. Pull by pull, she slides feet-first toward oblivion, until the firm floor beneath her disappears. Gravity grips the bulk of her and she drops like a sack of potatoes.

The rug cushions the blow of her head slapping the floor of whatever new space she's in, but it also fills her nostrils and mouth with hair and dirt when she gasps in surprise. Muscle and tendon strain and snap with the impact, and she lands with toes facing one direction and hips shifted in another. Her bubble of air collapses with the movement, and she fights to find space to breathe again.

There's no air in this space. She hadn't known what a luxury the gap between her chin and the rug's grisly fibers had been. Now it's gone, closing off any hope of returning to the world. The end is here, and Mac doesn't even have the will to fight it.

Her legs are hoisted higher again. Whoever is handling her drags her lopsided corpse onward, but when spots invade Mac's blackened vision and all her senses fade away, she realizes she doesn't even have the energy to care where they take her.

Over the years, she has stood above dozens of decomposing corpses, visualizing the circumstances that brought each individual to an early grave. Experiencing it firsthand is much, much worse than she ever imagined.

Nineteen

Josie reties her apron around her waist and carefully scrapes dinner's remains from the delicate China dish into a large, plastic takeaway container. Even cold, the food looks divine. Sam was right, she really outdid herself tonight. The food pantry will be delighted to receive such decadent meals, and she is sure Vernonia's townspeople will not mind having a couple of quiet days once the pantry distributes the meals and the rabble sleeps off the effects of their sedation.

Of course, if the food is given to children, it could be fatal. She looks at her reflection in the dark glass of the window and considers how this should bother her. She is a mother herself, after all.

Josie shrugs her shoulders and turns back to the task.

She is glad Richard is finally fully blacked out. It took more liquid ecstasy to knock him out this time than it has in the past. She is glad she thought to climb into bed with him for a few minutes after Carl and his hired men dragged him upstairs. He had stirred himself awake almost as soon as they had gotten him in bed. It would have been better for him to make it through the night and wake up in the morning to a clean house and even tidier story about how Mackenzie and Sam had gone home with no fuss at all.

But Mackenzie made things difficult for everyone. She had not eaten enough of the dinner that would have put her under, and even after being forced to swallow a straight dose of gamma-butyrolactone, she fought harder than Josie expected. The ruckus of the three hired men trying to get her into the SUV was enough to pull Richard from his stupor and Josie hopes her coverup story sticks once he wakes up.

A trickle of sweat slips down her forehead and she wipes it away with the back of her hand before sliding a casserole dish of chicken parmesan across the counter to a waiting line of empty takeaway containers. The spatula scrapes against the smooth dish while she divides up the portions, her divine purpose guiding her hand.

Once the last portion is set aside, the dishwasher churning loudly under the counter, Josie stacks the takeout containers in a pair of oversized grocery bags. She looks around the spotless kitchen, making sure she has not missed a smudge or fleck of blood from the evening's struggle, then carries the heavy bags towards the garage door.

She is nearly there when a noise upstairs causes her to cock her head to one side and listen. A floorboard creaks and something drops to the floor with a heavy thump. Has that bastard woken up again?

Josie hurries through the doorway and sets the bags beside her car before returning to investigate. The house is silent when she re-enters the kitchen, so she slips out of her shoes and tiptoes towards the stairway in the center of the house. Where is Richard now?

A sinful tingle of excitement stirs in her belly as the predator in her awakens. If all goes to plan, she will not need to kill Richard or Sam, but her well-laid campaign has been shoved off course; first by Mackenzie's refusal to pass out like she was supposed to, and now by Richard's defiant wakefulness.

She will have to call her supplier tomorrow and file a formal complaint.

Palms sweaty, Josie wipes her hands on her apron hem and quiets her breath until even she cannot hear it passing in and out of her lungs. Her toes search out the quiet edges of the stairway until she is high enough to examine the hallway. It is empty and she creeps the rest of the way to the top stair.

The shadows cast from the nightlight at the end of the hallway lean in on her, reaching across carpet and floral wallpaper like black fingers of death beckoning her forward. She tiptoes into the master bedroom and finds Richard crumpled in a heap, face-down beside the bed. Josie freezes where she stands, waiting to see if he springs to life, but he simply lies there, a pile of flesh and limb, their bed's wrinkled sheet draped over his left shoulder.

A few quiet steps are all it takes for her to reach him. She kneels to examine him. It looks like he tried to reach up for a blanket, but passed out again before he succeeded. Shoving him hard, she rolls him from his flopped over position onto his side. His face is slack; eyes rolled back into his head, and jaw hanging loose. He looks like a marionette with cut strings.

"Such a good boy," Josie coos. "You will not be any bother at all." She closes her eyes and inhales. Letting clean air in, and blowing out the darkness, she tucks the monster within back into its cage. There is no need to destroy her best alibi tonight.

Just as she has a hundred other nights, Josie pulls a pillow from the bed and tucks it under his lolling head. She pulls a thick quilt from the chest at the end of their bed and tucks it around him, smiling when she thinks of him waking in a few hours to the feel of the soft fabric around him. Even if he is on the floor, he will be appreciative of the care she has given him. One more stitch in a patchwork of events that have strengthened their bond over a lifetime.

A cellphone buzzes in her pocket and she hurries from the room, pulling the door closed behind her. She is moving down the stairs when she retrieves the black phone to answer. "Yes?"

"The husband is home. We left him parked at the end of the driveway with the motor running, so it looks like he pulled partway in and passed out." It takes Josie a moment to recall the voice speaking between heavy breaths. Javier. The second of Carl's hired hands. The crinkled sound of him jostling the phone makes Josie wonder if he is running.

"Have you heard from Carl?" Josie asks as she plucks her car keys from the rack in the kitchen.

"Not since we put the rug in the SUV. He was going to meet Father Roberts on the way. Want me to call him?" A door closes and Javier clears his throat.

"No, he will check in when he has time." Josie's lip curls into a Cheshire smile. It will not be long before Mackenzie and Oliver are reunited, outside the protection of steel walls and video cameras. "He is in for a long night. Let him be."

She ends the call and returns to her car, placing the packaged meals carefully into the trunk before getting inside to start the engine. She taps the button on the garage door opener, humming to herself while the door creeps upward. The street outside the house is deserted, peeling away the veneer of anxiety. None of her immediate neighbors has security cameras, so no one will see her leave.

It only takes a few moments to reach the end of the block, and only a few miles more until she is on the highway heading out of the city. She turns from the main highway onto a winding road, driving for an hour through thickening evergreens that blot out the moonlight. An hour later the faint lights of Vernonia creep through the trees and she cruises through town towards the church on North Street.

Before she gets there, she pulls onto a neighboring road, driving all the way to the turnaround at the termination of the dead-end street. She parks the car, watching her mirrors for movement behind her, counting the few lights left on by residents smart enough to be wary of what might lurk in the dark. She picks up the ski mask and gloves from the passenger seat and puts them on, zipping her jacket up to her neck and flexing her fingers in the gloves before returning down the street and driving the rest of the way to the church.

What is known as the food cabinet is a cooler built into a boxy framework. She parks beside the ramshackle hut and opens it up. The innards are in disarray. Empty wrappers litter the shelves, and a soda bottle left on its side has leaked its sticky contents, attracting an army of sugar ants.

"What in God's name is this? Do you people not clean up after yourselves?"

She swiftly cleans up the garbage, tossing it in the trash can chained to the side of the pantry, and collects a bottle of bleach and a rag from her supply box in the trunk to wipe away the soda and ants. Only after it is clean does she retrieve the food from her trunk, and soon the shelves are filled to bursting.

How happy the nearby beggars will be when they awaken to find meals waiting for their empty bellies. The thought makes Josie grin.

The phone vibrates in her pocket. Josie peels a bleach-soaked glove off to answer. "Carl. Are you unloaded?"

"Yes. There is a girl here. She says her name is Sarah. She has asked me to let her into the building."

Josie chuckles. "Yes, please do. There is food in the front office, and a cot. Get her settled for me, will you? I am on my way."

She ends the call. Her smile falters beneath her mask and there is a tug of discomfort in her chest. Oliver will be here soon. Tonight will be a rekindling of what they had before their mother sent her away. A conclusion to the dance they have performed with Richard and the FBI. A rebirth of their true selves, seen by no one but their victims and the inky black sky.

"It is the end of an era," Josie whispers to herself as she returns to her car. "May as well go out with a bang."

Twenty

Mac had been relieved when the explosions of pain faded into the serene release of numbness. Was thankful for the foggy bliss of exhaustion that triggered the collapse of her nervous system, shutting off the messages between her mind and the gaping wounds Oliver and Josie inflicted in the black of night.

Now, she sobs as warmth wriggles its way through the disconnected tissues of her being. If they find her alive, the torture will start all over again. All Mac wants is for it to stop. Forever.

The entirety of her body stings, as if she's been left to lie on a bed of nails. She can feel the thick crust of blood and vomit encasing her skin, cracking in places where she's been bent to someone else's will. The scent of gasoline and rusted steel weave their way through her sinuses, mingling with the bile and hammering the inside of her mind with each new beat of her heart.

She wishes her stubborn heart would stop beating and release her from her broken shell.

Although death would be a welcome visitor, she is inexplicably alive. She filters through the biting agony and takes an inventory of her surroundings. Quiet voices speak nearby, though she can't hear enough through the screaming impulse to flee to make out what they're saying. Straining to lift her head upward, she swings it to one side and catches the heavy rumble of a large truck passing by and opens her mouth to scream. They might be close enough to hear her. But her raw throat seizes, and her lungs burn with fire when she inhales.

The hinge of her jaw feels like broken glass, and the only sound that escapes is a hoarse gasp that sours before it crosses her tongue.

She concentrates on prying open eyelids crusted with dried tears and blood, heavy as concrete slabs, whimpering with the impotence of a deflated balloon as her eyelashes break apart, one by one. Her vision is foggy, an unfocused wash of yellow coloring the upside-down shapes around her. In the wavering light she can make out barren branches of a dead tree reaching for her prone frame.

Below her is the sky, broken in two. One side of the universe shrouded in darkness, stars too far away to cast their light on her, watching her die like curious strangers. The other half is a blur of colors; blue-green and burnt orange reaching out to cover her in a burial shroud.

Exhaustion shutters her eyes before she can make sense of what she's seen, and when she opens them again, the color brightens and spreads farther across the sky. Even through the slits of swollen eyelids, she's never seen anything so beautiful.

An excruciating pain, like the vertebrae separating over the edge of a dull knife pierces her neck when she tips her chin upward, hoping for a better look at a morning she never imagined she'd see. The movement throws her off balance, tilting her backward. Instead of being washed over with relief, water sloshes against her head, filling her nose and mouth with fetid sewage.

Jerking her chin toward the sky, through the pain, she forces herself upward, trying to find the strength to lift out of her topsy-turvy position. She needs to get the water out of her airway, breathe full, and clear her head so she can take stock of what little remains of who she was just the day before. Her limbs are locked in place, bound together in rope and some sort of harness. The rope winds around her, passing through a ring at her middle. A hook weighs heavy at her chest, its thick clasp fastened around the ring, and a second rope snakes upward from it, high into the branches above her.

The way she lays, bent backwards at an odd angle, is disorienting. The sky dips below her and muddy water looms above. She wriggles enough to tip herself towards her feet and realizes she's stuck high-centered with her back arched over the tangled knots of the tree's root, her body reduced to a bundle of dead weight at the end of a forgotten hoist. Like a ragdoll draped over a handrail, her body hangs backwards over the root, left for dead with her head and feet bobbing in the acrid water.

She struggles to sit up, teetering on the rough bark wedged beneath the small of her back, but she doesn't have the energy to move more than a few inches upwards. The momentum of her slight swing up draws her backwards again. Her toes reach for the sky while her head drops beneath the sour waterline, forcing the river to flow freely into her nose and mouth. The slick polluted water floods the back of her throat and when her body convulses to cough it out, the grisly sludge forces itself into her lungs.

Sparks of stabbing pain explode behind her eyes as she gags and splutters. Cold water runs deadly fingers through her unkempt hair like an unwelcome lover, frigid tendrils playing at her scalp and scraping her will to live from her brain.

The sounds of people and traffic that seemed so close a moment ago disappear beneath the water, smothered by the howling rush of the river in her ears. Spine tensing, chest heaving, she fights to lift her head above the surface, but she's so tired. The water pulls her downward, flowing into her and refusing to flow out again. The morning light fades above her and the cold fills her veins. The thunder of her panicked heart slows, the fire of survival flickers, and Mac understands it's time to move.

Death whispers to her, commanding her to join him, promising to rid her of the pain tethered to her being. She remembers Sam,

Ryan, and Robby. If she lets go of the world and tumbles into eternity, she will never see their faces again. The grip of nothingness tightens around her, the bite of Death's maw splintering bone and tendon. Hope fades like a dying flame, blown out in the breeze of a whispered secret, and there's nothing to do but surrender.

Terror bubbles away, filled with the calm end of the struggle. She fades into the dark, slips beneath the thin veil between life and death, and accepts the place where her bones rest, is on the riverbed. Her soul unwinds itself from her body one thread at a time, ready to float back to where time began.

The serenity of acceptance shatters with a jolting wrench so severe, it feels like she's being split in two. The river peels away from her skin while her corpse is yanked toward the jagged fingers of the tree branches. A breeze whips at her, stripping her of a layer of warmth she wasn't aware still sat on her bones. She teeters upside-down, the weight of her sodden hair pulling her back to the river while her feet stretch towards the clouds.

Blood flows from its still place in her veins, rushing to her head. She panics at the visions popping behind her eyelids and forces her eyes wide. Vision unfocused, she can still make out the fuzzy mud-slick shore. The breeze turns her lazily around until she sees the wavering lines of a narrow parking strip. The asphalt is cracked, upheaved in sections, and a glossy chunk of metal winks at her from across the lot. Her sluggish mind fights until it connects the boxy shape with that of a vehicle, but the association is lost with another yank upwards.

The rope at her chest heaves her upward again, swinging her another quarter turn. A building is nearby, bright in the morning sun, a long arm of canopy jutting from its side. Discarded hoses lay across the pavement like a half dozen black snakes, their nozzle-shaped heads reaching towards the riot of brambles invading the scene from every direction.

Upward and around, she moves through the air. The blinding sun lifting its head above the horizon, its light washing out the grime and grit with its joyous arrival. The sharp stabbing pain of her crooked spine screams for her to stay still, but she forces her neck to bend, her head to turn, to look at the trunk of the tree below her.

In the shadow of dead wood, there is a flash of one bright hand moving over another. The bulbous shape of arms setting their weight against rope, and the sickening feeling of her body being lifted upwards once more. Mac blinks furiously, willing mud and blood from her eyes, forcing herself to focus on the person braced against her weight.

At their feet, another body lies, blank eyes staring at nothing. The corpse's long, auburn hair erupts like a firestorm from the upturned collar of a long, muddied jacket. The bloodied hem of a blouse is ripped away from the body's waist, exposing the waistband of the slacks that bunch loosely around the body's legs.

Mac considers the glassy-eyed woman's attire. It's the kind of outfit she might find buried in the back of her own closet; not here, limbs splayed every which-way, sandwiched between the broken asphalt of an abandoned building and the muddy shore of a river crawling too-high up its banks.

The costume draped over the lifeless corpse is a corrupt glimpse of familiarity. The fit of the carefully selected fabrics hugging battered skin with deliberate care, seamlessly drawing Mac's eye along the woman's soft curves and long limbs with effortless design.

“Is that me?” The words leak from Mac’s lips, her voice settling on the breeze like cotton over broken glass.

There’s no answer but the tug at her ankle, a tight grip pulling her closer to the swinging haze of land. The length of rope that hoisted her out of the water angling itself as the living body at the base of the tree pulls her over solid ground. It’s unclear if they are her rescuer, or her assailant. The thrill and terror of both outcomes prod the corners of Mac’s muddled mind as she gazes down at the bulk of their hooded clothing, the dark fabric blending into the murky landscape and staggering bulk of the tree.

One length of rope at a time, the sky recedes, and the ground rises gently to meet her. The blood thumps in her ears but all her other senses are overwhelmed by a thousand different sensations. Is the flutter in her breast panic, or the woeful arrival of hope?

She touches land and those haunting eyes; at once Josie’s and Oliver’s, look her over from tip to toe. “Why won’t you die?” Josie whispers. “Let me help you.”

A knife appears in Josie’s hand, the flash of the early morning sun glinting across its blade before it snaps through the skin at Mac’s neck. A fresh dampness seeps across her chest, warm and thick like pancake syrup on a Sunday morning. Mac shudders a breath and closes her eyes. Behind her eyelids, Sam holds a baby, rocking it to sleep, humming *Origin of Love* softly. He looks up at her, smiles, and fades into the dark.

Twenty-One

Josie pours herself a mug of coffee and settles into her favorite chair. She tugs a blanket from the armrest and lays it across her lap, protecting her from the chill sneaking through the house. The patter of rain on the window mingles with the rustling pages of the newspaper she pulls from the side table, the night's events whisked away from her memory by a sharp, wild wind.

She props her feet on the ottoman and dismantles the paper, draping each section over her shins. The heavy stutter of Richard's footsteps on the stairs sends her glance to the clock to check the time. It is already half past ten, long beyond when he should have run off to work. Josie grins. The delay in his wakefulness gave her plenty of time to clean up from her nocturnal adventures.

"Good morning," she says when he shuffles into the room. She turns a page of her paper and lets her eyes drift across the page. "Did you sleep well?"

His tongue darts over his cracked lips and he wheezes a sigh. "Like the dead, I guess. I feel like I was buried six feet under and am just clawing my way back to the surface."

Josie tightens her face and finally grants him the courtesy of her gaze. "You drank more than you should have."

Richard scratches the grit of stubble along his jaw. He looks like he has aged ten years overnight. "The dinner went well though, right? Everyone had a good time?"

The tension in Josie's face loosens into a smile. He does not remember their conversation the night before… wonderful. "I have not heard any complaints."

"Good, good." Richard stretches his arms overhead and yawns. "What did you make of Mac and Sam's big announcement?"

"About the baby?" she offers as if they had said anything about it at all. "It is a surprise, certainly. But wonderful for them. Do you think she will stay on with the FBI?"

"Why wouldn't she? She's worked too hard to give up on it now." He cocks his head to one side with a curious expression and his eyes drift across the room while he thinks. When he focuses again, the whites of his eyes peek out from under droopy lids. "Oh, shit. You didn't tell me how late it is. I was supposed to meet her at the office hours ago. She's probably pissed."

"Since you are already running behind, you may as well take a few minutes to get cleaned up and eat some breakfast." Josie pretends to refocus on the newspaper while he considers what she has said and smiles to herself when he trudges towards the kitchen. He staggers like a drunkard, which is almost enough to make her believe he actually had gone too far with his drinks the night before. She sinks into her chair, allowing the padding to embrace her, and sniffs a chuckle of satisfaction.

Pounding on the front door rouses her from her contentment and she tosses the newspaper from her lap, drops her blanket to the floor, and is halfway across the living room before Richard makes it out of the kitchen. Josie swings the door open to find Sam leaning heavy against the doorjamb, his wild bloodshot eyes searching her face for answers to questions he has not yet asked.

"Sam! What are you doing here?" Richard crosses the room quickly, too lost in himself to realize he is sloshing coffee across the floorboards.

"I'm looking for Mac. Did she come back here last night?" Sam leans over the threshold and his head swivels like a marionette while he searches the room. His sour breath is overwhelming. It reminds Josie of the final, fetid exhales of her victims. She breathes in his desperation and steps back so he can enter, closing the door behind him.

She leans against the closed door and watches Sam hobble towards Richard. The pair of them look at one another, puzzled.

"Mac's not here. I was just about to call her to apologize for being late meeting her at the office." Richard's wild eyebrows knit together. "You look terrible. I'll pour you a cup of coffee and find my phone to call her."

"The office? Could she be there? But… how would she get there? Her car is at Becca's house." Sam shakes his head, like he is trying to knock something loose inside. “Where did she go last night?”

“She drove you back to your sister’s, didn’t she?” Richard asks. He looks at Josie with confusion.

“Yes,” Josie answers with a sharp nod. “Mackenzie said she was not feeling well after dinner. And I am afraid Richard shared a little more wine with you than he should have.” With this she tosses a cutting glance at her husband and enjoys the way he shrinks, taking a step away from her as if a mere gaze can cut him. “You were in no shape to drive, so Mackenzie drove you home.”

Sam lists to the left when he shakes his head again, but catches himself on the entry table before falls too far. “I woke up in the van because both our cellphones were ringing off the hook. Becca was calling since we hadn’t come home all night. We looked all over the neighborhood but didn’t find any sign of her. And my car was still parked on the curb, right where we left it last night. But Mac… she’s gone.”

Josie frowns. “That is strange.”

Sam casts his bloodshot eyes around the room once more. “I have to find her. I’m sorry to have bothered you." He stumbles out the door and onto the porch, Richard following close behind.

"Have you called the police?"

"Yes. They took a report over the phone and said they'd send someone out later today. Who knows when that will be? Becca said she'd wait for them and told me to check with Mac's friends, so I came here."

"You could have called us," Josie says as she touches Sam's shoulder compassionately.

Sam looks at her, face so full of worry that he does not appear to understand what she has said. "On the phone? Oh. Yes. Well…" He looks down at his own shuffling feet. "I'm not thinking straight, I guess."

"Go back to your sister's house, Sam. You don't look like you're in any condition to drive around on a wild goose chase. Get on the phone, call your family and friends. I'll check to see if she's at the office, then I'll touch base with you. If the police show up, file their report."

"She's not happy about being pregnant." Sam's face pales and beads of sweat form along his forehead. "You don't think she'd leave me, do you? Not like this?"

Josie wraps her arms around him, absorbing his misery. She keeps her features tense with worry, though the intensity of his victimhood feeds her soul. She knew he would panic but had not anticipated the vigor of this moment. His wide bloodshot eyes are like exquisite stained glass. The sweaty sheen of his skin like morning dew. She basks in the heat of terror that fills the air around him like a summer breeze.

"What if we can't find her? Something terrible might have happened." Sam's voice is weak and warbling, like a lost child at a festival, searching for his mother. His knee buckles and he grips the porch rail to steady himself.

"Do not say that," Josie says softly. She looks at Richard. "I will not let Richard rest until we find out exactly what happened to her."

Twenty-Two

Blinding sunshine streams through the windshield, cutting through Richard's retinas like knives while he waits for his turn at the guard shack. He grumbles as the gate draws nearer, knowing he'll have to remove his cap and sunglasses while the guard checks his ID. The black-on-black van ahead of him pulls to a stop and the guard waits for the driver to roll down the window.

Richard swipes his finger across the screen of his cellphone propped on the dashboard and rings Mac's desk phone one more time. Anxious disappointment sinks in his gut when the call goes to voicemail, and he disconnects just as the van crosses the threshold of the entry gate.

"Good morning, Inspector Douglas." The young guard leans against the frame of the open window. "ID please."

Despite the guard's acknowledgment of who he is, Richard lifts his cap from his head and removes his aviator sunglasses. He pulls his badge from his pocket and hands it over so the kid in a security uniform can verify it's authentic, the same way he does every day. A second guard walks the length of the car with a mirror and scent dog, checking under the chassis for tracking devices and explosives.

"Has Special Agent Jones come in yet?" Richard hides his anxiety behind a casual tone and the guard hands his ID back to him.

"Haven't seen her. But I just got back from my break." The guard looks over the grubby roof of Richard's ancient car at his partner, who is fiddling with something on the rear passenger door. "Jimmy, you seen SA Jones?"

"Don't think so," he answers.

A tingle of unease slithers across Richard's skin like a snake and spreads through him, invisible until it quickens his breath and brings on a cold sweat.

"What you got over there?" the guard at Richard's window asks. "Did you find something?"

Richard cranes his neck to look through the passenger window at the guard hunched over beside his car. His car has been checked at the gate for explosive and tracking devices every day for decades, and never before has anything ever been found on his car. A fleeting worry passes through his mind. Ollie is irritated at Mac's refusal to submit to his offer, and now she's missing. Does Ollie see her obstinance as Richard's fault? And if he does, how far will he go to punish the failure?

The pause in the guards' conversation sends Richard's heart climbing up his throat. This could be it. The silent Father of the Killers Club ending Richard's life with a bang.

"Gum," the second guard answers with a grimace. "The dog tried to lick it off the car handle, and now it's stuck in his fur. Damn dog. I just gave her a bath! The car's all clear though."

Richard's thoughts tumble around inside his head. If Mac isn't with Sam, and isn't at the office, where is she? "Maybe Jones is so stealthy, she snuck in when no one was looking." Richard lets the joke answer his own question.

"If anyone could do it, she could," the guard at the window says with a smile.

Richard puts the car in drive and touches his temple with two fingers in a goodbye salute as he's waved through. He parks in the first open spot he finds and trots across the parking lot, winded by the time he makes it through the front doors of the building. The morning light casts the lobby in a golden glow that might be inviting if it weren't for the phantom knife carving up the inside of Richard's brain. The lingering scent of stale coffee, half-smoked cigarettes shoved back into their packs, and cheap breath spray that hangs in the air aren't helping matters. It mingles with the tincture of aftershave and panicked sweat collecting on Richard's upper lip, and although he moves through the security queue quickly, it still isn't fast enough.

His lungs burn while he rushes through the building, brushing off greetings from people he passes and side-stepping anyone who tries to start a conversation. When he reaches the office he and Mac share, he rests his hand on the doorknob and freezes, whispering a silent prayer. He imagines her inside, pounding her computer's keyboard, deep in the business of solving the Vernonia murders.

The door's handle slips under his sweaty palm, and he grips it tighter, forcing it to turn. He pushes the door and steps into the office with a smile. "Good morning, Mac!"

Although the office lights are on and the air smells faintly of powdered sugar donuts, Mac's desk is empty. A half-empty tray of donuts sits in the trash, leftover from his snack run the day before. He steps to his workstation and flips through the mess atop his desk, hunting through the refuse for a note from Mac. When he doesn't find one, he turns on his computer, and checks his e-mail. There are a handful of messages marked urgent, and he promises himself he'll check them later. But nothing from Mac.

The message light blinks furiously on his landline, and he punches the code to check his messages.

Richard, this is Warden Darren Hazel from down in Sheridan. We've got a problem. Oliver Roberts is missing, and we haven't found an inmate willing to tell us where he might be. We're reviewing footage to figure out where he's hiding. I won't authorize a BOLO until we're sure he's no longer on the grounds, but given your closeness with him, and the threat he made to your partner, I figured I owe you a courtesy call.

Richard restarts the message and listens to the time stamp. The call came in at a quarter to eight the night before, right in the middle of dinner. Shit.

He scrolls through his contacts on his cellphone, looking for Detective Sharpe's number, but the phone on his desk rings before he finds it. He punches the speaker button. "This is Inspector Richard Douglas."

"Inspector, this is Detective Malone from Vernonia PD. I need you to come out and meet me and my partner. Another victim was called in this morning."

The niggling breeze of dread that tickled his nerves earlier escalates with hurricane force, nearly yanking him out of his chair. "I hate to tell you this, but your vic has to wait. Mac is missing. No one has seen her since last night." Richard pauses and an idea falls into place. "Unless she's already there with you. Have you seen her?"

When the line falls silent, Richard checks the call to make sure it's connected. Malone clears her throat. "I haven't been down to the scene yet. I only just got the description from the responding officer. But, Richard, when they told me what she looks like…"

"Yes?" Richard asks, tapping his foot with impatience to get through this call so he can get back to looking for Mac.

"I think it's her."

Twenty-Three

A low drone of music seeps into Mac's consciousness. The volume ascends through the void until Mac recognizes it exists somewhere above her, outside her. Out in the great, wide world. She gasps a panicked breath and is rewarded with a shot of oxygen, hot and stale, close and heavy like the unmoving atmosphere of a mausoleum. The stench of death and decay fills her nostrils and her swollen tongue sticks to the roof of her mouth with her own blood, thick and coppery at the back of her throat.

A sheet of rough plastic scrapes against her cheek when she turns her head. She twitches, confused by the sensation clenching her abdomen and reaching into the unknown. The ground drops beneath her, spinning the world abruptly as the weight of her bones slide through her skin to her left side.

Stomach twisting, sour vomit erupts from her throat. Adrenaline sharpens the fuzzy edges within her, bringing her to life. With flesh burning like fire, she gropes her surroundings. Her left hand refuses to bend, sending shooting pains from palm to skull. The fingers feel like flesh hung on bent wire, and she cups the palm instinctively close to her side, but when she tries to bend the arm to bring it closer, it won't move. The rope that bound her before still snakes around her, its rough fibers digging into her skin.

Her body feels broken, though her eyes are too watery and overwhelmed by the dim green light filtering through woven plastic to see how badly. The burn of her lungs explodes in a quiet gasp when she realizes she's lying beneath a tarp.

The notes beyond the cocoon change pitch, and the volume increases. A man sings with the radio while the momentum of the world slows to a stop. Mac straightens her legs, only for the balls of her feet to rest against something firm and unnatural. Could it be siding, or a hard plastic panel? The floor beneath her shifts while the man's baritone voice blends with the familiar rumble of wheels on asphalt.

Mac inhales slowly, attempting to keep the rising tide of panic bound inside her. Her ribs rake against her lungs like talons and she bites back a scream while silent tears collect in the papery folds of her cheeks.

She's bound, covered in a tarp, every inch of her seared in a pain unlike any she's ever known; a prisoner hidden inside a moving vehicle. The light bleeding through the tarp means there's a window out there somewhere. At least she's not suffocating in an enclosed trunk. Thank the universe for small miracles.

Wherever she is, the casual warbling coming from beyond the plastic means the crooner hasn't heard her move and isn't aware of her blooming consciousness. She doubts it'll stay that way for long, but for now she's alive, and that's enough. Knowing she has this small sliver of an upper hand eases her panic. If there's a way to get out of here, she'll find it.

The singer wanders through the scales and she strains to hear if the voice is familiar. A vision of Oliver Roberts carefully carving her skin within a dark concrete block building sends a shudder through what's left of her core. She blinks rapidly, erasing the image and refocuses on the singing happening here and now. The voice is too low, too garbled with road noise and the tune on the radio to make out clearly.

Moving backward through her thoughts, she tries to remember how she got here. There are flashes of recollection… She and Sam standing on Richard's front porch… Josie serving dinner… Mac's realization that Richard's daughters carry Oliver's features, and Josie revealing she isn't his lover, but his sister… The mud of a river… And then, the cinderblock hell where she was bound with another woman.

Josie and Oliver together, playing with her like a toy. Josie's joke that she and the other woman looked similarly enough to be twins. The murderous siblings slicing Mac and the other woman's abdomens open before shoving their hands beneath thin ribbons of skin.

The punishment Oliver dealt for Mac not choosing his side was brutal. Her body vibrates with despair as each memory burns through her, but she bites back the sobs trying to escape. She can't cry, not now, not until Oliver and Josie are stopped.

Mac shifts her weight slightly, attempting to move her right arm, and feels a faint stirring of muscle and sinew. It's painful beyond belief, but she can move it if she pushes herself hard enough. It's a marvel after what she's been through.

The vehicle leaps over a bump and her body bounces away from the floor. A flash of painful recollection courses through her; the memory of the moment she was dead washes over her like the very river that stole her soul. She clenches her working fist and holds her breath, willing the stabbing pain of her carved belly and broken ribs to work against the nausea threatening to boil over.

She didn't die, though she was sure she had. From her position stuffed in the cargo hatch, she's lucky her captors thought so, too. If they think she's a corpse, there's only one place the man crowing to Oh the Larceny can be taking her to. She's not lucky enough for a *Weekend at Bernie's* reunion, though if they propped her up against a jukebox and put a cocktail in her hand, she wouldn't complain. No, wherever they're going, it's bound to be somewhere he is sure she'll never be found.

The vehicle stops. The radio dies when the car is shut off, and Mac doesn't hear any movement. Then the floor beneath her adjusts with a shift of weight and she hears a door close. She hasn't heard anyone else in the vehicle, but that doesn't mean another person isn't sitting in the back seat, waiting to see if she moves.

Controlling her breathing feels impossible with the penetrating grip of her fragmented breaths digging into her lungs. She counts to ten, counts to twenty, and decides she can't wait any longer. She has no idea when that guy is coming back, and she needs to find out as much as she can about where she is before he does.

Her spine feels like twisted rebar when she bends her legs, tucking her knees as far beneath her as she can. Her hip erupts like a spilled bucket of hot coals when she wriggles herself to her side. Although she tries to keep her movements small, the plastic tarp crinkles and whispers with every motion. She freezes, sure some unseen enemy will realize she's alive.

Nothing happens. A low groan pushes through her clenched teeth when she tucks her knees closer. Ignoring the crumpling plastic, she hoists herself upward. She doesn't have the strength to get fully onto her knees but when the tarp shifts it creates a gap of open light. She cranes her neck to look through it. Her view is narrow, and she curses to herself, frustrated with how little she can see. A wall of thick, gray carpeting saturated in bright daylight is directly in front of her. A sliver of window spans wide above the sidewall.

A panel van would be more enclosed, and the window she sees is much too large for a work truck. She thinks about her minivan. It has large, panoramic windows, and a carpeted cargo space, smaller than where she is now. Could she be in an SUV?

Whether she's in a family van or not, she doubts the person carting her around is taking her to Disneyland. She's got to come up with a plan, and quickly.

Footsteps fall on gravel outside, slow and deliberate. They near the back of the vehicle, stopping just beyond her enclosure and she thinks she hears the rattle of keys. She drops herself low, biting her cheek to keep from yelping from the agony of the movement while the mechanism inside the rear door clicks in its housing.

The area around her brightens and the plastic tarp crackles with the change in pressure when the door opens. The air fills with mixed scents of dust and pine, and knowing she's close enough to freedom to smell it makes her muscles twitch.

Should she scream? Try to squirm through the open door? What if the person has a gun? Is there any way she can fight them with her arms tied to her sides, her ribs broken, her abdomen raw with scabbed-over wounds, and her ankles bound together?

She listens for the sound of people. If someone beyond the SUV can hear her, it could be worth blowing her cover. But the only thing she hears is the scraping of metal against rock and before she has time to understand the sound, something hard lands against her side.

They toss something small and heavy on top of her next. Its metal surface cracks the side of her head and stars flash behind her eyes. The throbbing inside her skull intensifies tenfold and it takes everything she has to not pass out. A sharp hunk of metal hits her side, but despite the fresh pain tearing through the throbbing misery dripping from her body, she stays quiet and doesn't react.

The door slams shut, striking Mac with fear like lightning. Tears spring anew and her tight lips tremble over her teeth. She missed her chance. She should have tried something… anything. She collapses the rest of the way to the floor. The tarp folds backwards, revealing the sharp edge of a shovel. Her situation is not getting any better.

"Shit," she whispers before a door in the front of the vehicle opens. The engine starts and the radio plays again. The driver puts the transmission in gear, and they move forward a few inches before a shrill jingle punctuates the cabin and the vehicle stops again. Jim Carroll's chorus of *People Who Died* is cut short when the driver kills the radio.

"Hello, Josie." Without the road noise and radio, the speaker's voice is loud, clear, and distinctively Oliver Roberts. There's a lengthy pause and Mac realizes he must be on his cellphone. "I'm about four hours away from camp. It's been a long time. I look forward to savoring the time it takes to get Mackenzie Jones in the ground. I do wish you'd come. We could make s'mores."

Being trapped in a vehicle, Oliver driving her to her final resting place, turns Mac to stone. This is much worse than him issuing instructions from a bank of phones in his prison pod in

Sheridan. He warned her that she'd pay the price for not agreeing to be his pawn, and here he was, delivering his promise in person.

Terror freezes the blood in her veins, and she sticks her tongue between her teeth to quiet their chattering.

She scrambles to think of where they're headed, but the Pacific Northwest is a serial killer's playground. And Oliver has picked his way across the landscape, keeping his favorite haunts secret for decades. He might take her to the coast, deep into the Olympic Peninsula, or to the northern Cascade Range. He's dumped bodies in the high deserts of central Oregon, and as far south as the Umpqua National Forest.

Mac dives deep, searching for some sliver of a silver lining surrounding the mind-shattering migraine pounding between her ears like a bleak thunderstorm. Oliver doesn't know she's alive. If she can keep it that way, she has time to plan her escape.

"Yes, yes. Of course. I'll see you in the morning. Love you, too." Oliver ends his call with a calm, brotherly farewell. It's as casual as if he'd been talking about where to meet for breakfast, instead of burying the corpse of an FBI agent somewhere in the wilderness. He skips through the radio stations a moment and settles on whistling happily along to the melody of One Republic's *I Ain't Worried.*

At least one of them isn't worried about what's coming.

The vehicle pulls away from wherever they've been parked. High branches pass by the sliver of window Mac can see through, and she wonders which of the thousands of neighborhoods with tree-lined streets they're leaving? A bump in the road shifts the metal tools atop Mac, and they clatter together like cymbals.

"Oh no you don't," Oliver says. He hits the brakes and pulls sharply to the right.

The moment they stop, he exits the driver's seat and hurries to open the rear hatch. Cool air tickles Mac's bare feet, begging her to fling herself outside. But before she can even consider it, Oliver's hand is on her, pushing her down as if he knows she's alive. She's sure he'll unwrap the tarp and strangle her. She'll never see her family again. Alarm bells rattle inside her and she opens her mouth to let them loose, to not go silently while he breaks the thin thread of life she's clinging to.

His hands move, separating the tools and tucking them around her more securely. “That’s better. Don’t need this beautiful drive ruined by that noise the whole way.”

He shuts the door, returns to the driver’s seat, and pulls into traffic. The radio clicks on and Oliver resumes his low sing-along. Under the protection of poppy music, Mac allows herself a quiet sigh of relief. He doesn’t know she’s alive.

Yet.

Twenty-Four

Richard has long been numb to the violence of most crimes but when Detective Sharpe emerges from the small, white tent behind the crime scene tape, the open flap revealing a body wrapped in a muddied black trench coat, his stomach bubbles and a brick of dread sits heavy in his chest.

He fumbles with his seatbelt as Sharpe saunters towards him, finally getting it to unclasp when the detective ducks his head into the open car window. "Thanks for coming out. They just finished with photos of the scene and the M.E. is getting ready to leave. Want to take a look before they bag her up?"

“Yeah,” Richard says with a nod. The way Sharpe talks about Mac like a bag of leftovers reminds him of all the times she’s urged him to speak gently with victims’ families, and he vows to do better. He peels his fingers from the steering wheel and forces the car door to open.

He feels like running away, though with legs that feel like they’re made of lead, he wouldn’t get far. Even if he did, Ollie would drag him right back here. He warned Mac that it was dangerous to ignore his friendship, and now here she is, dumped in the mud without even a fraction of the care he’d shown his other victims. This is more than murder, it’s a reminder to Richard to stay in line, or suffer the consequences.

A breeze comes off the river, lifting the sour smell of a nearby lumberyard and decomposing refuse shoved into the corners of the abandoned gas station lot. When the wind drops off again, the scent of wet wood and decay rolls over the asphalt in a putrid cloud. He releases the grimace from his face and breathes through his mouth to avoid the smell. Passing under the yellow tape Sharpe holds aloft, he shoves his hands in his pockets, cutting off the impulse to touch anything involved in the crime scene.

The forensics photographer pushes the tent flap out of the way and nods to Richard and Sharpe. Pins and needles prick behind Richard's knees and his heart climbs into his throat when he's let into the white canopy tent. He steps gingerly under the flap, casting his eyes away from Mac's body and inching forward like a child trying to find the courage to check for a monster under the bed.

He takes a bracing breath and turns to look at the body lying flat on her stomach, face obscured by her long, auburn hair. She's still dressed in the clothes she wore to dinner the night before. Did Ollie take her immediately after she returned to her sister-in-law's house? Guilt pierces Richard's chest when he imagines Ollie lying in wait in the bushes of a neighboring yard, jumping out at Mac after she pulled into the driveway, and forcing her out of the car.

An urge to comfort her settles into his bones. He wants to cradle her in his arms, the way he held his girls when they were young. To tell her he's sorry and wipe away the stain of fear he imagines in her eyes. He knows he can't fight the urge to reach out and feel her much longer. "Does anybody have any gloves?"

Sharpe pulls a pair of blue nitrile gloves from an equipment bag shoved in the tent's corner and Richard puts them on slowly before kneeling beside Mac's prone body. He pulls the hair back from her face and gags. She's battered and bruised, her features unrecognizable from the woman he's known for the past few years. Her mouth is open in a silent scream, cracked lips peeled back in an echo of the agony she felt in her final moments. The lower half of her face is off kilter, like her jaw was broken and left intentionally askew.

The paternal need to hold her is buried under the shock of brutality. Richard drops her hair and curls his hand into a fist, covering his mouth while he swallows a stream of vomit. He turns away and stands, stepping to the edge of the tent to spit on the ground. "It looks like her, but we should make sure," he says to Sharpe once he's recovered enough to speak. "Can you pull her left boot off?"

"They'll undress her when they do the autopsy," Sharpe says.

Though this isn't his crime scene, he knows how agonizing the wait for reports and confirmation can be. He bites back a snarky remark. "Humor me."

Sharpe considers him for a moment, then moves towards the body and crouches at the feet. He pushes the sodden pant leg up her shin to reveal the boot's mud-caked zipper. It takes a moment to work the zipper past the debris stuck in its teeth, but soon Sharpe peels the boot away, exposing the calf, shin, and ankle. The skin is a portrait of yellow and purple bruising, painting a map of the ordeal she's been through. But something is missing.

Richard's heavy breath is a mixture of relief and confusion. It's not her.

"Mac has sunflowers tattooed on the inside of her calf." Richard's finger trembles when he points it to the empty patch of skin where Mac's tattoo should be. "Whoever this woman was, they've done a great job of making her look like Mac. These are the clothes she wore to dinner with me and my wife last night."

"So they wanted us to think she was here, but took her to another location." Sharpe lets out a low whistle. He looks up at Richard, the boot still in his hands. "Does this mean she's still alive?"

Richard shrugs. His internal monologue struggles with itself, taking turns celebrating and mourning, surging with relief that this isn't

Mac's body lying in the mud, and drowning in despair that if she's not here, she could be anywhere. Ollie is on the run, and while it's possible he'll get in touch with Richard soon, there's no telling what he'll do to Mac between now and then.

Sharpe replaces the boot on the woman's leg and tugs the pants back into place. Richard steps backward as far as the tent allows when the medical examiner and her assistant duck inside to prep the victim for transport to the morgue. He watches them unroll the body bag and reposition the body to make it easier to move.

When they shift the body to hoist it into the bag, the jacket falls open across the woman's hips and the blouse rises above her navel. The change exposes a deep horizontal gash across the victim's abdomen and Richard's heart jams itself between his tonsils. Ollie isn't just making a statement about his ownership of Mac, he's claiming her embryo, too.

"Hey," the M.E.'s assistant says. "There's something here."

Richard was so distracted by the woman's desecrated abdomen that he hadn't even noticed the canary yellow envelope encased in a sealed plastic bag. It rests in the depression where the woman's body had been a moment before.

"That's for me. Can we open it?" Richard doesn't bother to hide the anxious creak in his voice.

Sharpe shakes his head and pushes the tent flap open. "Get the photographers back out here!"

Richard's eyes wander over the dead woman and the nearly perfect imprint of her body left behind in the sticky soil. It reminds him of old crime scene photos with bodies outlined in chalk and tape. He's spent decades following Ollie's tips, digging up the dead and locking up those few killers Ollie has deemed too uncontrollable to be left wandering the world. He justified the arrangement when he was the only one who gave a rat's ass about serial murders, but when Mac came on, she complicated everything.

She wasn't content to clean up Ollie's scraps. She wanted to do real investigative work, and left to her own devices, she could have done some real good. Deep down, Richard had been proud of her for being the one person strong enough to say no to Ollie.

But maybe if she'd been weak like him, this woman would still be alive, and Mac would be home with her family instead of…

"Richard?"

He snaps his attention back to Sharpe. The detective stares at him expectantly. "I'll make sure this is a number one priority and have the lab send you photos the second they open the envelope." Sharpe touches Richard's arm as the photographer drops an evidence tag next to the plastic encased envelope and snaps photos. A tech pinches the muddy packet with a pair of tweezers and drops it into an evidence bag, sealing the letter inside before Richard can manage to get the words out to stop him.

"Don't worry. We'll find her," Sharpe says.

Richard watches as the evidence bag with the cheery envelope is rushed out of the tent. "Unfortunately, Detective, if that letter says what I think it does, I don't think we will."

Twenty-Five

Josie listens to her voicemail with her cellphone wedged between her ear and shoulder. As usual, Richard is tied up with work and it looks like she will have to attend the Vernonia homeless shelter fundraiser alone.

She hangs up and drops the phone on the mattress. Her poor husband is worried about his partner. He asked her to call if she gets any updates from Sam on the progress of Mackenzie's missing person report, but Ollie has picked out such a special spot for her corpse that no one will ever find it.

The devilish red lipstick Josie applies plays across her full, relaxed smile. Mackenzie Jones is gone for good.

Josie perches on the edge of the bed and carefully pulls on a pair of stockings. She typically skips the nylons, even for formal events, preferring to show off her flawless, slender legs. But Mackenzie and that homeless bitch were a wily duo. She tugs a stocking up over the ugly bruise that sits above her knee.

It is an unsightly reminder of Mackenzie's fighting spirit. She never knew when to give up, even when drugged and hanging from the arms of a tree.

The dress she has chosen is modest enough, aside from the clinging red fabric that accentuates her curves. Josie dabs perfume on her neck and inhales the crisp scent of tulips and thistle, so different from the sour smells of rot from the night before.

Dipping her toes into a pair of killer heels, she turns to admire herself in the full-length mirror in the corner of the bedroom. She sucks in a hiss of frustration. The wide purple bruise from Mackenzie's punch to her nose is visible under her makeup. It takes a few minutes to blend another layer of concealer over the mess and smooth the few flyaway hairs from her French twist. She reaches over to the nearby jewelry box to retrieve her necklace. It is a simple chain with a small silver cross. A gift from Sarah, the young woman whose corpse filled Mackenzie's boots.

The drive through the woods to Portland's distant bedroom community in Vernonia is uneventful until she reaches the tight network of blocks that stitch together to form a flood-soaked downtown. Traffic slows when the silt-coated roads narrow to one lane, and she uses the opportunity to look over the people huddled behind cardboard signs on the muddy corners.

The little town is busy with people hurrying past the beggars, outstretched hands remaining empty while those who could fill them rush to reach their destinations. Two worlds sharing the same patch of concrete.

At the single blinking stoplight, Josie spots a woman about her own age huddled beside a small suitcase belted to a broken stroller. The woman could easily be as pretty as Josie is; if she had a shower, and clean clothes. The soiled rags that hang from her frame do nothing for her gangly figure, and her hair is as dirty and matted as a stray dog's.

Glancing up and down the sidewalk, the woman's wide eyes look for something. Help? Danger? Probably cops. She turns her head and leans back until the stroller partially obscures her from people at the other end of the sidewalk. From where she waits in her car, Josie sees the woman press a glass pipe to her lips.

Disgusting.

Josie flips on her blinker and turns the corner, parking in the first open spot she finds along the curb. Thankfully this section of sidewalk is higher than the river's fingers reached during the flood, so her high heels click against the concrete. Across the street, a man stares at the way her dress swishes across her hips. She smiles at him and marches around the corner to find the woman with the stroller.

"Excuse me," Josie says when she sees her. "I could not help but notice you while I was driving by."

"Who the fuck are you?" The woman spits the words. Her pupils are like black holes, sucking life out of the world and turning its vibrant colors to ash. Her skin stretches across jagged cheekbones like leather over a steel drum, and her breath is so sour Josie fights the urge to twist her nose in revulsion.

Josie unclips the gold clasp on her Alexis Bittar clutch and pulls a gold-embossed business card out of an interior pocket. "My name is Josie

Douglas, and I am helping the city of Vernonia open a new women's shelter. I believe we all deserve a second chance. An opportunity to offer ourselves to a higher purpose."

"Oh, really? And you thought you'd just pop on over and save me, did you? Listen, bitch, I ain't some lost puppy you can put a bow on and take home." Yellow teeth protrude from her grimace, and she shoves Josie's hand away.

"A puppy, no. But lost?" Josie softens her face, letting her eyes pool with practiced tears. "Maybe." She bends her knees and waist, letting her dress drip onto the dirty concrete while she lowers herself to the homeless woman's level. The smell of sweat, tooth decay, and unwashed skin sends a thrill dancing up Josie's spine.

"You do not have to accept my help today. But maybe one day soon, you will run out of drugs and realize how alone you are. How broken. Deep down, I know you want off these streets and I am someone who has the means to help you." Josie imagines the woman, flayed skin and broken bones, pleading for her life. "I hope one day you will beg me to stop your misery. I will be waiting."

The whispered promise penetrates the glossy haze of the woman's high. Her eyes sharpen, zeroing in on the card. "I ain't some kind of fixer upper."

"Of course not. But I can take all your worries away, by one means, or another." Josie's cheek tugs at the corner of her mouth.

The thrill of victory bubbles inside her chest when the woman plucks the card from between her fingers. She has seen the hungry look in her eyes a hundred times before; the manic way she chews her lower lip, and erratic bouncing of her nervously bobbing leg.

This woman is ripe for the picking.

"Just think about it," Josie coos. She unfolds herself, standing tall and straightening her dress before walking away.

Before she rounds the corner, she looks back down the block. The woman is staring at her with hungry, wanting eyes. All it takes is a bit of kindness to hook someone like her on the idea that she can still be saved. She will be Josie's next conquest, there is no doubt about that.

Twenty-Six

The radio announcer mumbles something between songs while the vehicle winds its way uphill. Mac is glad Oliver has the radio on because although she has difficulty understanding the garbled words of the disk jockey, the flow of music gives her a method to keep track of the time. She's counted thirteen songs since they've been on the road. The music fades to static and he flips through to another station.

Each time Oliver has cranked the music louder, belting out songs in perfect tune, she's used the cover of music to attempt wiggling free of the bundle she's buried under. She thought if she could get loose, she might flag someone down at a stoplight, but they must be on the highway because Oliver hasn't tapped the brakes once since she came up with the idea. The sepia tone of the clouds passing beyond the window tells her the windows are tinted, so it's possible no one would see her waving outside the back window, anyway.

The tools shift atop her when the sound of tires crawls to a stop and the radio turns off. Oliver shuffles around in the front seat so quietly, she can hardly tell if he's still in the vehicle, but the door lock at her feet jumps in its housing. She hears the driver's door open, and close, and then he's at the rear of the vehicle. She holds her breath; thankful she hasn't managed to unbury herself yet when he opens the rear door and pushes the tools around.

He tucks the loose end of the tarp tight around her face, blocking what little view she had of the outside, and pats the tarp where her shoulder rests. "Sit tight," Oliver says with a low chuckle and closes the door. The locks engage and the weight of his looming presence fades away with the crunch of a few footsteps over gravel.

Mac waits in her plastic cocoon, too afraid to move. Without knowing where they are, or what obstacles she's facing outside her makeshift burial shroud, she's petrified of what might happen if he discovers she's alive.

But this might be her only chance to gain her bearings and make a real plan for escape. Her ribs clamp around her deep, haggard breath and the sharp pain forces a memory from the night before to the surface. She sat in a building, propped against a metal post. A long pipe slammed repeatedly into her side. The memory is so vivid, she flinches from the echo of the strike. It's a reminder that while every inch of her hurts, it will get a lot worse if she stays here.

Rolling her neck and flexing the fingers on her still-operable hand, she manages to loosen a fold in the tarp. Even this small motion grinds at her joints, muscles cramping with the effort. After a lot of painful wiggling, she's able to pull the tarp downward enough to uncover her head. A sleeping bag, metal chest, and tools rest around her.

The area above her head is open, and by pressing her feet against the rear door and straightening her legs, she's able to inch her way through the tarp's opening like an earthworm. Her shoulders breach the opening and she's careful not to lift her head higher than the edge of the cargo area's sidewalls. She can see so much more out the back window. Freeing her head, neck, and shoulders is exhilarating, and she takes her first unobstructed breath in hours.

Her eyes well with tears. She can see so much more from here; the tops of green pine trees reaching toward the bright blue sky, the red-tiled roof of a nearby building. She listens to the world outside and doesn't hear any movement, so allows herself to crane her neck a little higher.

The SUV she's in is parked at the edge of a narrow parking lot near a narrow, two-lane highway that hugs the curve of the forest. A half dozen buildings stand just inside the tree line. A sign stands at the edge of the lot and she blinks her watery eyes against the bright sunshine to focus on it. A covered wagon trundles across the words, "Barlow Trail," and Mac glances back to the highway where an RV ambles up the hill.

Her heart stutters. She knows exactly where she is. She and Sam bring the kids up to hike and camp on Mt. Hood every summer, and they've stopped at the Barlow Trail Roadhouse in Welches at the start of each trip, for years.

Emboldened by the familiarity of the space, Mac shoves her torso against a bag of tent poles, knocking them over, and wriggles her shoulders to get out from under the sharpened blade of a flat-nosed shovel. A moment later, she's free to the waist and she heaves herself upwards to look over the edge of the SUV's rear seat.

It has to be a rental, not only because Oliver doesn't own a car but also because the interior is spotless. He parked nose-in to a space near the building, within sight of the restaurant's row of square windows and front door.

Oliver is nowhere to be seen. He must be inside.

Without a second thought, Mac grits her teeth against the pain of her bones grinding under her skin. Her head feels like it's being split in two, and the throbbing ache of her shorn abdomen tempts her to give up before she's begun. She woozily shifts her shoulders to the side, kicking her feet to shove tools and plastic away from her. In the struggle, her right hand slips from its binding and she uses it to grab the headrest behind her, hauling herself upwards until she can scoot her knees under her.

It's the first time she's been able to look herself over, and if it didn't hurt so much, she'd gasp at what she sees. She's nearly naked, aside from the bloodied bra and panties caked to her torn skin. Bruises crisscross her skin, everywhere she looks a brocade of red and purple. Though she doesn't remember being beaten so severely, it's evident she was manhandled long after she lost consciousness. Deep cuts ramble through her skin like canyons and every inch of her limbs rage with invisible fire, but she won't let it stop her from taking this chance to break free from Oliver.

Searching the empty parking lot, she realizes trying to flag someone down from the back of the SUV is out. But if she can get outside, figure out how to get onto the highway, or run into one of the sleepy businesses…

She scrambles to work herself free from her bindings. She's too weak, and doesn't have enough functioning fingers to work the knots loose, but a set of landscaping shears among the pile of tools make quick work of cutting through the ropes.

Unbound, she runs her hands along the inside panel of the SUV's door, looking for a button or emergency release, and curses to herself when she doesn't find one. She will have to go out the front, which seems far less convenient from where she sits huddled against the back door.

She drags herself back to kneeling behind the rear seat and tests her legs. When they were tied together, they had enough force to push and kick, but apart they tremble and quake like a newborn fawn. It takes everything she has to wrap her arms around a headrest and climb over the backrest and into the rear seat.

The second her knees touch the upholstery, the restaurant door opens, and Oliver emerges, holding a plastic sack in one hand and a Styrofoam coffee cup in the other. He holds the door open with his elbow, distracted by someone talking to him from inside. A woman meets him in the open doorway, holding a piece of paper that looks like a receipt.

Mac scrapes at the SUV's rear passenger door, fighting to get her stiff, swollen fingers under the handle. Her hand slips across the smooth plastic and she glances up to find Oliver halfway down the restaurant steps, one foot freezing in the air mid-stride when his eyes lock on Mac in the backseat.

Oliver blinks and Mac springs into action. She screams with rage as she shoves her broken fingers under the door handle and Oliver trips over the last step, dropping the sack and cup to the ground.

The damn door won't open, and Oliver is charging across the parking lots empty spots towards the vehicle. His hand dives into his jacket. If he gets at Mac without anyone seeing, this really will be the end. She'll never see her family again. Sam. The kids.

The kids.

Fucking child safety locks!

She slams her fist against the door and howls, looking back to find Oliver standing next to the SUV. He points the hard nose of a Beretta pistol into the backseat with one hand while he fumbles in his pockets with the other.

"Where's the goddamn key?" he yells.

Mac throws her body between the front bucket seats and slams her fist against the horn. The sound cuts through the chaos of the moment and she slaps her palm against it again.

She doesn't see him lift the handgun to the window, but the deafening sound of the shot shattering glass overwhelms the pealing horn and drowns out Mac's screams. The bullet tears a riot through her hip, still wedged in the back seat. Mac is stuck, her broken ribs jammed against the center console, shoulders wedged between the two front seats, and she can't even roll away from the second shot that rips through her side.

Maybe it's Mac's pounding on the steering wheel, the seizing of her bleeding body, or the force of the gunshot through the glass, but now a loud, repeating squeal reverberates through the SUV.

Thank God Oliver opted for a model with a car alarm.

Mac grips the steering wheel with both hands and yanks herself forward. Through the windshield, she sees faces in the restaurant's picture windows and the woman who'd helped Oliver with his forgotten receipt peers through a crack in the front door, her expression wild with terror.

"Help me!" Mac screams. "Please!"

Oliver's eyes widen, the whites shining against his flushed skin. He wheels the pistol towards the restaurant. "Get back inside!"

The woman disappears, leaving Mac bleeding out over the upholstery alone. No way out. No one to help her. Oliver shoves his free hand back in his pocket and he grins. He extracts the key fob from his jacket and presses a button, unlatching all the doors with a deadly click.

Rather than silencing the alarm, the pitch changes. The new whine is faint and off-beat, but it grows in volume until Mac feels like her head might explode. She screams when he pulls the handle and she reaches for the door, clawing at the interior handle and trying to hold it closed. He is so much stronger than her, but she has the advantage of her dead-weight being wedged between the seats. Though he yanks the door open a few inches, it slams shut again the second his grip falters. As long as Mac doesn't let go, he can't get in.

Oliver's eyes are sinking black holes of rage above the flush of his puffed cheeks. He pulls his arm back and punches the window. The glass merely bounces in its frame, refusing to break. He howls with rage, shaking his injured hand and spits on the window. "You can't keep me out forever, you slippery little bitch!"

He's right. When he yanks on the door, it opens an inch, letting light spill around the frame. Mac tugs on it, but the strength in her arms is already fading. He loosens his grip to look at the highway beyond the parking lot. The alarm grows louder, less distant, and Mac realizes it's not an alarm at all. It's the sound of sirens.

Oliver smacks the window with the butt of the gun and yanks on the handle. This time she lets it slip open and he takes the bait, shoving the handgun around the door frame and in through the gap. Mac yanks backwards with all her might, willing the door to break his arm in two.

He screams at her through the closed window, trying to pull the gun back outside, but his unintelligible voice is cut off by the crack of a shotgun. Mac cranes her neck to look over the dashboard. Standing on the restaurant's uppermost step, a heavyset man holds a shotgun aloft. He fires a second shot over Oliver's head and Mac seizes the opportunity, letting go of the door and snatching the handgun from his loose fingers.

She fumbles the Beretta, turning it around clumsily and dropping it in the driver's seat. Oliver's attention is split between her and the man with the shotgun, and he reacts to the dropped pistol a second too late. Mac scoops it up and shoves two fingers into the trigger frame, pointing its barrel squarely at Oliver's chest, yanks back on the trigger once, twice, and a third time before she has time to breathe.

Oliver stops his struggle and looks at her, his face knitted together with disbelief. He takes a step backwards and blood seeps from his chest, dousing his white t-shirt with an expanse of lifeblood. He drops to one knee, dipping below Mac's view behind the door. She shoves the door open and trains the gun on Oliver where he kneels. He looks at her, an expression of bewilderment written in the wrinkled lines of his aged face, then slowly drops to his hip and falls to his side. Her cracked lips break into a smile when the sound of sirens reaches a fevered pitch and she catches the reflection of red and blue light in the rearview mirror.

The life in Oliver's eyes fades, and when they stare blank and vacant into the sky, Mac's last drop of energy evaporates with a final maniacal laugh. She lets go of the gun and collapses against the center console, tumbling into the darkness of unconsciousness.

Twenty-Seven

Richard slams the brake to keep from ramming the nose of his car into Sam and Mac's garage door. He had already been to Becca's once today to tell Sam they'd found a dead woman wearing Mac's clothes. It was the worst victim notification he'd ever done.

He'd apologized to Sam, not only for bringing the bad news, but also because deep down Richard knew he was responsible for this whole situation. If he hadn't made friends with Ollie all those years ago, if he'd treated him as a real criminal and worked to solve his cases, none of this would have happened.

No sooner had Richard ridden this emotional roller-coaster with Sam than the call came in from the Oregon State Police. They'd found the real Mac Jones, mostly naked, and mostly dead, trapped in an SUV off scenic Highway 26 in Welches, nearly a two-hour drive from where they'd found the decoy's body in Vernonia.

Richard rubs his face. They'd given Ollie copies of the case files, and he had said he'd been recruiting… Richard buries his fists in his eye sockets and stars burst behind his eyelids. He's in it deep, this time.

Now, he kills the car's engine in the Jones family driveway and flings the door open. His feet hit the ground running. He makes it to the front door at a run, reaching for the handle with too much momentum and slamming into the locked door before pounding on it. "Sam! It's Richard! Your sister told me you're here. Open up."

He's greeted by the click and slide of locks turning cautiously in their housing, and the door opens a crack, held fast by a security chain. Ryan peers out at him. "Inspector Douglas? What are you doing here?"

"Where's your father? I need to talk to him right now."

"Shower," says the teenaged boy. "Hang on."

The gap closes and the chain scrapes with painstaking slowness before Ryan opens the door to let Richard in. His brother, Robby, lies limp on the nearby sofa like a stain dissolved into the cushions. "What's going on?"

"I need your dad. Which way to the bathroom?" Richard takes a step towards the hallway.

"He'll be out in a while," Robby says, the crack of uncertainty in his voice. "You can wait if you want."

"We can't wait. They found your mom and I need to take your dad to her before…" Richard almost blurts out that they need to talk to her before it's too late. From the description he heard from the trooper, Mac should have already died.

He pushes past Robby and barrels towards the back of the house where he thinks the bedrooms are. The kid's eyes are round as saucers when he stumbles out of the way, but Richard is already peering into the rooms on either end of the hallway before he realizes he's bowled the kid over. He makes note of the boys' bedrooms before he finds the bathroom. Water runs through the wall and a low warbling that sounds like crying leaks through the door. Richard knocks heavily.

"I'm still in here!" Sam's voice croaks.

"Get out here. We have to go!" Richard shouts the order and when a response doesn't come quickly enough, he turns the handle and barges inside.

Sam pulls the shower curtain back a few inches. He peers out with eyes swollen and bloodshot, his face half covered in shaving cream. "What are you doing in here?"

Richard grabs a towel off the rack and shoves it through the gap in the curtain. "Shut off the water and get dressed. They found her."

"When? Where is she? Is she okay?" Sam's face contorts in a range of emotions. All at once he looks sad, relieved, vindicated, and scared shitless. He takes the towel and shuts off the water.

"She's being taken to a hospital in Gresham. Get dressed. I'll meet you in the living room." Richard leaves the bathroom, closing the door behind him. When he turns around, Ryan and Robby stand frozen in the hallway. "Get your shoes. I'll drop you off at your aunt's on our way out of town."

Richard shoves past them and collapses on the sofa. He can't believe she's alive. He's walked through the aftermath of Ollie's particular brand of torture enough times to know whatever she's been through should have ended her. The Oregon State trooper he talked to said she was only alive enough to not be declared dead, but that could change with a bump in the road if the ambulance driver isn't careful. Richard taps out a rhythm on his thigh. What will happen if she regains enough lucidity to recount how she survived? And if she dies, will things go back to the way they were before?

He'll have to find someone else to take over as Ollie's arm in the world, and that could take years. Time enough for Ollie to make a claim on them and turn them into puppets, just like he'd done with Richard. Like he'd tried to do with Mac. His gut twists and he feels sweat pooling at the small of his back and under his arms.

He's not sure he can live with the weight of that again.

Sam emerges from the depths of the house, pushing the boys out the door ahead of him. They drive to Becca's house in silence but the second the boys pour out of the car and scramble to their aunt's front door, Sam presses for answers.

"What happened to Mac?"

Richard turns around in his seat, looking down at the empty neighborhood street as though worried about his blind spot. What kind of answer can he give?

"You know something. I can see it in your face."

Richard's grip tightens around the steering wheel until his knuckles are white. "A waitress saw Mac in the parking lot of a diner in Welches and called the police. The owner went out with a shotgun, and it sounds like there was a back and forth and Mac got hit."

"But she's alive?" Sam grips the thigh of his jeans with clenched fists. He stares through the windshield with a hard glare and Richard's gut twists when he sees the light dim in Sam's eyes.

"She was when they found her. But she's in a bad way." Richard is glad Sam isn't looking at him as he answers. There's no way he can keep the severity of the truth from being written across his face.

"Do you think she'll pull through?" Sam's question comes out in a childlike whisper.

"She's a tough girl," Richard says without answering the question. They're silent for the remainder of the torturous hour-long drive. Every mile feels like a hundred, and any relief Richard felt at Mac's retrieval sinks beneath the dread that she might have been found too late. And while the search for Mac is over, the real nightmare of what she's endured is just beginning.

And with Ollie involved? There's the whole mess of his reputation to consider.

By the time they pull into the hospital parking lot, Richard's heart is in his throat and his stomach is lost somewhere around his ankles. He pulls into the first spot he finds and rushes through the hospital entrance with Sam hot on his heels. A nurse at the front desk checks Richard's badge and calls security to escort them back to where Mac is being treated.

They're led to a room in the rear of the emergency department where an armed guard sits at the door. Mac lies in the metal framed hospital bed like a mummy in a sarcophagus, hooked up to a vitals machine. An IV drips fluid from overhead, and the little Richard sees of her face is swollen and painted in such dark bruises that she's unrecognizable.

She looks like death, but the buzz of the equipment and numbers flashing across the vitals machine assure him that she's still very much alive.

Sam collapses into a chair beside the bed with a mourning roar. He smears tears across his cheeks with his palms and rocks back and forth in grief at what is left of his wife. Richard opens his mouth, about to ask the guard for an update on Mac's situation when Sam's voice cracks.

"She's alive." He reaches towards the pile of bandages but stops short, as if he's afraid touching her will be the end of her. He looks up at Richard with watery eyes. "But what about our baby?"

Twenty-Eight

Mac swims through the weight of nothingness toward a brilliant white light shimmering overhead, like an actress answering a stage call. She slips to the surface, pushing aside the fuzz of a medicated high, only to find her eyelids are glued together and her head feels like it's full of cement.

She sucks in a mouthful of air and gags on the taste of old blood and fresh antiseptic. Pain stabs her insides like an army of hot pokers, and she tries to escape the torture of her own body only to find herself trapped flat on her back, encased in gauze and with a myriad of tubes pulling at her veins.

The excruciating pain forces her eyes open as wide as they'll go. She's barely able to see through the paper-thin slits, but everything is too bright and covered with a screen of fuzzy wool. When she blinks, the blurriness only seems to worsen.

A pillar of shadow moves between herself and the light. It must be Oliver, back to kill her for good this time. Her heart bashes the inside of her chest, but the rest of her body doesn't move an inch. All the adrenaline that pushed her to survive has been used up. She collapses under the unyielding weight of her own skin and bones while the figure leans over her.

"Mackenzie, are you awake?"

Sam's voice is so unexpected, Mac doesn't believe it's him. Maybe she really is dead, and a vision of him is greeting her on the way to hell.

"If you can hear me, I want you to know we're doing everything we can. You're in a hospital. The doctors and nurses are taking good care of you. It's all going to be okay."

Her heart leaps again, but now it's jumping for joy instead of terror. Although her body feels like it's shattered into a million pieces, she's safe. Tears stream from her eyes, soaking into the gauze at her cheeks, and she tries to acknowledge him in some way. But her body won't respond, she can't even turn her head to nod or wiggle a finger to tell him she understands.

Beyond the exhausted frustration of him being so close, but so unreachable, she hears voices, muffled and far away, intermingling with the buzz and beep of machines nearby.

There's a knocking sound and Sam's shadow pulls away. Mac wishes he wouldn't go.

"How are we doing?" a feminine voice asks.

"I think she might have woken up."

The other figure leans over Mac. The slow, intentional pressure on her face says they are probably being as careful as possible, but it still feels like glass clawing through her skin. "Hello, Mackenzie. I'm Doctor Landess, but everyone calls me Gail. You've been admitted to a medical center and I'm so glad to see you today. You've been through quite an ordeal. I know everything hurts, but we're doing everything we can to help you feel better.

"Do you think she'll pull through?" The apprehension in the question cuts like a knife.

"It's too early to tell," Doctor Landess says. "But I think it's time we talk about your wife's pregnancy."

The tone in the doctor's voice ushers a pallor of dread into the room, and Mac silently pleads with her to not go on. Ever since she found out about her pregnancy, she's fought with herself about what to do about it. Whether she could up-end her entire life to accommodate another child, returning to the solitude and depression of a life lived entirely for someone else. Whether to terminate the cells multiplying and clustering inside her. And now, she knows Oliver and Josie have ripped the decision out of her.

"I'm sorry, Mr. Jones. Even if your wife recovers, she's suffered irrevocable damage to her reproductive organs."

A sharp, pinching feeling tugs at Mac's scalp and she's vaguely aware of someone stroking her hair. A wave of pain pours over her, a howling reminder of the horrors she's endured. She sinks like lead into the sea of darkness, her mind filled with questions and her heart heavy with grief.

Twenty-Nine

"I can't believe you already have a place for me. I've been waiting on Section 8 housing two years."

The woman fidgeting in Josie's front passenger seat is wild and high, her movements jerking and erratic. Josie loves playing with them when their senses are enhanced, their excitement and eagerness mingling with the drugs. A recipe for bad decisions.

She never knows how they will respond once they realize what they have done, and the not-knowing builds her own anticipation of what is coming as if it were the first time all over again.

"It is almost too good to be true, is it not?" Josie pulls her eyes from the roadway and glances at the woman with a half-smile. Ollie will be thrilled at her catch when he returns from burying the FBI woman's remains. They will play with her, and then escape to start a new life together. Brother and sister free to hunt and play across the ocean where hardly a soul has heard of *The Godless Killer*.

"My boyfriend will be excited when he finds out I've got a place." The woman freezes like a film put on pause and the smell of nicotine infused nervous sweat fills the car.

Josie wrinkles her nose, and the woman breaks free of her freeze-frame, running her tongue over her teeth. "I won't have him overnight or anything. I know how it is in these housing programs. No overnight visitors, right?" When Josie does not reply, the woman nods in answer to her own question.

"But if my boyfriend does visit, just for the day, is there a pool or something?" She sniffs and rubs the raw skin of her nostrils with the back of her hand.

"No pool. But it is right on the river." Josie grins, imagining this woman's body dunked head-first in the river, drowning under the boughs of the massive dead tree.

“Right on the water? You’re joking me.” The woman’s eyes narrow and her shoulders tense.

“It is only temporary.” Josie’s reply is cool and detached. “It might not be what you were expecting, but trust me. It is a nice place to land.”

The woman squirms in her seat, pulling the shoulder strap of her seatbelt loose and hanging it like a snake in her lap. Her tongue darts between her lips. “It’s too quiet in here. Mind if I turn on the radio?”

Josie shrugs, and she flips the stereo on. The woman grimaces at the classical music that bleeds through the speakers and scans through the stations until she finds one playing a modern tune. They only catch the last few seconds of the poppy music before the twangy beat and sultry words of *Body Count* slinks through the airwaves.

Palms tingling, Josie turns the steering wheel to pull from the main road onto an overgrown drive. Tendrils of Oregon blackberry creep from where they have been knocked back by the heavy traffic of the previous day. A curtain of yellow caution tape waves as she pulls past. She pulls onto the jagged concrete pad where gas station pumps used to stand and puts the car in park. She is about to shut the car off when a voice comes on the radio.

We interrupt this program to bring you breaking news. Notorious serial killer Oliver Roberts was captured earlier today after a shootout with multiple law enforcement agencies in Welches, Oregon. Roberts and an unnamed victim have been transported to Mount Hood Medical Center...

Josie's heart sinks as the report plays on. She remembers the night before, his sharp features and piercing eyes flowing with delight as they played together for the first time in decades. She swallows a knot of emotion and kills the engine.

"This doesn't look like an apartment." The fidgeting woman's raspy voice grates through notes of confusion.

"It is one of those industrial conversion projects. Come inside. You will love it." Josie lets herself out of the car and moves to the trunk, Oliver's capture heavy on her mind. It had been his idea to lead the police here, to play with them. She had known this would be her last time to work this sacred ground, but she had expected to leave here with her brother. To follow the horizon until they found a new place to settle.

She expects the police have picked the interior of the building clean after finding the discarded copy of Mackenzie Jones, but the loss of her equipment and tools does not matter. She keeps a second set in the trunk, for special occasions. And this being her last session in this quaint little town most certainly qualifies as an occasion to remember.

The woman slowly extracts herself through the passenger door and stands next to the car. Despite the warm evening, she wraps her arms around herself and shivers. Josie hoists her tool kit to her shoulder, shuts the trunk, and leads the way to the ramshackle building.

Yellow tape crisscrosses the narrow service door and Josie rips it from the doorframe. She tugs at a silver chain around her neck and the key slithers from under her blouse.

"D'you have one of those for me?" The woman asks.

Josie does not bother responding. She leans forward, spinning the key in the lock and pushing the door open. Taking a step backward, she gestures to the building's dark interior. "After you."

They cross the threshold, and the woman sniffs the thick air. "What's that smell?"

"Bleach." Josie closes the door and locks it before reaching for the switch box hidden in the shadows on the side wall. The click of the switch is loud in the tight, empty space.

The overhead bulbs sputter, and it takes a moment for the icy white light to glow freely. Once the light is on, however, Josie can see the whites of the woman's wide eyes. The vibrancy of her fear entwines with Josie's building rage at Oliver's capture. The mixture rumbles within Josie like a monster come alive, and she knows there is only one way to sate the hunger for violence.

The air shifts around them while the woman takes in their surroundings. An empty metal table, too heavy for the police to have removed, remains bolted to the floor. Her face blanches when she looks down at the ring of bloodstained concrete surrounding it. "What is this place?"

"My workroom." Josie sets her bag of tools on the floor beside the table and kneels to unzip it. She does not bother worrying about her strung-out victim. She has pressed herself into a corner, eyes darting around the space like a wild animal. Josie had planned to savor dismantling the woman, tickling her flesh with the end of a knife, peeling her apart an inch at a time. But now her presence serves a new purposc; to absorb Josie's frustration that Oliver has failed to live up to her expectations.

Josie feels around in the bag, retrieving a pair of nitrile gloves and slipping them onto her slender hands before retrieving a tin of no-bake cookies. "Are you allergic to peanuts?"

"Wh-what?"

The lid pings when the thin metal tabs pop loose and the weight of the goodies inside shifts in Josie's hands when she tilts the tin towards the woman so she can see. A half dozen gooey cookies rest on neatly trimmed slips of parchment paper. "I made these for you. But they do have nuts in them. Is that a problem?"

"I don't want cookies, thank you." The woman spits the words out dangerously. Her tongue darts out between her lips three times, like a snake tasting the air.

"They are awfully delicious." Josie slides a gloved hand under the parchment paper and lifts a cookie from the tin. She sniffs the edge of it, relishing the way the sugary scent of molasses and ground peanut butter masks any hint of sedative.

A mixture of fear and hunger fill the woman's watery eyes and she shakes her head. "I don't want one."

"Suit yourself." Josie shrugs. She savors the tension between them. The way the power flows through the air like a river, transferring completely into her control. She slips the cookie back into the tin and reaches into her bag again, pulling Richard's gun from its folds.

"What the fuck, lady!" The woman shrinks deeper into the corner, feet and hands scrambling backwards against the concrete as though the concrete blocks that press against her back will crumble against her weight.

Josie rises and steps towards her, offering the tin of cookies with one hand and tightening her palm around the hard curve of the pistol's backstrap with the other. "You have two choices. Enjoy a delicious homemade snack or find out how a bullet tastes after it is shot out of a gun."

The woman hesitates, wide, black pupils darting back and forth between Josie's offerings. She takes the tin of cookies gently between her hands and scoops a cookie up to taste. Josie lowers the gun, watching the woman chew and swallow with maternal interest. “See? They are good, right?”

“Yes, thank you.” She sets the tin on the floor and Josie lifts the gun to point at the woman’s chest.

“Eat them all. Then, we will get started.”

Thirty

The phone clicks in Richard's ear, then Josie's voice repeats the same voicemail message he's heard half a dozen times already. He ends the call and looks at the smudged glass of the phone's screen as if it holds some answer he can't discern.

"Still not picking up?" Sam hands Richard a paper cup filled with coffee and settles into the chair on the opposite side of Mac's bed.

"I guess her fundraiser ran over." Richard slides the phone into his pocket and lifts the cup a couple of inches in Sam's direction. "Thanks for this. I needed it."

Sam takes a quick drink of his own coffee and grimaces. "Don't thank me until after you taste it. I don't think they've cleaned that coffee machine in a while. It's a little sludgy."

Richard runs a thumb along the edge of the cup's lid. Josie keeps her phone off most of the time, so not answering isn't unusual. She's always been independent. It's one of the things he admires about her. But something about today feels off. All the years he's been buried in his work, traveling the country, hopping from one crime scene to another, she's never complained. Never asked him to quit. Never worried over him as if she's afraid today will be the last day she'll see him.

Seeing Sam, petrified of losing Mac… isn't that what love is supposed to look like? The thought picks at a scab of loneliness in his chest, and for the first time in years he feels like he might crawl out of his skin if he doesn't hear her voice.

He sets his coffee on Mac's bedside table, fishes the phone back out of his pocket, and tries to call her again.

"Oliver Roberts was your big break when you started with the FBI, wasn't he? Must feel strange to find out he's dead." Sam watches over Mac when he asks the question.

Richard wonders how much Mac has told Sam about their work and a wave of guilt swells behind his lungs. Ollie wasn't just his first capture; he was the entire job. Everything Richard had ever accomplished had been because Ollie allowed it. Sure, there were a handful of cases that hadn't had the Killers Club brand all over them, but they'd been few and far between.

The fact was, Ollie had turned serial killing into a socially structured event, and Richard was simply there to clean up any messes that seeped outside Ollie's authorization.

"Yes. Ollie made me famous. And if—" he catches Sam's flinch from the corner of his eye. "When Mac pulls through, she'll be famous too. The one who finally got the best of The Godless Killer."

"She has her own brand of fame." Sam's voice is firm in its conviction, but the edge of his words carries the weight of his grief. "Governor Carter's daughter went to the same summer camp as Ryan, when he was little. That's why Tarrell came to her when his daughter went missing. He believed in Mac. Knew she'd piece together what happened and find his daughter, because she's done it before." Sam looks up with glassy eyes. “Mac has made a real difference in the world, hasn’t she?”

“She has, and my guess is she’s not done yet.” He knows saying the words won’t ease Sam’s pain, and the guilt wrapped around his spine tangles itself around his lungs until it’s hard to breathe. He’s failed Mackenzie in so many ways. The first time Ollie told him to bring her for an introduction, he knew a day would come when there would be a reckoning between them. But he convinced himself she could be swayed, that if she just spent enough time with Ollie that she’d see how things worked, that she’d fall into line and continue the legacy that had benefitted Richard so much.

“I hope you’re right,” Sam whispers. He stares at the rippling coffee in his trembling hands.

“She’s a tough one.” Richard nods towards the bundle of bandages sunk into the mattress between them. While he’s bit back countless lies over the decades, he knows this statement is true. “She’ll pull through, you’ll see.”

Sam nods though he looks unconvinced. Richard doesn’t blame him. If something like this happened to Josie, he’d be a wreck.

Josie. The thought of her makes the phone in his pocket weigh a hundred pounds. He pulls it out and unlocks the screen to see if she's messaged him back. There's no text from her, but there is one from the office asking him to check in. "I should probably get going."

Richard gets up and Sam walks him to the door. They hesitate together and Sam opens his mouth as if he wants to say something but can't find the words. The dark circles set under his eyes make him look older. Richard pats him awkwardly on the shoulder and puts his hand on the doorknob.

A gasp from Mac's bed is followed by a mountainous groan. Richard feels his eyes widen in sync with Sam's and they blunder against one another in the small space when they rush to opposite sides of her bed.

The pillowy length of an arm unfolds from under the covers and flops toward her mouth. She rubs her jaw with the stub of the cast, a signal of life that is strange to behold after watching her corpse-like body for so many hours.

"Mac," Sam croaks while he leans over her, searching her face.

Her breathing shifts from the nearly motionless silence of near-death to a rasping shudder. Her head jerks to one side and Richard sees she still hasn't opened her eyes. Sam reaches out to touch her arm, but stops short, looking at Richard with a helpless expression and fresh tears welling in his eyes. "What do we do?"

"I'll call a nurse." He rushes to the door, yanking it open without hesitation this time and calls down the hallway for a nurse. A man in scrubs looks his way and sets down his clipboard, taking a step towards Mac's room. It is enough acknowledgement for Richard. He ducks back into the room where Mac splutters a cough and lurches forward, lifting off the pillow a few inches before collapsing again.

Bandaged arms and legs are flailing now, splints hitting the side rails and tossing the blankets aside. It looks like she's trying to claw her way out of a nightmare, and Richard supposes that's exactly what she's doing. Sam's hands hover over her, looking like he wants to hold her down, but unsure of how to touch her without bringing her more pain. She flops towards him, but Sam is too slow to move out of the way and she socks him in the eye socket with the heft of her cast.

The nurse rushes into the room, taking in the scene. Richard's hands are out, trying to keep Mac's flailing arm from banging against the metal bedrails while Sam has fallen into the chair beside the bed and cups his face. Mac groans like the undead.

"I don't know. She just started fighting!" Richard leans backward when Mac's arm swings wide, clipping the edge of the bedside table and tipping it so the cup of coffee spills.

Delicately, the nurse makes his way around the room to the IV. He makes an adjustment and leans over Mac, pressing firmly on one of her shoulders with a practiced hand. He gestures to Richard to back away. "It's alright, Mrs. Jones. You're safe in bed. Your husband and friend are here watching over you. We're taking good care of you. Everything is going to be okay."

Mac's groans turn to sobs, and then to soft, whimpering cries.

"She needs rest," the nurse says.

Sam helps the nurse tuck Mac into a bundle of blankets, adding pillows to the edge of the bed to pad her from the handrails. Once the room is calm, the nurse leaves the room and Sam falls into the chair beside the bed. Richard fidgets where he stands in the corner. He wants to run away, to get as far from here as he can, but feels a responsibility to Mac to stay.

"Where am I?" whispers from beneath the covers. Mac's eyes flutter open and she rolls her head towards Sam.

"You're in the hospital, sweetheart. They're getting you all fixed up." Sam inches forward to the edge of his seat until it looks like he might fall off.

"What happened?" Her brow furrows.

"You were kidnapped." The words come out of Richard's lips like poured gravel. He shoves his hands into his pockets while a pang of guilt spreads through his chest.

"You were so brave, fighting your way out. We thought we'd lost you for a while." Sam's bloodshot eyes well with tears and his lip trembles.

Mac nods and her eyelids lower halfway as if she's about to fall asleep. "She tried to kill me." She lies there, a pile of bones and grey skin beneath the bandages, looking like her soul was wrenched from her body. She lifts her head an inch to look at Richard. "Oliver was going to bury me somewhere no one would ever find me."

"He's dead." Richard finds the strength to move to the side of the bed so she can see him better. "You fixed it so he won't hurt anyone ever again."

"She?" A crease forms between Sam's eyebrows. "Did you say 'she' tried to kill you?"

Mac nods and licks her cracked lips. "Josie."

"What about Josie?" Richard tilts his head and frowns.

Mac coughs, grimacing with the jolt to her chest. "She did this."

"You're not making any sense." Heat builds under Richard's collar and the muscles across his shoulders tighten into a bed of ropes. "Josie made us dinner before you disappeared. Ollie is the one who took you."

The mottled bruises around Mac's sunken eyes crease with worry lines. She blows a sharp breath. "You really don't know?"

"Know what?" Richard's voice comes out too loud. A lump of fear slides from the back of his throat into the pit of his stomach. "Is Josie in trouble?"

The intensity of Mac's eyes on him sends a chill down his spine. "Oliver and Josie did this… together."

"That's not true." Richard shakes his head. His wife wouldn't hurt a fly. She's a saint of a woman, always there to set things right when the world has all gone wrong. At this very moment she's off on a crusade to raise money to build a homeless shelter. He bets she'll even stop by a camp on her way home, connecting with the women who will benefit most from the money she's raised.

Mac trembles and her pale skin between the bruises flushes bright red while she pushes herself up from the pillows. "It is true. I thought she was following Ollie, but it's the other way around. She's worse… So much worse than her brother."

"Josie doesn't have a brother." Richard crosses his arms over his chest. Whatever happened to Mac made her lose her mind. "She's an only child. Raised by her aunt and uncle."

"Oliver's sister." Mac gasps for air. She looks like she's about to keel over, but she inches closer to him like the ghost of Christmas yet to come. "The aunt and uncle died, and his sister disappeared. File shows it was a botched robbery and the girl was kidnapped, but they were wrong. Josie killed them and ran."

Mac's sunken stare bores into Richard's soul and his skin erupts in a wave of gooseflesh. "What the hell are you talking about, Mac?"

"She wasn't Josie then," she wheezes. "She was Kristin Roberts."

Sam's chair slides backwards and he lurches forward, grabbing the bedrails. He struggles to his feet and repositions the chair, a flush of embarrassment on his cheeks. "Sorry. I slipped. What's she talking about, Richard?"

"Oliver isn't the man behind the curtain," Mac croaks. "It's Josie. She hit your car during your first case, and you took her to coffee. She's been with you all these years, helping Oliver stay one step ahead of you until she wanted you to catch him. She's orchestrated the whole thing."

Richard wants to ignore what Mac is saying. To dismiss her as just another unreliable witness. But Mac is as reliable as they come. Smart, and sharp as the crack of a whip. He bites the inside of his cheek, realizing it's impossible to ignore the truth when it lands at your feet.

Thinking back over all the family dinners he's missed because Ollie called at the last minute. The way Ollie skirted around his investigation in the early days, always seeming to know Richard's next move before he made it.

"Josie taught him when they were kids," Mac rasps. "She's still killing now. Right under your nose."

Thirty-One

He should have called it in.

Richard guns the engine and races through the traffic crowding the highway. It's a ninety-minute drive from the Mount Hood Medical Center in Gresham to the tiny town of Vernonia and he overtakes yet another lumber-laden semi-truck while the voice inside his head–Mac's voice–chides him for not making the call. A lot of anything can happen in ninety minutes.

But Josie is his wife. She can't possibly be the monster Mac is making her out to be. She's the woman of his dreams. The mother of his children. The mystery he could never unwind… but hadn't that been part of the romance of her?

Her fundraiser ended hours ago, but she still isn't picking up the phone. She could be anywhere, but he hopes she simply forgot to check her messages when the event wound down, and started her hour drive home without calling.

He swings into the next lane, cutting off a white sedan, and ignores when the driver blares their horn at him. He calls the church where the fundraiser was held again, and swerves around a red and black motorcycle while it rings.

He's been listening to the ringing of Josie's phone so long that he's shocked when someone answers. He over-steers and his tires hit the row of reflectors at the edge of his lane.

"North Street Church, Candace speaking. How may I be of service?"

"This is Richard Douglas. I'm looking for my wife, Josie. Is she still there?"

Traffic slows to a crawl and Richard slams on his brakes to avoid rear-ending a maroon SUV. It's a similar make and model to the one police pulled Mac out of and he sees a phantom of her wild eyes peering at him out the back window. He forces his eyes shut, and when he opens them again, the specter is gone.

"Oh, Josie." The woman's professional tone slips into one of disappointment. "Yes, I know her. She was supposed to buy me a drink if we hit our fundraising goal today, and we did, a whole hour before the event ended. But you know how she is… she said she'd found a young woman who needed a place to stay, so she skipped out to help the poor girl."

"She didn't even show up?" Richard feels the blood drain from his face. "She had to be there. You don't understand how important it is that she was there."

Candace's smile bleeds through the phone. "It's okay. So she missed one more fundraiser. Her heart's in the right place. I'm sure she'll swing by with an apology and a trunk full of donations in a day or two. That's Josie, you know?"

Everything Mac said in the hospital clicks together neatly in Richard's brain, like puzzle pieces finding their home at last. If Josie is the killer Mac says she is, and she's found another victim, she wouldn't bother wasting time with charity. He has to find her before another lifeless corpse washes up on the shores of the Nehalem River. But where would she take her victim? She wouldn't be bold enough to take her back to the place where the vic dressed like Mac was dumped, would she?

"Thank you, Candace. You've been a great help." He ends the call and dives out of his lane, gunning it down the shoulder and passing traffic at a dangerous pace. Mac's voice echoes in the back of his brain, screaming that he's compromising everything by handling this himself. *You have to call this in.*

But Josie is his wife. Maybe Mac, and the cold chill running through his belly, are wrong. Josie wouldn't be rooting around the Vernonia homeless camps searching for easy prey. Maybe she helped the woman find a safe place to stay the night and went home.

The exit for home races towards him. It would be so easy to hop off, drive home, and make sure that's where she is. Of course she's there… cookies in the oven while she knits, phone shut off to avoid distraction. Or maybe a symphony playing loudly while she soaks in an hours long bath, phone ignored while her stress steeps into the bathwater.

He passes the exit and counts four more, merging from interstate to highway, pointed in the direction of Vernonia. It's only another hour's drive to Vernonia. He may as well check it out for himself. Make sure everything is fine. No need to call anything into the office until he has evidence that something is happening.

Besides, what kind of husband would he be if he interrupted her quiet evening with a manhunt?

He comes around a bend in the highway. A tunnel bottlenecks traffic, and he slams his brake as the vehicles lined up in front of him come to a full stop. The flashing lights of a firetruck fill the void within the tunnel, swirling red lights erupting from the space like lava from a volcano.

"Shit." Traffic stacks up behind him like a brick wall. There's no telling how long he'll be stuck on the one-way section of highway. He picks his phone up from the center console and breathes deep while he dials.

"Vernonia Police Department. Detective Malone speaking."

"Inspector Douglas from the FBI calling. I've got a tip I need you to check out."

Thirty-Two

Josie backs away from her worktable to admire the full scope of her efforts. The woman's breathing is labored and wet, nothing like the life-giving inhales and exhales of a whole being. The muscles in her neck are strung tight, and the skin wraps over tendon and sinew like wet tissue paper. A vein pulses under a patch of unmarred skin, evidence of the still-beating heart. It is faint, erratic even, but still present beneath layers of flesh that Josie has yet to unravel.

Josie sways to the music playing through her phone and steps toward it to adjust the volume. A drop of blood glows atop the light of her phone's screen. She removes the bloodied glove from her hands and picks up a towel from her work satchel to wipe it away before turning the volume up a few clicks.

Light piano notes sing through the phone's nearly invisible speaker, increasing in a dramatic crescendo while she dances with herself around the table.

"Do you know this song?" Josie asks. The woman's tongue twitches in her mouth, beautifully grotesque. Josie pulls on a fresh pair of gloves. "You are probably too young to remember it, but it was my brother's favorite when we were young."

Josie lifts a hand in front of her as if being led by an invisible stranger. A fire of violence blazes up within her, burning up her insides until she cannot fight it any longer. She spins, limbs aflame, and grasps a knife from where it lays. She plunges the blade into the woman's thigh, and all the heat and horror bleeds out of her through the tip of the knife. The woman's scream soothes Josie's soul, bringing her back into herself.

"It might still be his favorite. I would ask him, but he is not here. All because of that bitch, Mackenzie Jones."

Blood gurgles in the woman's throat, an acceptable reply and a sound nearly as sweet to

Josie's ears as Sinatra's voice. His crooning words from *One for My Baby* fill the air between chords. Josie checks the result of her handiwork while the woman's head bobs slightly, lips twisted in a grimace Josie could almost mistake for a smile.

"You are so beautiful. My brother would have loved you." Josie leans down and kisses the woman's forehead.

Tears pink with blood roll down the woman's temples and trace her earlobes. She shudders in a sob that has the same wet grind as a broken garbage disposal. Although a few hours ago she had thrashed against the cuffs, now her wrists merely twitch where they were bound, too tired and broken to fight back.

"Shh, shh." Josie brushes a sweat-soaked lock of hair from the woman's forehead. She twists the sticky hair into a neat bundle and ties it with a pale pink ribbon, snips the bundle with a pair of rose-gold scissors and holds her prize up to the light. She tucks the lock of hair and scissors into her apron pocket and leans into the woman's ear. "It is nearly over now. I will rescue you from this horror and bring you peace. I promise."

Josie stands upright, stretching the soreness from her arms while she stares down at her captive. She has been a fun little plaything, an angel of catharsis, and a funnel for Josie's pain. But now it is time for her to go. Josie adjusts her grip on the knife, testing its weight in her hand one last time. She admires the shine of metal beneath the combination of flesh and dried blood.

It is time to end this, to pack up her bags and drive off into the sunset while this corpse floats downriver. She frowns, wishing she could drag the experience out just a little while longer.

"This one is for you," Josie whispers. She raises the knife, inhaling deeply while she steadies herself for the final blow. Her fingers tighten around the handle, met by her other hand high overhead. Her forearms scoop backwards another few inches.

Three loud bangs, the sound of a fist against metal, erupt through the room. Josie peers left under her lifted arm. The light leaking beneath the gas station's battered door is broken by a shadow.

"Josie Douglas, this is the police. Open up!" The voice is muffled, but the words are clear and the flicker of pleasure dancing through Josie's belly ignites into rage. How dare these idiots interrupt her? After all she has done for this shitty little town. She lowers her arms, pride setting her shoulders and indignance lifting her chin. She marches to the door, knife leading the way, ready to slice through whoever is on the other side.

She only makes it two paces when the door springs open and reaches the limits of its hinges with a bang. A rush of cool air bursts in from outside, punching a hole in the comfort of the death-infused atmosphere of her workshop. Josie takes a sharp breath of the fresh, clean air before a man bursts through the opening and tackles her to the ground. He lands on top of her, the heft of his right shoulder pounding her into the floor and knocking the breath from her chest.

Her head hits the concrete with a sickening crack and the world swirls with black streaks while the man squirms atop her, dragging the rough fabric of his uniform across her face. Blood pools in her mouth and her ears ring while the world explodes around her… boots pounding the ground and angry shouts filling every inch of the space.

The knife is pried from her fingertips and the man holding her rolls her to her belly. He forces her arms down and together, binding her wrists with thick plastic ties.

"Oh shit… Bring in the medic!" someone shouts.

Josie blinks the spots in her vision away and cranes her neck, turning her head to see the woman on the table. Her glassy eyes are open, staring unseeing from the table's edge. An officer dressed in black pumps up and down on her chest, but the blood that splatters is dull and thick. The freshness of it curdling as the minutes pass. Josie grins.

Two medical technicians rush into the room, the blue star of life emblazoned on their uniforms turning black in the low light. The officer steps back and one EMT touches the body gently while the other unloads equipment from the bag.

They tried to stop her, but she took what she came for in the end. And if her brother taught her anything over the years, it is that a prison sentence is simply another new beginning.

Thirty-Three

"Mac?"

She keeps her eyes pressed closed, mind wandering in the dark. She marvels at how remembering your own name is an automatic thing. You are you, and that's it. But there are moments where you become different. When you become someone you don't yet recognize.

It took a kidnapping, a partial drowning, and the loss of an unwanted pregnancy for Mac to lose herself. She'd thought she'd been lost before, wavering between the life she had and returning to one she didn't want, but now it felt like she was ten-thousand specks of sand scattered across a coastline. A stone so dismantled that it could never be made whole again.

A hand squeezes her shoulder. "I heard you sigh when the door opened. I know you're awake."

She peels an eyelid open to find Sam leaning over her. Behind the veneer of concern is an unmistakable pity in his eyes, and she hates him for it. Never before had she been so weak and broken. From the first day they met, he's been in awe of her, treating her like an invincible force without needs or limits. Even with all their problems, she was his equal before. And now, she's something less. An invalid.

"How are you doing?"

Mac tries to lift her shoulders in a noncommittal shrug, but a stabbing pain rips its way down her left side. It takes everything she has not to cry, but she swears if she loses it in front of him one more time, the pain will take a distant backseat to the erasure of what little pride she has left. And the last thing she wants to do is make Sam's pity more solid.

"I'm fine," she croaks.

The truth is, every time she gets tired enough to sink into sleep, she feels like she's drowning all over again. Rest has become the weight of water closing in around her, bearing down on her chest and filling up her lungs. She gasps for air and struggles to fight her way to the surface, and once she breaks through, she awakens to the horrific realization that she got her wish.

Her pregnancy ended, but she is alive. The weight of facing this barrenness is a grief no amount of FBI training could have ever prepared her for.

Sam pulls the worn hospital chair closer to the bed. "I don't know why they keep pushing this thing into the corner. I'm just going to keep coming back and dragging it beside you again." He settles into the thin cushions and reaches for the cast around her arm. "I found something you'll want to see." He pulls his phone from his pocket and flips the screen open to a website emblazoned with *Breaking News*.

Mac looks past the screen, avoiding looking at the photo of the abandoned gas station. "What does it say?"

"They captured Josie, while she was holding another victim hostage. They life-flighted the woman to the hospital. She's in critical condition, but she's alive, Mac." Sam's face loses its sheen of hope, and he frowns. "I can't believe Josie did that. She was such a nice lady."

The soft disbelief in Sam's voice is genuine, but the "they were so nice," comment is such a common bullshit statement that Mac snorts a laugh. She regrets it immediately and her eyes water while her sinuses come alight with infected fire. Sam hurries to collect a wad of single-ply tissues and dabs the tears from her eyes.

She side-eyes him. "You do know it's *always* the nice ones that are the worst criminals, don't you? 'He was such a quiet boy. She was such a pleasant neighbor; always had their hedges trimmed just so.'" She lifts her working hand to open and close her fingers through the air in a slow scissoring motion.

The pity in Sam's eyes fades when he smirks at her. "Nobody suspects a thing until they invite you to dinner and try to kill you. Is that how it is?"

Mac clicks her tongue and points at him with a finger-gun. "Now you're getting it, Chief. How did they know where to find Josie?"

Sam scans the article, swiping his finger to advance the page. "Says they received an anonymous tip."

"Had to be Richard." Mac sets her lips in a line. He came through in the end, and she hopes that counts for something. "Have you heard from him?"

"No, but the end of the article says an agent involved in the case has been suspended pending an investigation."

"Really?" Mac mulls the information over. She suspects if they dig too deep into Richard's dealings with Oliver that they'll find something unsavory. But even if his hands are somehow clean, being married to a homicidal homemaker, and secret sister of the serial killer he built his career around, won't be good for him. "I wonder if Richard will finally retire."

"What about you?" Sam's voice breaks and he hangs his head. "I know this job has been your purpose in life the last few years, but we almost lost you out there this time. I can't sit around and watch you tear yourself apart over this job anymore. It's too much."

His hands shake and she knows he's not just talking about the mess she's in right now. She's been struggling for years between the job and trying to be a half-decent wife and mother. When the chips are down, and she has to choose, it's become natural to pick the job over her family. But now that there's a gaping wound within her where guilt and relief mingle, she's not sure she made the right choices.

Intrusive thoughts bounce around her fractured skull, all of them echoing that she should have died along with the embryo she hadn't wanted.

"Everything hurts too much to think about." She closes her eyes and wishes it were as easy to shut off the voices in her head.

Sam is quiet for a long moment, then exhales a heavy breath. "You're here with us now, and that's all that matters. We'll give it some time, and things will feel better again."

They sit in silence together, each lost in their own thoughts. Mac doesn't know what will come. If surgery and therapy will bring her body and mind back. If she'll ever get to sleep again. But she does know she can't keep going the way she has been. Not just because of how deeply her entanglement with Oliver has scarred her family. But also, the chunks of life cut away by late nights, unpredictable travel, and constant threat that every new day might be her last.

"This job isn't worth dying over, Sam. I need to quit," she murmurs. He kisses the patch of her forehead that isn't covered by bandages, and she knows there's so much she needs to say to him. But she doesn't know where to start. "I'm sorry. For everything."

"You have nothing to be sorry for. You wanted to make the world safer, and you have." He tangles his fingers gently in hers.

She remembers the first time she held Sam's hand. The moment their skin touched, it felt like coming home. Now, the way his fingers tremble against her own feels like everything they've lost. Peace was wrenched from their lives, and she's not sure she'll ever feel at home again.

Thirty-Four

Richard's cheeks burn with embarrassment at having an Uber drive him home from the office. His gruff attitude is quick to make the young woman driving skip any small talk, which is a relief. With Josie's arrest, and his own suspension, complaining about the price of gas and talking about the weather with a stranger feels like torture.

When he turned in his badge, and his car, his director warned him against visiting Josie until after the investigation into his conduct is complete, saying it would only fuel speculation that he's been her inside eyes to FBI operations. So now here he is, pulling up to the curb of his cold, empty home in the cramped backseat of a Chevy Bolt.

He tells the Uber driver he promises to give her a five-star review, though he has no intention of doing so, and hauls himself and the cardboard box containing the remaining shards of his career up the driveway. He props the box on his hip while he unlocks the door and goes inside, dropping it in the foyer with a thud.

The house feels vast and empty without Josie in it. There's a hollowness in the rooms that rattles Richard's soul, as though he's stepped into a museum of their lives together; silent and expansive.

He stops to pour himself a nip of whiskey in the kitchen, then wanders the rooms and observes the furniture they bought together. Framed photos that document the family they've raised, despite their newly discovered circumstances. He stops in front of their wedding photo in the dining room. A much younger Richard, and timelessly radiant Josie stare back at him, standing together at an awkward angle. Not really joined at the hip as partners, so much as posed on stage by a photographer talented enough to make strangers look like lovers.

He should call the kids to tell them what happened. The thought tightens his chest. He hasn't talked to the girls in ages. How can he call them up and explain the accusations their mother is facing?

Fuck it. He'll call tomorrow. For now, another drink will do.

The table whiskey in his glass isn't strong enough to cut through his misery, and his mind turns to the bottle hidden in the desk in his office. He steps across the bright-white carpet in his muddy shoes, feeling rebellious in the moment, uncaring about the hell to pay when Josie finds the trail he's tracked through the house.

He laughs. "What the hell is she gonna do about it from jail?"

Unlocking his office door, he flips on the light and settles into the chair behind his desk. He drains the rest of his drink in one gulp and opens the bottom desk drawer where a twenty-year Glenfiddich waits for him. He fills his glass to the brim and leans back in his chair, looking around the room. Trophies of his career line every surface; award certificates hung in identical frames fill the walls, ribbons of commendation and pins of appreciation fill the gaps between them.

It's all very impressive, if you don't look too deep. But how many of these awards would he have been clever enough to earn if he hadn't sold his soul to Ollie?

Even Josie, his own wife, was a trophy he won through his deal with the devil. He takes a long drink and ponders her. Josie is a confident, yet solitary woman. Busy, dependable, but always with that light in her eyes like she's holding back some deep secret.

Well, Richard supposes that cat is out of the bag, now. The sister of a serial killer, and a killer herself, married to a bumbling man who hunts murderers for a living.

Richard turns in his chair, and he isn't sure why, but he stops to stare at the lock on his office door. Even living for decades under the same roof, he and Josie have always kept separate lives. He always had a deadbolt on his home-office door, a necessary security measure for his work. But Josie has her own room. A craft room he rarely felt brave enough to enter. The kids, too, always knew not to enter their mother's space.

She's not here now, and although the wheels of the warrant to search the home are turning slowly, it's only a matter of time before someone comes to tear the place apart looking for clues. His director warned him against coming home, told him to stay at a hotel, but the house hasn't been declared a crime scene yet, and it is still his home. If anyone is going to start digging around Josie's things, it may as well be him.

He takes a long drink, letting the burn of the alcohol warm him from the inside-out. A little liquid courage to bolster the bravery he needs to venture down the hallway to Josie's room. Once he's standing at the threshold, his knees lock and all he can do is stare.

He can't shake the feeling that once he steps inside, he'll never be able to face her again. There's an ominous force deep inside the tidy room that will trap him in the truth of this moment, forever.

The lump in his throat doesn't bulge, even when he tries to swallow it down with another gulp of whiskey. He takes a tentative step inside and stops beside a wall of fabric, running a hand over the bolts carefully organized by hue and print on the shelves. At the center of the room, an arrangement of silk flowers holds court on an otherwise spotless craft bench, and Josie's collection of thimbles and spools of thread line pegs beneath the window.

It's too neat. Too perfect. As if it's a set in a cozy movie, and Josie was never really here at all.

He's not sure how long he stands there, breathing in Josie's scent, before he finds the will to do more than observe her space from a distance. He wishes she were here right now, not locked in a booking cell an hour away. If she were, she'd shame him for second-guessing her loyalty.

But for the first time since they moved into this house, he's taking it all in. The carefully refinished furniture and handmade decorations feel lifeless without her fiddling with them. His eyes wander to the narrow writing desk in the corner, and he finishes his drink while he observes its simple design. It's well made, carved maple, and polished to within an inch of its life. In all the years they've been married, Richard has never seen inside the little desk. Thinking back, he can't even remember ever seeing Josie use it.

Curious, he runs his hand along the lid and tries to open it, but it's locked. He searches briefly for a key, but comes up empty-handed. Back through the house he goes, dipping into his office to retrieve a lock-picking kit collecting dust on a bookshelf.

He returns to the desk with tools in hand and after some fiddling with the rarely used tools, unclasps the lock. He curls his fingers under the lid in triumph, "Well, let's see what's inside."

Any delight he expected at peeking into his wife's secret space turns to ash. The inside of the desk is meticulously organized, and its contents are laid out so they are immediately recognized.

To one side lays a stack of canary yellow envelopes, and the same stationary Richard has found tucked away in recent crime scenes. Beneath the stationery is a tattered photo album with a faded polaroid of Josie as a child glued to the cover. Richard digs in his pockets for the disposable gloves he keeps there, and he pulls them on before picking up the album. He's afraid to open the cover, to see the truth inside. But he has to know.

He flips open the cover and as the first page comes into view, his heart sinks to his knees.

There, staring back at him, is a young Josie. She's no more than two years old, sitting on an orange and black checkerboard sofa with her chubby arm hanging lazily across the shoulders of a baby. A bubble of acid climbs the back of Richard's throat. He's seen this photo before. Well, half of it, anyway.

Ollie had torn his sister out of his copy of the photo long before anyone thought to comb his property for evidence in a string of murders.

Richard thumbs through the small book's pages, finding several more pictures of Josie and Ollie together as children. There's a shared darkness in their eyes that sends chills across his skin. And then, on the last page, there's a picture that's larger and brighter than the rest, as if it has been blown up and restored. Josie grins at the camera with a gap-filled smile. Her arm is around Ollie in this photo too, but her grip on him looks dangerously tight. This young, less ominous version of Ollie looks wide-eyed at the camera, his hands braced against his sister's torso as if he's trying to escape her, and his mouth turned into a small 'o' of fear.

Josie holds a kitchen knife in the foreground. There's blood on the blade, and a pattern of rust-colored stains splotch the front of her dress. Although Ollie looks like he's terrified of the girl beside him, he appears unharmed. Richard searches the picture for signs it was Halloween, or that they are on the set of a play. Maybe the blood draping over Josie's hand and staining her dress is fake?

He scours the picture, and then he sees something in the background that would look out-of-place even on Halloween. A brown and black chicken hangs upside-down from a board of the white picket fence in the distance behind them. A river of dried blood coating the boards below the slaughtered bird.

The album snaps shut in his hands, and he trembles where he stands. He drops it into the desk when a geyser of bile rises to meet the back of his throat and the room tilts beneath his feet. He doesn't want to believe it, but the evidence is right here, hidden in the only piece of furniture Josie brought into their marriage. The only remnant of her childhood that exists.

Josie truly is Kristin Roberts, reinvented.

The drumming of Richard's heart between his lungs is enough to take his breath away, and he bends over, bracing himself with his hands on his knees. He shakes his head, bewildered with the heaviness of knowing. He peers again into the open desk, and something tucked in the back corner catches his eye.

He gently retrieves the yellow cigar box and opens it. The second he recognizes what's inside, he bursts into tears. It's filled with locks of hair, each tied tightly together with a different colored ribbon. There are dozens upon dozens of them in every shade of blonde, brown, auburn, and black. Some are a bundle of curls while others lay flat and lifeless in Richard's palm.

Richard has walked through countless murder scenes, each one more vicious than the last, but he can't tear his eyes away from the neatly tied bows and colorful hair. This isn't some stranger's murder scene. This is his own life turned into a nightmare slowly and all at once. A bundle of black curls falls from his trembling fingers and spirals to the ground, the terrible reality of what Josie is capable of… what she has done… hits him like a pigeon in a hurricane.

Knees buckling, he sinks to the floor, back hunched and face buried in hands filled with death. He thought he knew her. Thought she loved him. But he was wrong.

Dead wrong.

Josie is a monster. And he's been living with her, sleeping in the same bed, fathering her children. How could he have been so blind?

Thirty-Five

The minivan's dinging is driving Mac crazy. She pinches the bridge of her nose between her thumb and forefinger, trying to still the pulse of her migraine with every ping of the alarm. Sam's voice has become a constant stream of curses and grunts, the wheelchair rattling in time with each yank and pull while he tries to wrestle it out of the cargo hold.

She can't take the noise anymore and snatches his keys out of the ignition. "Is everything okay back there?"

"Almost got it." He shakes the chair back and forth so hard, it makes the whole van lean from side to side.

Exhausted, sore, and out of patience, Mac opens the passenger door and lowers her feet gingerly to the driveway one at a time. She gasps at the pain shuddering through her while she works her way to standing, and leans against the road-grime encrusted paint while shuffling towards the trunk.

Sam's face knits itself in incredulous knots. "What the hell are you doing? You're not supposed to walk around!"

"I'm helping." She reaches over and flips the handle on the chair, disengaging the closest wheel's brake. Sam frowns and unlocks the other side, and a light turn of the freed wheels brings the chair rolling smoothly over the cargo hold's lip.

With a grunt, Sam pulls the chair the rest of the way out of the van and settles it on the driveway. He jabs a finger at the seat. "Get in, wiseass."

"My hero." She flutters her eyelashes, rests the back of her hand on her forehead, then drops the damsel in distress act and frowns at him. "I can walk. It just takes a while."

"What's the fun in shuffling around like an old lady when you have this sweet ride?"

Mac lowers herself into the chair with a pained sigh and Sam pushes her up the newly installed wheelchair ramp that connects to the front door. She's glad to be back at the house, even if it has to be like this.

He reaches over her shoulder to open the door. It swings wide and half a dozen voices cheer. "Surprise!"

Mac grins at the sight of family and neighbors crammed into the living room. She feels the sting of tears in her eyes, and for once doesn't bother to stop them. "You didn't have to do this."

"Are you kidding?" Sam wheels her into the center of the living room. "We've been dying to throw you a 'welcome home', slash, 'thanks for quitting your job' party."

"Thank you. It means a lot." Mac looks around at the banners and streamers, her kids, her parents and in-laws, and friends all wearing colorful party hats. "You went all out."

"You needed a proper party," Ryan says, leaning down to give her an awkward hug.

"And we wanted to make sure you got cake this time." Robby hands her a plate with a giant piece of cake, topped with dog-shaped sprinkles.

"No cake for Bruce this time?" Mac winks at the boys. "You guys are the best."

The group mills around her, conversations ebbing and flowing in a pattern of well-wishes and thanks-for-comings. Mac has difficulty engaging until Tarrell approaches from the far corner of the room.

Mac may be the one fresh out of the hospital, but the governor is a shadow of his former self. His enigmatic smile has been replaced with a stiff-set jaw, and the light of his eyes has dimmed. "Special Agent Jones," he says in a low voice while he bends over to give her a one-armed hug. "I can't stay, but I wanted to see you home."

Mac sets her cake in her lap and wraps both arms around him, pulling him close. Her throat tightens and tears spill from her eyes before she has a chance to fight them. "I'm so sorry I didn't stop them in time to save Jacqueline."

Tarrell leans into her, and his shoulders jump in a silent sob. He drags a heavy breath in, then pulls away from her embrace and wipes the dampness from his eyes. "You did enough. It almost killed you." The room has gone silent around them, and the stillness seems to make

Tarrell even more uncomfortable. “Thank you for your service to my family. I won’t forget it.”

He pats her on the shoulder before walking away, letting himself out the front door. The gravity of the room loosens the moment he leaves, and soon conversations between the other partygoers begin anew.

Each person’s voice slips into the next, their faces blending together in a flurry of activity she can’t keep up with. Beneath the gratitude of being back among people she cares for, a storm of guilt and disappointment brews.

No one brings up Mac’s pregnancy. They don’t ask about her kidnapping, and no one aside from Tarrell mentions her almost dying at the hands of the Roberts siblings. The longer the details of her ordeal remain unspoken, the darker the monster of grief becomes. The guilt of surviving, the anger of a world pretending none of it happened, the sadness of losing her independence, it all swills together, creeping under Mac’s skin like a virus. She returns friendly smiles, nods her head in all the appropriate places, and shakes hands, but the longer the party drags on, the closer she feels to erupting.

She turns to ask Sam to send everyone home, but he's walking away and doesn't turn back when she calls his name. He disappears into the kitchen and Mac sits, silently pitying herself while everyone celebrates around her, until he returns with a package wrapped in pink and blue paper.

"The kids and I wanted to get you something."

"Thank you." She receives the package and forces a smile.

She carefully unwraps the paper, revealing a wooden frame with a photo of the kids and Sam. The three of them huddle around an empty stroller, smiling. A sign propped on the stroller's seat reads, *In loving memory of Baby Jones.*

"It's beautiful," she says through the choke of tears. She hiccups a grief-stricken sob that she's been holding inside for weeks. Sam wraps his arms around her, and she cries into his shoulder.

She leans as far into him as the chair allows, so grateful to have him as her husband. Even after all these years, all the petty arguments, and heartache they've shared, she knows he will always be there for her, no matter what.

When the tears dry, she's so exhausted, she can almost sleep right where she sits. Sam ushers the partygoers out the door. When the last person is gone, he kneels at her feet. "Ready for bed?"

Mac checks her watch and sighs. It's only a quarter to eight. If she goes to sleep now, she'll be awake again at two in the morning. "Not yet. Do we have any coffee? I want to stay up a while."

Sam frowns. "No coffee. I'm not spending all night carrying you to the bathroom every forty-five minutes because you need to pee. But I do have something else that will keep you up for a while."

He walks to a pile of mail sitting on a side table and retrieves a pair of tattered looking envelopes. When he hands them to her, it's apparent they've been opened and resealed. They're addressed to her office, a stamp from Sheridan's prison yells at her in red ink from the smaller envelope. The second one is larger, heavier, from the detectives in Vernonia.

"These came for you a couple of weeks ago." Sam follows the statement with a resigned sigh when she opens her mouth to ask why she's only getting them now. "We all agreed I shouldn't bring them up to the hospital. They would have interfered with your recovery. But I know if I don't give them to you now, you'll never forgive me."

Mac cradles the envelopes like they might explode if she squeezes the paper too hard. "How did you get them?"

"Richard brought them the day after he was suspended. He said you'd want to have them."

The envelope from Sheridan opens easily and Mac finds a single sheet of lined paper inside. Her hands tremble while she unfolds the letter and smooths it in her lap. The handwriting is neat, deliberate, and uncomfortably familiar.

Dear Mac,

I've been thinking about what you said the night I was arrested. I didn't know what to say then, but there is a lot I wish I'd told you.

Rumors are going around that you got caught up in some shit, and I'm not sure you'll be around to talk again. But if you make it, I'd like to try. I'll be here. I've got nowhere else to go.

- Henry "Peter" Roberts

Mac stares at the letter, reading it again. She'd told Peter that if he ever wanted to talk about Oliver, she would be there to listen. She wasn't sure if the fact that she shot his father and been one of his aunt's victims would make that easier, or harder. But it was interesting.

She slowly folds the letter and slides it back into the envelope and tucks it into the side of the wheelchair. It's interesting that Richard read it and gave it to Sam instead of passing it on to someone else in the bureau. This could be the opening she's been waiting for ever since she first met Peter. An invitation to know the full truth about Oliver Roberts and his network of connections in and outside of prison.

The second envelope is the size of a file folder. She opens the end, letting a sheaf of photographs slip out. The first set are familiar. A photo of the envelope found in her bathroom, and a letter laid out on a lab table.

Dearest strong-willed Mackenzie,

I respect that you have made your decision. But it is the wrong one.

Blessings on your way to hell,

Oliver

Mac shudders at the way she can hear his voice, smooth and crisp in her mind when she reads Oliver's words. It's as if he's standing beside her, reading the words aloud. "I'll see you there, asshole," Mac mutters.

Sam raises an eyebrow. "Is that something I want to see?"

She shakes her head and pushes the reminder of their serial-killer inspired home invasion back into the envelope, wishing there were a way to speed up the process of putting his reign of terror behind her. But beneath the photographs of her note from Oliver is another set of pictures. A canary yellow envelope wrapped in plastic, in the mud. That letter opened on another lab table.

To my constant Richard,

Thank you for your service. I have decided to move in a new direction. Best wishes on your retirement.

All my love,

Oliver

Mac's mouth drops open, and she looks at Sam. "You said Richard gave these to you?" Sam nods and Mac shakes her head, turning the photos over in her hand to see if she's missed anything, then holds the letter up for Sam to read. "What does this look like to you?"

"That's basically what my boss told me when I was laid off a few years ago. 'We've decided to take this project on a new path. Please clean out your desk immediately.' So that's what? Oliver firing Richard?" Sam lifts an eyebrow.

"I guess he wasn't planning on granting Richard any more visits down at the prison, since he broke out." Mac shakes her head again, thoughts tumbling through her mind of what this could mean. A weird cult-leader's way of parting as friends? Or something else? Something darker?

Sam watches her with knowing eyes. He crosses his arms over his chest and lowers his mouth in a frown. "You did just quit your job today. That means it's not up to you to solve all these mysteries anymore."

"You're right." Mac slides the photos back into their parcel and tucks it into the side of the chair with the other envelope. She gives Sam a reassuring smile. "I'm keeping my end of our bargain. Rest and relaxation until the doctors say I'm well enough to terrorize the world again. If somehow, I do talk to Peter or Richard between now and then, it will just be to talk. Might be good for the three of us to process what we've been through, you know?"

"Mmmhmm. Absolutely not a ploy to unearth even more of Oliver and Josie's secrets." Sam sniffs a sharp breath. "It's never just a normal conversation with you."

The gears of her mind break loose, threads of thought coming alight as she considers what reconnecting with Richard and Peter might reveal. She scribbles invisible notes inside her mind, ticking boxes and making lists of questions that only those two men can answer.

Sam clears his throat, startling her from her thoughts. "You're already breaking your promise to rest, aren't you?"

The excitement of the moment dulls the pain in Mac's shoulders enough for her to lift them in a casual shrug. She tilts her head, feeling the light gleam of mischief in her eyes. "I admit nothing. But you were right, these letters did work better than a cup of coffee. Wheel me into my office, will you? I think I'll be awake for a while."

About the author

D.K. Greene is an Amazon bestselling author of gripping psychological thrillers and mysteries hidden in the landscape of the Pacific Northwest. She's the wife of a painter and the mother of a social and environmental activist, but is also a backyard farmer, midnight crafter, a fan of geeky conventions, and is always on the lookout for unexpected adventures.

Greene is the author of the Killers Club series, The Mommy Mysteries, and the Pace Morrow mystery series. You can find the growing list of her work at https://KawaiiTimes.com/d-k-greene/

Series by D.K. Greene

The Pace Morrow Mysteries

The Mommy Mysteries

The Killers Club

Sign up for the D.K. Greene newsletter and **download a free e-book**! Grab your copy now at https://kawaiitimes.com/book-promotions/